Hilary Mantel was born in Derbyshire. She was educated
at a ... in Africa and the Middle East, she returned to Britain in
1985 to make a career as a writer.

Visit www.AuthorTracker.co.uk for exclusive
information on your favourite HarperCollins authors.

By the same author

Vacant Possession
Eight Months on Ghazzah Street
Fludd
A Place of Greater Safety
A Change of Climate
An Experiment in Love
The Giant, O'Brien
Learning to Talk
Beyond Black

NON-FICTION
Giving Up the Ghost

HILARY MANTEL

Every Day is Mother's Day

HARPER PERENNIAL
London, New York, Toronto and Sydney

Harper Perennial
An imprint of HarperCollins*Publishers*
77–85 Fulham Palace Road
Hammersmith
London W6 8JB

www.harperperennial.co.uk

This edition published by Harper Perennial 2006
2

Previously published in paperback by Penguin Books 1986

First published by Chatto & Windus Ltd 1985

A catalogue record for this book is
available from the British Library

ISBN-13 978-1-84115-339-1
ISBN-10 1-84115-339-7

Set in Sabon

Printed and bound in Great Britain by Clays Ltd, St Ives plc *to the Bevington-Levitts*

Two errors; one, to take everything literally;
two, to take everything spiritually.

PASCAL

Do not adultery commit;
Advantage rarely comes of it.

A. H. CLOUGH

CHAPTER I

When Mrs Axon found out about her daughter's condition, she was more surprised than sorry; which did not mean that she was not very sorry indeed. Muriel, for her part, seemed pleased. She sat with her legs splayed and her arms around herself, as if reliving the event. Her face wore an expression of daft beatitude.

It was always hard to know what would please Muriel. That winter, when the old man fell on the street and broke his hip, Muriel had personally split her sides. She was in her way a formidable character. It wasn't often she had a good laugh.

Click, click, click, said the mock-crocs. They were Mrs Sidney's shoes. She passed without mishap along the Avenue, over that flagstone with its wickedly raised edge where Mr Tillotson had tripped last winter and sustained his fracture; they had petitioned the council. Mrs Sidney's good legs, the legs of a woman of twenty-five, moved like scissors down the street. Her face was white and tired, her scarlet lips spoke of an effort at gaiety. She had carried the colour over the line of her thin lips, into a curvaceous bow; she had once read in a magazine that this could be done. Of what lies between the good legs and the sagging face, better not to speak; Mrs Sidney never dwelled on her torso, she had given it up. She stopped by the house called 'The Laburnums', by the straggling privet hedge spattered white with bird-droppings and ravaged by amateur topiary; and tears misted over her eyes. She wore the black coat with the mink trim.

Arthur had been with her when she bought the coat. It was budgeted for; the necessity had been weighed. Arthur had been embarrassed, standing among the garment rails; he had clasped his hands behind his back like Prince Philip, and with his eyes elsewhere

7

he tried to look like a man deep in thought. She had not trailed him around the shops, she knew what she wanted. 'A good coat,' she said to him, 'a good cloth coat is worth every penny you spend on it.'

She had tried on two, and then the black. The salesgirl was sixteen. She was not interested in her job. She stood with one limp arm draped over the rail, her hip jutting out, watching Mrs Sidney push the laden hangers to and fro. She did not know anything about the cut of a good cloth coat. Mrs Sidney removed her gloves, and her fingers stroked the little mink collar appreciatively. She had tried to engage Arthur's attention, but he was not looking, and for a second she was shot through with resentment. Carelessly she tossed her old camelhair over a rail; until this morning it had been her best coat, but now it seemed shabby and inconsiderable. She unfastened the buttons carefully, slipped her arms into the silky lining. Turning to see the back in the long mirror, she smiled tentatively at the salesgirl. 'Do you think the length . . . ?'

The girl raised her thin shoulders in a shrug.

By now Arthur stood smiling at her indulgently, his hands still clasped behind his back.

'I will take it,' Mrs Sidney said. She minced towards Arthur.

'Very nice, dear,' Arthur said. 'Are you sure you've got what you wanted?'

She nodded, smiling. He would have been willing, she knew, to pay twenty pounds more, once he had agreed on the economy of a good cloth coat. Arthur did not stint. The girl laid it out by the cash register, flapped some tissue between its crossed arms and slid it, folded, into a big bag. Arthur took out a virgin chequebook, and his rolled-gold fountain pen. Precisely, he unscrewed the cap; smoothly, the ink flowed; with care, he replaced the cap and returned the pen to the inside pocket of his lovat sports jacket. Then, with a single neat pull, he removed the cheque and handed it courteously to the girl. Mrs Sidney was proud of that, proud of the way the transaction had been carried through; how they did not pay in greasy bundles of notes like plumbers and housepainters. The carrier bag was heavy, with the good cloth coat inside it, and Arthur reached out without speaking and took it from her. He asked about a hat, so anxious was he to have everything correct; but she told him that people do not go in so much for hats nowadays. To be truthful, millinery departments intimidated her. The assistants looked at you scornfully, for so few of the people who tried on hats ever made a purchase; they had lost faith in human nature. She was happy. They had a cup of coffee and a cream cake each, and then they went home.

That night Arthur had his first stroke. When she got up in the morning, all the right side of his body was paralysed, and his mouth was twisted down at the corner; he couldn't speak. By eight o'clock he was lying on a high white bed at the General. She was sitting outside the ward, drinking the strong tea a nurse had given her out of a chipped white cup. All she could think was, you can get these cups as seconds on the market. Could that be where they get them? A hospital, could it be? He's on the free list, the nurse said, you can come at any time. When she went to see him he moved restlessly those parts he could move; he never again knew what day of the week it was, or anything at all about the world in the corridor or the market-place beyond. He suffered his second stroke while she was there, and they put lilac screens around the bed and informed her that he had passed away. She wore the black coat to his funeral.

Mrs Sidney raised one elegant knee a little, to prop her bag on it, fumbled inside and took out a pink tissue. Standing by the stained and formless privet, she dabbed her eyes. She looked for a litterbin, but there were none in the Avenue. She screwed the tissue back into her handbag and scissored along the street.

The Axons' house stood on a corner. There was a little gate let in between the rhododendrons. No weeds pushed up between the stones of the path. And this was odd, because you would not have thought of Evelyn Axon as a keen gardener. There was stained glass in the door of the porch, venous crimson and the storm-dull blue of August skies. Mrs Sidney stopped a pace from the door. She feared her nerve was going to fail her. Again she fumbled with her bag, patting for her purse to make sure it was still there. She did not know whether Mrs Axon accepted payment. A small tickle of grief and fear rose up in her throat. She arrived at her decision; Mrs Axon would already be watching from some window in the house. She placed her finger on the doorbell as if she were buttonholing the secret of the universe. It did not work.

But somewhere, in the dark interior of the house, Evelyn moved towards the door. She opened it just as Mrs Sidney raised her hand to knock. Mrs Sidney lowered her arm foolishly. Evelyn nodded.

'Come in,' she said. 'I suppose you want to speak to your late husband.'

It was a nice detached property. As soon as she entered the hall behind Evelyn, Mrs Sidney's eyes became viper-sharp. She took in the neglected parquet floor, the umbrella stand, the small table quite bare except for one potplant, withered and brown.

'Nothing seems to survive,' Evelyn said.

Mrs Sidney took a tighter grip on her bag.

'And into the front parlour,' Evelyn said.

Then she kept her eyes on Evelyn's fawn cardigan, the bulky shape moving weightily ahead. It was a sunless room, seldom used; at this time Evelyn lived mostly at the back of the house. There were heavy curtains, a round dining-table in some dark wood, eight hard chairs with leather seats; a china cabinet, and two green armchairs placed at either side of the empty fireplace. 'You'll want the fire,' Evelyn said; she was nothing if not a good hostess. Mrs Sidney took one of the armchairs, knees together, her handbag poised on them. Evelyn shuffled out and left her alone. She stared at the china cabinet, which was quite empty.

Evelyn returned with a little electric fire, two bars, dusty, the flex fraying. 'If you don't mind,' Mrs Sidney said, 'that's dangerous. Bare wires like that.'

Evelyn slammed the plug firmly into the socket. As she stood up, she gave Mrs Sidney what Mrs Sidney called a straight look, the kind of look that is given to people who speak out of turn. 'Make yourself comfortable, Mrs Sidney,' she said.

Once again, Mrs Sidney was struck by the cultured tone of Evelyn's voice. She was, had been, what old-fashioned people called a lady. She and her husband had lived in this house when these few dank autumnal avenues were the best addresses in town. The Axons had always kept to themselves. For years the neighbours had complained about Evelyn's ways, about the odd times at which she hung out her washing, about her habit of muttering to herself in the queue at the Post Office. Yet, Mrs Sidney thought, she was a cut above. In a way she was a very tragic woman; Mrs Sidney had a nose for tragedy these days, alerted to it by her own. 'You'll have to excuse my not providing tea,' Evelyn said. 'It's not convenient. I'm not going into the kitchen today.' Mrs Sidney blinked. For want of reply, her eyes slid back to the empty china cabinet.

'Smashed,' Evelyn said. 'All smashed years ago.'

Evelyn went over to the sideboard. It was, Mrs Sidney noted, the most modern piece of furniture in the room. It had one of those compartments for drinks, and a flap that came down to serve them on. Evelyn pulled it down. Mrs Sidney gaped. She could make out the labels from here; baked beans, salmon, ox-tongue. Evelyn reached into the back and took out a half-full bottle of orange squash. From a cupboard, she took two glasses and poured a careful measure into each. On the table stood a jug of lukewarm water. Evelyn set down one of the glasses by her guest's side, and took the armchair opposite.

'I expect you will want to talk about him a little,' she said. She sat upright and alert, watching her visitor, noting how the face-powder had caked at the side of her nose, how the open pores of her cheeks shone, how the body mocked the pretty, lively legs. And suddenly Mrs Sidney crumpled, as if she had been dealt a blow; her bag slid from her knees to the floor, her shoulders sagged, great gouts of grief came dropping from her mouth. Yes, Evelyn thought, how they steer you to cheerful topics; how after twice meeting they cross the road and pretend that they didn't see you so that they can avoid the whole embarrassing encounter: a widow. There is, Evelyn reflected, a custom known as Suttee; to judge by their behaviour, many seemed to think its suppression an unhealthy development.

She watched. Mrs Sidney's mouth worked, and the scarlet line of lipstick above her top lip contorted independently of the mouth, so that her face seemed to be slipping in and out of some grotesque and ludicrous mask. The woman lurched forward; her hands scrabbled for her bag and she scrubbed at her face with the pink tissues and dropped them in sodden balls on the carpet and on to the chair. Evelyn reached for her orange juice and took a sip. She put down the glass carefully, on a mat with a fringe. 'Mr Sidney was a good husband to you,' she suggested.

Mrs Sidney talked about the buying of the coat, of the cakes they had eaten, of the vast corridors of the hospital with its draughts and swinging firedoors; the stained walls, the starched impatience of doctors' coats and the dreadful grimace of his paralysed mouth. As she talked she gasped and retched at the memories, but in the end she calmed herself, sat upright and shaking on the edge of the chair, her legs crossed tightly and her eyes formless and red. She was ready to begin.

'Mr Sidney's line of work was with the Transport Authority,' she said carefully. She spoke as if each of her words was a precious crystal glass coming out of a crate; one slip could shatter her again.

'You mean the Bus Company?' Evelyn said.

'It was a kind of insurance work. When – if, you see, there was an accident, someone was in an accident on the bus, he would be finding out what happened and deciding how much the Bus – the Transport Authority – ought to pay out for it. He was called a Claims Investigation Agent.'

'Yes,' Evelyn said. 'He was a clerk. I understand. Now I will tell you, Mrs Sidney, sometimes I meet with success and sometimes I don't. If you would call it success; I would say, results. It appears that they tell some people that all is very beautiful on the ninth plane and that there are flowers and organ music, but they never said that to me, and if they do say it I think they must be confusing it with the funeral. It would be a natural mistake. On those grounds, I hardly approve of cremation.'

'But do you ever', Mrs Sidney hesitated, 'do you ever speak with your own husband?'

'Clifford died in 1946,' Evelyn said. 'He was a quiet man, and I suppose we have less in common than we did.'

'What did – did he pass over suddenly?'

'Very suddenly. Peritonitis.'

There was a silence. Mrs Sidney broke it with difficulty. 'Do you use a wineglass?'

Evelyn snorted. 'If you want that, you get it at parties, don't you?'

'I'm sorry,' Mrs Sidney said. She stood up. 'Mrs Axon, I'm sorry, I don't think I should have come. If my daughter knew she'd kill me.'

'And your curiosity would be satisfied,' Evelyn said. 'How old are you, Mrs Sidney?'

'Since you ask, I'm sixty-five.'

Evelyn sighed. 'Not a great age, but you ought to know what to expect. If I were you, I'd sit down, and we can get on.'

Mrs Sidney sat. She stared about her, hypnotised by her own temerity, by Evelyn's watery blue eyes, by the dull sheen of the afternoon light on the hard leather chairs.

Presently Evelyn leaned forward, her hands clasped together, her eyes closed, and scalding tears dropped from under her lids. Mrs Sidney watched them falling. Her heart hammered. Evelyn's mouth gaped open, and Mrs Sidney dug her nails into her palms, expecting Arthur's voice to come out.

Evelyn dropped back in her chair. Her pale eyes snapped open, and she spoke in a perfectly normal voice.

'I told you not to come to me for reassurance, Mrs Sidney. Go to the Spiritualist Church if you like. It's in Ruskin Road. They have a cold buffet afterwards.' She got heavily to her feet. Mrs Sidney lurched after her, past the empty china cabinet and the dead pot-plant, stumbling to the door.

'Mrs Sidney,' Evelyn said, 'your husband Arthur is roasting in some unspeakable hell.'

She closed the door. I shall give this up, she thought. They come here, for a Cook's Tour of the other world; as if it were in some other but accessible place, they use me like an aeroplane, like a cruise liner. But it was here, a little removed yet concurrent; each day some limb of the supernatural reached out to pluck you by the clothes. I shall give it up, she thought, because it is making me ill; if one day I took some sort of fit and were laid up, what would happen, who would look after Muriel?

AXON, MURIEL ALEXANDRA
DATE OF BIRTH: 4.4.40
2 Buckingham Avenue

Miss Axon was visited at her home by Miss Perkins of this Department on 3.3.73 and subsequently by CWD on 15.3.73. Client lives with her widowed mother, Mrs Evelyn Axon. Her father died in 1946. They are resident in a comfortable detached house with all usual amenities. Client attended St David's School, Arlington Road, 1945 – 1955, but her attendance seems to have been nominal as her mother states she was 'more often absent'. Mrs Axon states that she was informed about 1946 or 1947 that Muriel did not seem to have the normal aptitude for her age-group, and she was kept behind a class for two subsequent years. At this point it appears client should have been designated ESN under the provisions of the 1944 Act, but this was not done and it is suggested that at this point in time she appeared in a borderline normality situation. Mrs Axon states that she considered that client had been adversely affected by her father's death at six years old and that 'she would not have benefited' from special provision. During the years following Mr Hutchinson, then School Attendance Officer, visited the house on several occasions but unfortunately these records cannot be traced in the files of the newly-constituted Education Welfare Department. (Query check County Hall.) According to Mrs Axon client was referred (by Mr Hutchinson) to the Gresham Trust which prior to the takeover of its functions by the Local Authority dealt with the welfare of the subnormal in the community. Client was visited by a caseworker of the Trust, a Miss Blackstone, and Mrs Axon states that tests were given to the client but that she refused to participate in them. Mrs Axon states that the visits of the Trust ceased after one year and there appear to be no records of client as it does not seem to have been the policy of the Trust to keep records for more than five years.

Client appears physically fit. Mrs Axon states that other than the usual childhood illnesses she has never been seriously ill, never been hospitalised, and has not had occasion to visit her GP in the last ten years or possibly more. Mrs Axon is in general very vague about dates. Mrs Axon states that Muriel is able to wash and dress herself but will 'put on anything' and that she has to supervise her washing and also her meals as she will eat unsuitable food. However she is able to help in the house though Mrs Axon states she is not very willing. She is sometimes taken shopping by Mrs Axon but not frequently. Mrs Axon states that client is not able to go out alone because of various incidents that have occurred in the past, but she would not go into any further details about this.

Mrs Axon is extremely uncommunicative in herself and this is seen as a problem in assessment. According to Mrs Axon client is able to understand everything that is said to her but often does not answer when she is spoken to. She has no hobbies or pastimes. Difficulties in this case are increased by the uncooperative and almost hostile attitude of Mrs Axon, who seems to resent any intervention by welfare agencies. Client's environment seems to be unstimulating and Mrs Axon seems to be ashamed of her to the extent that she is unwilling for her to be seen by neighbours. Her attitude to her seems to be one of basic contempt and that client does not have ordinary feelings, for instance she referred to client in her hearing as a 'hopeless idiot'. It must be said that client appears to be adequately fed and clothed and that although Mrs Axon's standards of housekeeping are not high she does attend to client's physical welfare, but she seems to have a negative attitude to client's mental and emotional development and it is unlikely that any significant improvement will take place unless Muriel is encouraged

to mix a little more with other people and acquire social confidence.
Recommendations: Multi-professional assessment
Day care

C. W. D.

Department of Social Services
Wilberforce House
15th April 1973

Dear Mrs Axon,

You may remember that I visited you on March 15th to discuss your daughter's case and we agreed then that it would be helpful to Muriel if she could attend a day care centre where she would be enabled to mix with other young people and take part in group activities. I have looked into the possibility of this but unfortunately there is a waiting list for our Community Daycare Centres and I have only been able to arrange for Muriel to attend initially for one afternoon a week. However, I feel sure she will benefit from this, and we do look forward to extension of our provision in the near future. She will be able to take part in informal activities like community singing, and she will also be able to try her hand at crafts such as pottery and basket weaving. Our Community Daycare Centre is situated on Calderwell Road. Muriel will be collected by minibus from the corner of Buckingham Avenue and Lauderdale Road, and will be returned to the same point. The hours of our Daycare Session are from 1.30 p.m. to 4.30 p.m. and she should be at the collection point by 1.15 p.m. There is no charge for transport. A nominal charge of 15p is made for tea and biscuits. Her first session will be on Thursday 25th April.

Unfortunately because of pressure on our facilities I have not yet been able to arrange for Muriel to be seen by our psychologist, but I assure you that this will take place at the earliest possible opportunity.

Yours sincerely,
CATHERINE W. DAWSON

One year on; noises from above. They are hard at work again, always at work. Sometimes, as today, in one room of the house, shrieking with laughter and tossing her possessions. Or following her from room to room.

Pulling her fawn cardigan about her, Evelyn lumbered over to the calendar. Woolly lambs pranced in a meadow impossibly green, roses bloomed around the door of a thatched cottage. She searched for the month. All the Thursdays were ringed in red; it was a task she had set herself when this last bout of interference with their lives began, over a year ago now. And today was Thursday.

Now for the hallway. She flicked on the light. It seemed empty. As she moved to the foot of the stairs something grazed her sleeve, and she pulled away. Go, go, she thought savagely; I did not invite you here. A bloody handprint stained the cream emulsion, the leprous skull grinned behind glass. Mr Sidney's twisted mouth, in another place. Never again.

She mounted the stairs heavily. Her rheumatism was worse this year, in the raw damp April weather; every day sodden petals from the flowering trees flurried across the window, and thrushes sang in the neglected garden. I am sixty-eight, she thought, I am feeling my age this year.

'Don't you know it's Thursday?' Evelyn said sharply. Muriel raised her head. She nodded. Evelyn appraised her; the lank black hair cut straight across her forehead, the coarse flaking skin, the ungainly legs and large red hands. Whatever they say, she thought, she has not improved. Whatever they say, is rubbish. 'Well, then, we must sort you out some clothes.'

A sign of animation crossed Muriel's face. She got up. Crossing to her chest of drawers, she proffered Evelyn her pink cardigan of fluffy wool. Evelyn nodded without interest. 'If you like.'

Something caught her eye. She plunged her hand into the drawer and delved for the metallic glint. She held it in her palm as if it were contaminated; a tin of furniture polish, half-used, its waxy rag still stuck inside it.

'Did you put it there?'

Muriel's pale grey eyes gazed at her. She showed neither guilt, nor fear, nor surprise. Evelyn believed her. Muriel never did anything of her own volition; Muriel never lied.

'They've been in here, then?' She reached out to grasp Muriel's arm above the elbow, squeezing it hard. She was a strong woman. Her fingers bit into the flesh. Muriel blinked at her. 'Did you see them?' She shook her daughter's arm. 'Tell me what they did.'

Evelyn's pulse raced. Until now they had never been in this room. But now here was the proof of it, the tin taken some weeks ago. It was always the same kind of trick; the spilt sugar, the small thefts, the china they had smashed piece by piece. She let Muriel's arm go and it fell limp at her side.

'I could move you from here. But where would you go? They are always getting into my bedroom.'

Muriel said that there was a third bedroom. Evelyn stared at her. She could feel again her heart hammering and pounding in her throat. The woman had made a shocked face when she had called Muriel an idiot. She, Evelyn, lived with the daily confirmation of her idiocy. Only a hopeless idiot would suggest she took up residence in a room already tenanted; and such tenants. 'Wash yourself,' she commanded her. She went downstairs.

At ten past one she called up to Muriel. Muriel came down. She wore the fluffy pink cardigan and a red skirt. She showed none of the caution Evelyn used when she moved about the house. Sitting on the step next to the bottom, Muriel put out her feet for her shoes to be laced, her legs stiff like a child's in the dentist's chair. There was something almost sly in Muriel's face. But Evelyn never troubled to interpret her expressions; she could speak, if she wished, she could make herself clear.

'If you can make baskets, why can't you tie your shoes?' Evelyn said brutally. Probably, she thought, the reason is that she cannot make baskets; if the other week's example is anything to go by. She took Muriel to the door. She had only to walk fifty yards, along the bushes, around the corner to Lauderdale Road. Let her do that by herself, the Welfare woman had begged; to give her a little sense of independence. She had looked at the woman with contempt. In those days she had been very high-handed with them. She had underestimated their persistence. They had kept coming back. Now she was ready to do anything they said, to make the sacrifice of Muriel, if only it would stop them coming to the house, enquiring into the arrangements she found it necessary to make, the shifts and expedients by which she kept them washed and fed and warm from one day to the next; sniffing around with their implications that life could be improved.

She held the door open to watch Muriel out of the gate. Florence Sidney was passing, a stout, well-set-up woman. She had the house, now that her mother had been taken away to a home. It was Florence Sidney, Evelyn thought, who reported us to the Welfare. As if persons in our class of life needed the Welfare. Miss Sidney turned her bonneted head curiously, and Evelyn drew back and slammed the door. She turned to the house, alone; so often, in the 1940s, she had wished she were alone, and now her wish had come back to mock her, to gibber and tiptoe and hiss.

They had not eaten lunch. That was Muriel's punishment for not speaking when she had been asked about the visitors to her room. Whether something she had seen had terrorised her into silence . . . Evelyn wondered if she had been unjust. It was too late. Still, she would have her tea and biscuits.

On the floor of the hall lay a crumpled piece of paper. Evelyn's gorge rose. Low stinking entities, she said to herself. Once she had been able to smell them, but her senses were becoming blunter with age. Increasingly they were choosing this method of communication, this, their tricks, the sharp raps on the wall from different rooms of the house, warning her off by their noises or luring her by their silence. She stopped. Her face twisted. She tried always to avoid showing that she was in pain. It was agony for her to bend to the floor, they must know this. Evelyn looked around. She took her umbrella from the hallstand, and with it fished for the paper, dragging it from where she could not reach, like the intelligent ape in the experiment. From her feet, she scuttled the paper ball to the first stair, from there to the second. She picked it up and straightened it out. The wavering great letters were familiar by now, fly-track thin: GO NOT TO THE KITCHIN TODAY.

Evelyn's heart sank. Like this, they prolonged her existence. They could take her at any time, kill her (broken neck at the foot of the stairs) or leave her a shell without faculties. But they preferred to watch her fear, her pathetic ruses, her flickering hopes which they would dash within the hour; that was the only explanation. Disconsolate, she entered the front parlour. There, placed precisely in the centre of the circular table, lay a tin-opener.

At once she thought, how provident. It was a matter in which she had been careless. She did not touch it, examined it with her eyes. It did not belong in the house, she had never seen it before. Carefully, she picked it up. It was new, quite new. It was the first time they had left her a gift.

She lowered the flap of the sideboard and took out a tin of baked beans. I must make better arrangements, she thought. The days when they forbade her the kitchen were becoming more frequent, they were driving her increasingly to the front parlour with its hard chairs where she had seen the dead. Perhaps, she thought, a paraffin stove. She opened the tin, and cast around. To hand came the heavy glass ashtray, unused since Clifford died. She emptied the cold tan slime into it and sat eating the beans with her fingers. When she had finished she put down the ashtray and sat resting for a moment. Now where would she go, until it was time for Muriel again? The blue light bounced off polished wood. The air was silent, serene. Evelyn breathed deeply. All their ingenuity had satisfied itself, for the afternoon. Travelling around the room searching the corners, her eye fell on the basket which Muriel had brought home two weeks ago from the Handicapped Class. It was a very ill-made basket, very mis-shapen. Evelyn could not think what use to put it to. Because she was very considerate about Muriel's feelings, she had not discarded it. Now she took it and hobbled out with it to the hall, where she placed it on the table, for display. As an afterthought, she lifted the dead plant in its plastic pot, and placed it inside.

AXON, MURIEL ALEXANDRA
III/73/0059

Client has attended the Calderwell Rd Day Centre once weekly for three months. Whilst we await a comprehensive appraisal, it must be stressed that the ongoing observations of the Day Centre staff have had a great part to play in analysing the client's difficulties, as in applying multifocal measurement tests it is essential to take into account the degree of emotional retardation probably partly induced by her home environment.

Preliminary estimates suggest that the client has an IQ of around 85 on the Stamford-Binet scale, and that therefore her potential and capabilities are somewhat greater than we were led to expect from History III/73/0059. Whilst the need for special facilities may have been indicated at an earlier date, it is suggested that client when in contact with education professionals suffered from a degree of retardation not readily distinguishable from borderline normality, and thus was not brought to the attention of the Social Services; however, due to impoverished environment her emotional condition has worsened and she is now subsisting at a marginal level of social adequacy.

Client has achieved basic literacy, but as she lacks concentration and motivation no occupational adequacy is envisaged for the future. In carrying out simple mechanical tasks, which are well within her capacity, her lack of sustained self-direction is seen. A marked flattening of affect may give rise to the suspicion of a schizoid or sub-schizoid state. Emphasis must be given to social adjustment and interpersonal relations, and inculcation of a maximum degree of self-direction, and efforts must be directed towards helping to attain a satisfactory level of social independence. Subaverage intellectual functioning may be compensated for in this case by sequential development of self-help skills.

M. S. BYRNE, MA
Community Daycare Supervisor

Dear Jacki,

Sorry to bother you on this one but since my transfer has come up so suddenly Norman suggested I dump this one on you, and you do a home visit this week. I should warn you that in my opinion the old woman is completely gaga, but I don't see what we can do.

Cheers,

CATH DAWSON

III/73/0059
Home Visit, 23.9.73.

Explained to Mrs Axon that Miss Dawson had been transferred. Client appears well. Mrs Axon stated that she was dissatisfied with client's progress, but that she had not expected her to make any progress. Explained to Mrs Axon the various activities in which client participates at Community Care Sessions. Enquired why she had not told Miss Dawson that client able to read and write. Mrs Axon stated 'Because it would have been a lie.' Explained to her that client's achievement was on a basic level. Nevertheless this was a very praiseworthy attainment and client should be given every encouragement to use her skills. Asked client if she would show her mother how she could write. Client agreed that she would do this but when supplied with paper she scribbled on it. Mrs Axon stated 'It is plain that you are all fools and fools in charge of fools.'

Introduced the subject of client's longterm care. Mrs Axon expressed the idea that client would be left alone in the house (presumably meaning after she herself was dead). Mrs Axon did not appear to be able to verbalise the idea of her own death. Explained to her that Muriel had been placed on the waiting list for five-day care at the Centre and that in the event of her decease a place would be found for her in a residential institution or hostel. Mrs Axon stated 'Do you mean Holloway?' and when this queried stated 'She has murderous inclinations.' Did not clarify this statement. Asked Mrs Axon about her own physical health and whether she felt able to care for Muriel as of the present time. Mrs Axon stated that her own health was excellent. Suggested that client might be able to do more for herself if encouraged. Surprisingly in view of her previous statement Mrs Axon said that client had always been a good and obedient girl and that she had never been any trouble from her birth. Suggested to Mrs Axon that Muriel was no longer in this position now i.e. no longer a girl. Mrs Axon stated that if Muriel was 'any trouble' she would hold caseworker responsible.

Mrs Axon's attitude on this visit was most unfriendly.

J. S. S.

Dear Sister Janet,

When you come on duty will you try if you can stop Muriel putting her hand in the tea-money again. M. S. Byrne MA says she had a need to do this as in the present state of her she needs to take things not be given as part of her identity, or autonomy, one of those. It isn't her first time thieving so if I were you I'd bring the box at half past three and lock it in the medicine cupboard till you see the back end of her, then she can have her autonomy on Mpoe's shift next week.

Love,
NORAH

Muriel is walking along Lauderdale Road. Muriel is observing Muriel walking along Lauderdale Road. Off the bus; like puppets of wood the people on the bus nod their heads and jerk their arms at her. She understands it to be their ceremony of farewell. Rigidly, as if saluting some dictator, she raises her right arm in imitation. Always she finds the outward forms the best, the safest. The people on the bus seem perfectly satisfied. She smiles to herself.

Off the bus at the junction of Buckingham Avenue and Lauderdale Road. This is the blind side of the house. Along Lauderdale Road to the end; cross the road; turn. Back along the opposite side. Along the road, in at the gate. No purpose in the detour, except that Evelyn will never know. But wait:

There basking in the weak sunshine is the dog known as pedigree wire-haired fox terrier. Between its paws, a big bone licked clean.

23

Muriel stoops. As her fingers creep towards the bone, the dog wakes and leaps to its feet, a growl in its throat. Muriel extends one of her stiff legs and lace-up shoes and kicks the dog in the ribs with all the force she can muster. The dog known as pedigree wire-haired fox terrier flees, yelping. Around the corner. In at the gate.

Evelyn opens the door without speaking. She shuffles towards the back of the house. The living room is safe then, Muriel thinks sardonically. Muriel stares at the dull floor, at the table. I could be that floor, she thinks, that very floor to walk on; things placed upon it. I could be the thing that is placed. The familiar panic begins to rise up inside her. As her fingers close over the bone in her pocket, her heart slows.

That morning Evelyn had shouted questions at her. Evelyn had taken by the arm and shaken the girl known as Muriel Alexandra Axon. Whenever this happens, Muriel creeps out, a midnight flitter; she watches from the other side of the room. Evelyn thinks she knows who she is talking to; she does not know that she is shaking a table or a floor, a dead planet, a pebble on a beach. It is most satisfactory. It shows how little Evelyn knows of the true state of affairs.

Once, some years ago now, Muriel realised that her mother could not read her mind, or not all of it. She tested this. She thought certain thoughts, like: I will kill you. Then many times a day Muriel would think thoughts, rejoicing in the deception. I will trip you down the stairs and break your neck. Mother mother mother. Muriel eat your soup spilling it like that. Clumsy girl. From thoughts, short steps to action. Evelyn did not know that she had walked along Lauderdale Road, that she had a bone in her pocket, or five coins from the tea-money. Unless . . . still, Muriel was not sure how much she knew. This was why, when Evelyn spoke to her, she became like an empty cavern. Muriel Alexandra's body stands irreproachable like a guardsman on parade, while her thoughts slip off to gambol and strut, enjoying their own existence.

GO NOT TO THE KITCHIN TODAY.

Evelyn explains. They go into the front parlour, and drink the cordial with the lukewarm water. Tomorrow, Evelyn thinks, if there is no message, I must remember to fill the jug. Or I could take it upstairs, and fill it in the bathroom.

Muriel remarks that the orange juice is very nice. Evelyn says kindly. 'You are a good girl, you appreciate what is provided for you.'

And again Muriel smiles. The orange juice is revolting; she thinks so. She marvels constantly at how easy it is to deceive. She wants one of the tins of meat; all evening she cherishes her longings and her hunger, the feelings she has that Evelyn does not know about. At eight o'clock Evelyn says, 'We could have a tin of meat.'

Inside, Muriel squirms in pain. Her thought has been read again. Dragged, filleted, out of her living head. But she struggles to keep the smile on her face; and Evelyn thinks she is pleased at the suggestion. Muriel is beginning to feel the victor; she can keep changing the rules, Evelyn cannot win. Unless . . . still, it might be possible that she is Evelyn. That Evelyn is growing inside her. Go, go, she thought savagely: I did not invite you here.

Nine o'clock; Evelyn nods in her chair. She is growing deaf, Muriel thinks, old and deaf. Stealthily she moves out to the hallway. It is not until Friday morning that Evelyn goes through her pockets. First she takes the money, spreading it out on her palm; five, five pieces of money. Then the letter in its brown wrapper. Where? She looks around. Her mouth twists. She puts her hand to it in alarm. That was Evelyn's mouth twisting, Evelyn growing inside her.

In panic she spreads out the money and counts it again; five. And there is the dead plant, all its leaves gone now, nothing but the brown withered stalk, standing in a basket made by a person they have taken to be Muriel Alexandra Axon. Carefully she lifts out the plantpot; folding the letter in half, she places it in the bottom of the basket. (And you be sure you give it to your mother, won't you now, Muriel?) Back goes the plant. She takes the bone. It is still slimy from the jaws of the dog called pedigree wire-haired fox terrier. Outside the door of the front parlour she listens. Only

Evelyn's breathing; she snickers in her nose, her lower jaw droops on to her chest. Muriel enters the kitchen. There is the teapot from this morning, the breakfast toast, all the remains from before Evelyn received her message from the spirits. Muriel picks up the box of matches, selecting carefully the one that will do the job. From the drawer she takes three tea-towels; white and blue check, white and yellow check, sights of Southport. She puts them in the sink to burn them. The first match goes out, and the second. But she has seen a man, when he lights his cigarettes, shielding the flame with his hand. She takes pleasure in the fact that no one will ever know where she learned this trick. In time she can throw the charred debris on the floor, surrounding the bone. And the pedigree wire-haired fox terrier will never complain, she knows that; when she walks along the Avenue again, she will see the resentment locked in its yellow eyes, and the dumb unproductive movements of its jaw.

Evelyn wakes with a start at Muriel's hand on her shoulder. 'Yes, yes,' she mutters, 'it's time we were getting to bed.' She takes up the poker which she always carries with her when she moves about the house after dark. All the lights will be left burning tonight; that is the least discouragement one can give them, she tells Muriel. Muriel mounts the stairs behind her. Muriel's shoulders droop. Her knees stiffen, her hand quivers for support on the banister. At each tread she feels pain, she grimaces, she gasps a little. All her resources for today are played out. She is becoming Evelyn, for the night.

Department of Social Services
Wilberforce House
1st May, 1974

Dear Mr Byrne,

You will be pleased to know that we have persuaded Tarleton's Hardware not to press shoplifting charges against Miss Muriel Axon, regarding the removal of a tin-opener which occurred when a small party of clients was taken on a shopping expedition last week.

Fortunately Mr Tarleton was most reasonable when the situation was explained to him. However we cannot count on meeting this forbearance from shopkeepers on other occasions. I should therefore be obliged if you would request your staff to exercise great vigilance when taking clients out of the Day Centre grounds. This type of incident, if publicised, can have a very unfortunate effect on public relations between the department and the public.

The caseworker involved here tells me it would be unwise to let Miss Axon's mother know of this incident, as she appears to be a woman of exceedingly old-fashioned moral values and her already extremely negative attitude to Miss Axon is compounding our difficulties in this case.

I should also be obliged if you would not mention this to the nursing or other care staff.

Sincerely,

SUZANNE CLEGG
Principal Social Worker

Dear Sister Janet,

This is just to tell you that Muriel got let off the bit of thieving she did when Mpoe took them out the other week to have their autonomy. I know because I heard M. S. Byrne MA bawling Mpoe out for not keeping her eyes open when they came out of the Chocolate Kabin, I think he's had a rocket from Clegg. What the devil do you think she wanted a tin-opener for? Between you and me I wouldn't mind if we could lose Muriel when we get demolished.

Love,
NORAH

And Thursday.

'This day last week some beast was murdered in the kitchen,' Evelyn said. Oh, can they die, Muriel asks. Evelyn tries, without much hope, once more to explain to Muriel. There is more than one set of persecutors. There are the tenants with their constant jibes, their petty destructiveness; it was not (she pats her daughter's arm) a human creature. It is possible to see them, quite possible, but they are very quick. You must learn to look for them out of the corner of your eyes. If people did learn to look out of the corners of their eyes, they would see a great deal that at present they miss; and most of it would be to their disadvantage.

But the other inhabitants, their effect is more – she presses her hand to her ribcage. In the soul, she wants to say, but she wonders if Muriel has a soul; if she had, and they took it away. I fear ... her seamed face works a little in distress at her thoughts. She makes a gesture like someone erasing the writing on a blackboard; after which, the board itself remains.

She looks different, Muriel notices, more harassed, more starting and looking in corners. Since last Friday's discoveries.

She is fumbling in her purse now. She lays out certain coins on the kitchen table.

'For your tea and biscuits,' she says.

Muriel lets them lie for a time. She practises fixing her eyes on Evelyn but looking straight through her to the wood of the cupboard at her back. She practises wiping all thoughts out of her mind. At the same time she must watch Evelyn, to see that she is still mumbling over her own concerns, not looking up with the comprehension she dreads. Finally, when Muriel can bear the suspense no longer, she snatches up the coins and holds them in her hands. Evelyn lays out more on the table. 'For the milk-money. Tomorrow.' Evelyn shuffles out of the kitchen, but in a moment she is back. 'My envelopes,' she says, her voice querulous. 'My white envelopes for putting in the milkbottles. They have torn them all.' She opens the kitchen drawer where she keeps her ration books and ends of string, her paper bags and cotton reels and farthings.

'Lock and key,' she says. 'I shall have to buy more and keep them under lock and key.'

She tears the corner of a paper bag and puts the money into it. She folds the remainder of the bag and puts it back in the drawer. Once again tomorrow he will take the money and go away, without having to knock at the door; when the price goes up he will put a note through the letterbox. They have teased her so often with their rappings that she tries not to go to the door for any unnecessary reason; tries not to set the precedent of being in a certain place at a certain time, in case they set traps. Suddenly vindictive, she turns to Muriel: 'I think of stopping you going to these Handicapped Classes. What good does it do? I think of stopping you.' In a monotone, Muriel begins to repeat her words. 'Stop it, stop it,' Evelyn screams at her. There is terror in the girl's face. Evelyn waddles from the room.

And once more: the match rasps against the box, the flame wavers up; Muriel watches her flesh shrinking away from the heat, and feels pain. She allows the flame to play over her wrist until it burns out in her fingers. Feels, feels. Taking the scissors, uses the point to draw blood. Again, feels.

'If you're going, if you're going at all, it's time you got ready. Are you listening to me?'

Muriel sits with her arms clamped down to her sides, willing her mother to turn. The blisters are forming now on her raw skin, the blood has dried. Evelyn shows no signs of recent pain.

'Here.' Evelyn goes to the chest of drawers and impatiently wrenches one open, tossing a cardigan and a pair of thick woollen stockings on to the bed. Her water-eyes darting, Muriel sees that Evelyn's forearms are unmarked. So however it came about that her thoughts were read again (as good as read), even if half an hour ago Evelyn was thinking in her brain, she has not been in all parts of her today. Still, unless . . . unless the marks will show up later. Evelyn turns, and sees only her daughter's shuttered face with its habitually blank gaze. She begins again to grumble about the trouble it gives her, getting Muriel ready for the class and setting her going. Only the thought of the Welfare people coming to the house stops her from keeping Muriel at home. 'What do you want to go there for anyway? Going on a bus with a lot of other people with things wrong with them, cripples and people not right in the head. One day they'll put them on that bus and take them and gas them, and then you'll wish you'd stayed at home with your mother.' She knows

Muriel is not listening to her. She is looking sceptically at the clothes on the bed. She goes to her drawers and hunts through for the pink fluffy cardigan.

'Grey with dirt,' Evelyn says contemptuously. 'If you won't give it me to wash I won't let you wear it again after this week. They will suppose I don't see to your cleanliness.'

She gapes. Her jaw unhinges and her eyes grow round. Muriel is not in any doubt now. Evelyn has not been in her body today, not even very much in her brain. She is completely surprised, Muriel thinks. To be helpful, always to be helpful, she holds up her arms for Evelyn's inspection. A low moan comes from Evelyn.

'They have been torturing you,' she says. 'They have been here in your room, torturing you.' Moaning again, she washes her arthritic hands together. Could you not cry out? You have gagged me, Muriel thinks. Up the stairs you would have come, rushing to take my pain for yourself. With what? Sharp blades and fire, Muriel says, in her casually dead voice. Now Evelyn is smashing her way out of the room and along the landing, quite heedless of the usual mockery as she passes the door of the spare room, and Muriel can hear her retching behind the closed bathroom door. Putting her hand to her belly, Muriel feels a little wash of the sickness to come.

Now Lauderdale Road, homecoming. Screened by the high bushes, Muriel takes out her coins to count them. Some of them have gone. Spent, she thinks dully, expended. What are these heads, she wonders, whose are these heads upon them? She slips a hand in her pocket and takes out the little looking-glass that she picked up from where it was lying on a counter in a shop. She presses the sides of her skull, to keep in her memory the places she has seen.

Evelyn drives questions into her like hooks. Did they see, did they remark upon your arms, what people were there, were there baskets made at that place, was there singing of songs, of what type and number, kind and shape, were the biscuits you ate? Of the tea, was it pale or brown, is there sugar in that tea, do they give you the sugar as you are accustomed, in lumps or spoons from basins, and do they place it there for you or do you yourself take what you suppose you need? Of the singing: is there piano or other instrument to accompany it? She knows nothing, Muriel thinks with contempt. She makes her face frozen up.

'Oh, you are stonewalling again,' Evelyn says furiously. That night when she enters her room she will find it almost festal, the pieces of the torn envelopes littering the carpet and sibilating in the draughts, like confetti.

Department of Social Services
Wilberforce House
3rd May 1974

Dear Mrs Axon,

This is to advise you that the Daycare Sessions attended by Miss Axon will be temporarily suspended for a short period only, due to the demolition of the premises in Calderwell Road, from the Thursday after next. However our sessions are to be resumed at a much better equipped centre at The Hollies, Vernon Road, and you will be advised presently of the new arrangements for transport and etc. If you have any enquiries please contact Miss J. Smith at the address above or telephone.

Yours sincerely,

M. CARTWRIGHT
Social Work Assistant
p.p. *Director of Social Services*

If they had not been pushing her about that morning, if they had not been trying to do her bodily injury, she would not have smashed the plantpot or found the letter underneath, in the bottom of the basket.

This is old, she said to herself. It has been here for some time. This was May, it is now late June, therefore certainly there have been Thursdays when . . . there was time unaccounted for. Yet time in the house was moving now at its own speed, in fits and starts. Food decayed on the plates, insects bred in the dark. The place was more and more crowded. Useless to try to talk to Muriel, to ask her for some account of the letter. Muriel rarely spoke now; it was like going back to her childhood. More and more, when Evelyn was in a room with her daughter, she felt as if no one was there.

Department of Social Services
Wilberforce House
3rd July 1974

Dear Mrs Axon,

   Mrs J. Smith visited your home on behalf of the Department last Friday, but was unable to gain admittance. The reason for her visit was to ascertain whether Miss Axon had been informed of the new arrangements for attendance at The Hollies, since she has not been present at Daycare Sessions since they resumed. If Miss Axon is ill, perhaps you would be kind enough to notify us, and let us know when she will resume attendance. If you have any problems, please don't hesitate to contact us.

   Jacqueline Smith is now on maternity leave, and I shall be dealing with Miss Axon's case in future.

                              Yours sincerely,

                                             CAROL TAFT

At first, Evelyn had said, 'Perhaps you need not go to this new place. They won't want you. They are always saying there is pressure on their faculties.' She was afraid that they would call, and when the knocking did come, at an unaccustomed time of day, she had taken Muriel into the back room and made her sit quietly until the caller had gone away. That morning she had not felt like seeing anyone, combating them, dealing with anyone at all. It had been enough of a shock to find that morning's trail of messages. First the little mirror that she had never seen before lying on the hall table, a tawdry affair of pink plastic, and the twist of papers round it with the insect capitals: LOOK AT YOUR FASE.

   Then she had hunted them through the house: THERE ARE MANY PEOPLE IN THIS PLASE and YOU ARE PUTING IN MY PLASE and SHE

SHALL BE PUT IN HER PLASE and, last of all, ANOTHER IS IN HER PLASE.

The day she received the second letter from the Welfare had been much calmer. There had been no messages lately, no buffetings on the landing and stairs, no thefts of her property. It had been Muriel's problem that was uppermost in her mind; or Muriel's condition rather. She strove to keep it in perspective. The invention and ingenuity of the parallel world had amazed her in recent months, its many and new manifestations, the closeness of its stinking breath on her neck. Periods of calm followed by new alarms, the torturing of Muriel, the closing off to both of them, permanently now, of certain parts of the house. In the circumstances, Muriel's pregnancy could only be felt as a lesser shock.

'Both mad, if you ask me,' Florence Sidney was saying. 'You might as well try to fly through the window as help either of them.'

She was standing by the window, which had perhaps helped to indicate the improbability to her mind; she was looking out at her nephew and her nieces, playing among the windfalls in the disarrayed late summer garden. 'I haven't seen Muriel for – ' She turned her head. It was painfully evident that her sister-in-law was not listening to her. Sylvia was launched on a series of questions.

'And may I ask what you intend to do with yourself now?'

'Do now? Well.' The questions seemed to make no sense. What does anyone do now?

'With your life. With the rest of your life. That's what I'm talking about, Florence.'

'Well, I'll do the same as everybody,' Florence said. Limp on, eyes front, towards the grave.

'I mean, it's no kind of life, is it? For anybody?'

'What had you in mind?'

'You want to put the past behind you. Get out and live a bit. You want to join some Societies. Get yourself a new girdle.'

Florence didn't speak. She came away from the window; she

never admitted it, but the antics and the shrieking of the children got on her nerves.

'The trouble with you is that you don't make the best of yourself,' Sylvia said. 'I'm not running you down, I'm only telling you out of the kindness of my heart. You're no beauty queen, but you could do yourself up.'

'What for?' Florence sat down by the tea-trolley.

'For the fellers,' Sylvia said conspiratorially.

'I don't know any fellows.'

'Well, and you never will, will you, if you keep mouldering in the house? What's stopping you now? Your mother's been put away, you don't have to stop in and mind her any more.'

'I wish you would not use that expression,' Florence said. Any of those expressions really; redolent of your time at the cooked meats factory. Sylvia laughed; she patted her hair, puffed out and lacquered in a style that had passed its apogee some years before. It was impossible to imagine her without this hairstyle; like a helmet, it covered her weakest point, the head. She was, Florence thought, a strange blend of savage self-assertion and abject dependence; pathetic and ferocious by turns. Florence knew so little of the married women of her generation that she imagined Sylvia to be unusual.

'It is a home for the elderly,' Florence said. 'A sanctuary for the twilight years.'

'Get away,' Sylvia said. 'Your mother's off her rocker. Colin doesn't keep any secrets from me.'

'Really?' Florence said. 'By the nature of a secret, you would not know if he did.'

'You've room to talk, about the folks round the corner.'

'It wasn't idle gossip. I haven't seen them for some time. They are old neighbours, though they are not people whom we have known. I am concerned.'

Sylvia yawned, leaning back and allowing her fingers a token flutter before her mouth.

'You want to be concerned with yourself. I'm telling you. Smarten

34

yourself up and get out a bit. The trouble with this family, it's too introvert.'

'Oh, is that Colin's trouble?', Florence asked.

'Well, he *was* introvert.'

'But you remedied it.'

'What kind of a life is that?' Sylvia asked. 'I had other offers. I could have got married four times over.'

'That might have been unwise,' Florence said gently. 'You know, you've changed, Sylvia. You will have your opinions now. I remember when Colin first brought you home.'

Sylvia blushed furiously. So she remembers too, Florence thought. Father had been alive, of course, quite hale and hearty. Mrs Sidney wore a new Crimplene suit in powder blue with bracelet-length sleeves. She herself put on a beige jersey wool. There were fruit scones and a Victoria sandwich. Mother's gimlet eyes spotted a traycloth insufficiently starched, and (although often they were not starched at all) she whisked it off. As she waited to meet the girl her son intended to marry, one pointed finger rubbed and rubbed at a spot on the wooden arm of her chair. It had been summer, a day very like this. Sylvia's substantial black brassiere had shown clearly under her short cotton frock, and she had emitted great guffaws of nervous laughter whenever she was addressed. Father had been exquisitely civil. Colin had not known where to look. Florence and her mother had agreed later that, seeing her in the setting he was used to, Colin would be sure to see that he was making a mistake. But he hadn't.

'I let your blasted mother put on me,' Sylvia said. 'I'd know better now.' From upstairs came the sound of the lavatory flushing.

'Unfortunately it isn't given to any of us to have our opportunities over again. Or what would you do if you could? Perhaps since you are now so dissatisfied with your life, you ought to have looked the other way when you saw Colin on the tram.'

'I can assure you,' Sylvia said, 'that I didn't meet Colin on any tram.'

'It would be nothing to be ashamed of if you had.'

'I assure you.'

'She couldn't have,' said Colin, coming in. 'It's not possible.'

'I understood you met on a tram. I'm not saying anything against it.'

'Couldn't have been on a tram,' Colin said. 'I'm not saying we wouldn't have been on a tram, either Sylvia or myself, but I happen to recall that the trams had stopped running some years previously. It was on the railway station that we met.'

'I knew public transport was involved somewhere,' Florence said.

'And what have you got against it?'

Florence smiled faintly. 'Nothing.'

'Only I was going to say, your father made his living out of it, didn't he, people falling off buses.'

'Yes, my love,' Colin said. 'We are all staunch supporters of public transport in this house. Perhaps that's why you caught my eye. You so clearly approved of it too.'

'You were a while,' Sylvia observed, 'in the toilet.'

'Allow me a few moments' privacy,' Colin said. 'Confine your interest to the children's bowel movements, not mine.'

'The topic of romance on trams has worn thin,' Florence said. 'I see that we must have something else. Sylvia sees it too.'

Defiantly, Colin took out a cigarette and lit it. Love is blind, Florence thought: for a year or two.

'Unhygienic habit,' Sylvia said. 'I gave it up when I was pregnant with Suzanne. I read it in a magazine. Smoking and Pregnancy.'

'Sylvia takes magazines devoted to housewifery,' Florence said. 'Does she have recipes making use of frozen chicken which are both tasty and economical?'

'I know what you eat,' Sylvia said. 'Bread and jam.'

'In its place,' Florence murmured.

'Tea,' said Colin.

'I know. And tomato sandwiches. I don't think Colin had ever had a proper meal in his life until we got married.' She got up. 'We'll be off, Florence.' She went out through the kitchen to the back door. 'Come on, you lot, we're off.'

An argument ensued. Florence could hear the protests of the

children overridden by Sylvia's firm flat voice. It made her nervous. If they wanted to stay, it probably meant that they were engaged in some form of covert vandalism. 'The roses,' she said nervously.

'Roses.' Colin put his head in his hands. 'You ought to get some cabbages in. The cost of living being what it is.'

'Oh, I couldn't. They were Father's roses.'

'Grub them up,' Colin said. 'That's it. Grub them up.' He groaned quietly, then stood up, stretching himself. He was a man on poor terms with his clothes – his shirt always coming out of his waistband, his trousers shooting up around his calves as he sat; it was difficult not to see this as a symptom of a more general failure of control. He had once been remarkably good-looking, but now his looks had faded, as if his features were doubtful of their application in his current circumstances. His habitual expression was one of anxious astonishment, like that of a man who has been stopped in the street by a policeman and finds he has forgotten his name. 'Where's my pullover?' he said, looking about. He hauled it over his head and smoothed his thinning fair hair.

'You're ageing, Colin,' Florence said in a low voice.

'Ah well. At my back I always hear time's wingèd chariot etc. It's been ten years you know, me and Sylvia. I should have thought the amusement would have palled. You hurt her, you know. She cries. She isn't entirely the jolly factory lass you take her to be.'

'Come on, Colin.' Sylvia was standing in the doorway holding the hands of her two younger children. 'Thank you very much, Florence. Say thank you to your Auntie for the nice tea.'

Freeing their hands, pushing past Florence, the children whooped out to the car. Sylvia followed them.

'I wanted your opinion,' Florence said. 'About Mrs Axon and her daughter.'

'I have no opinion,' Colin said. 'Mrs Axon has lived around the corner for as long as I can remember without having done anything to warrant my having an opinon on her.' His shirt had come out again; he was stuffing it back, hauling at his belt. 'You know, Florence, Sylvia's quite right. You've got to make a life of your own.'

Outside, Sylvia wound the car window down. 'Colin, are you coming?'

'Anon, good Sylvia, anon. You see, the problem is, you were geared up to years of self-sacrifice, looking after Mother. Now all that's aborted . . . well, you know what I mean. Eh, old girl? Pop over next Sunday.' A peck on the cheek. She stood in the porch watching Sylvia wind the window up again. There was something incongruously patrician about Sylvia's averted profile, her mouth was set, her chin sagging. Colin hunched himself into the driver's seat.

'It's a flaming bloodsport,' Sylvia said.

'Sorry, love,' On a sudden whim Colin transferred his hand from the knob of the gearstick to her knee. He patted it. 'You mustn't let her get you down. She's lonely, you know.'

Sylvia sniffed. 'Come on, let's get home.'

Colin steered along Buckingham Avenue with his usual caution. The little saloon forced him to drive with his arms stiffly extended, as if he were fending off the week ahead.

'You were getting at me,' she said.

'Well, just a bit.'

'Florence sets you off.'

'I said I'm sorry. Can we have a bit of peace? I said,' he raised his voice for the children in the back, 'can we have a bit of peace?'

The most difficult thing was not knowing: how many months. Evelyn took down the calendar and pored over it. You could not be positive that the missing Thursdays were implicated. That would be a jump altogether too far ahead.

'Do you want to go to the doctor?' she said. 'It would cost.'

Muriel said that it was free now.

'Free? Nothing's free. What sort of stupid talk is that?'

She didn't know what was going on in the world, Muriel said craftily. Craftily, because it was Muriel's scheme to have her inadequacy prick her, so that she would buy a television set. Evelyn wouldn't have one in the house, not while she was alive; and after her death she expected to exercise some sway. After all, they hadn't missed the radio when it had broken down, and they didn't feel the lack of newspapers. Soon after the last war Muriel had been sent with the month's money to the newsagent's. It had been wrapped up in a piece of paper, and she had lost it. Evelyn couldn't see her way to finding the money twice over. So the shop had stopped delivering. Evelyn had never read them anyway. All the news was the same, and all bogus. The papers took no cognizance of the other world, except when they found some cheap talk of poltergeists or table-turning to fill the pages up.

'And where do you go?' she demanded of Muriel. 'Where do you go, that you know so much?'

Muriel didn't answer that question. Either Evelyn knew where she had been, and was mocking her, or she did not; in which case, her powers were on the wane, the long battle was drawing to an end. They tell you what's free at the Class, Muriel said. They tell you what you can get for nothing.

It was strongly in Evelyn's mind now that it must be someone from the class who was the father of Muriel's child. But it was no use bothering Muriel about it, no use trying to get anything out of her. It did cross her mind that something malign in the house might be responsible for the girl's condition; but she had to admit that in her extensive experience she had not heard of such a thing. There were unnatural unions, but did they come to fruition? Muriel looked as if she would come to fruition, quite soon. No, surely her first thought was right. The lax Welfare had turned their backs. Some half-wit had prevailed on a quarter-wit. Only one thing she would have liked to find out; was he in some way deformed?

Social Services Department
Luther King House
Tel: 51212 Ext. 27
10th October 1974

Dear Mrs Axon,
    I must apologise for the delay in contacting you, but Miss Axon's

file was mislaid when the Department moved to new offices recently, and has only just come to hand.

As Miss Axon has not attended our Daycare Sessions since the move to The Hollies, we are anxious to know whether any difficulty has arisen. Miss Taft of this Department wrote to you on July 3rd, but you may perhaps have overlooked this letter. If it is convenient for you, I will call at your home on October 15th at about 3 pm, and I will hope to see Miss Axon then and have a chat with her. If this date is not convenient perhaps you would kindly telephone me at the number above.

Miss Taft is now attending a course, and as she will be away for six months Miss Axon's case has been handed over to me. I hope to be able to help you with any problems that arise.

Yours sincerely,
ISABEL FIELD

CHAPTER 2

'Isabel,' Colin said. 'Isabel.'

'Don't slobber, Colin.'

'You are unkind.'

'Oh?'

'You are vastly too good, Isabel. You make it plain.'

'Yes.' Isabel wound down the window of the car. A dank semi-rural darkness entered. She lit a cigarette.

'Colin, why do you always lock the doors?'

Heaving and sighing.

'The car doors, Colin, why do you insist on locking your passengers in? Oh, come on, Colin. A bit of coherent conversation.'

'The A6 murder,' Colin said.

'What?'

'This. Murder. Similar. Circumstances. Night, a field, or a tract of, I don't remember, some open ground, I suppose, by the side of the road. Hanratty. Before your time.'

'Oh, Colin.' She put out a narrow cold hand to find his face. 'Colin, you are a worrier.'

'Personally, I think the conviction was unjust,' Colin said. 'I'm against capital punishment. The truth is, Isabel, now forgive me, it's rather maudlin I know, but the truth is Isabel, I'm against death. Death in any form.'

She sighed, in the damp darkness of the passenger seat.

'Sylvia,' he said. 'Sylvia is forbidding me eggs. My arteries. She read these things. Aagh.' He let out a long breath, releasing his tie further with one hand. He heaved across to her, wet and sweating. 'Do you know, sometimes I feel very much like suicide. But I had a good idea the other week. I thought I would buy myself a record of the Marches of Souza. And if I felt really tempted to suicide, I would play it. You wouldn't kill yourself after that – after you'd marched about a bit. It would be too ridiculous. Isabel, Isabel.' He pressed his face into her neck. It was a source of constant amazement to him that she did not pull away; not every time.

This is October. Isabel is just a name on a letter, received by someone else.

This is Colin off to his evening class. Sylvia is clattering the dishes together in the sink, slamming them with dangerous force on to the stainless-steel draining board. It is clear that she thinks Creative Writing a waste of time. Early evening bouts of violence echo from the lounge; the air hangs heavy and blue with gunsmoke, the children squat before the TV set, their mouths ajar.

'You see nothing of them,' Sylvia says. (This conversation has been held before.)

Colin reverses himself and strides back into the room, swerving to avoid cracking his shins on the coffee table. Blocking the TV he treads the carpet before his offspring like a Lippizan stallion; but not very like.

'They,' he reports, 'see nothing of me.'

'What?'

'I wafted in there and stood in front of the television. They didn't address me by name. They saw me merely as an obstruction to their view.'

'Waft?' Sylvia says. 'You couldn't waft. Never in a million years could you waft.'

'They're in a state of advanced hypnosis. Deep Trance. Tell me,' he says, 'why couldn't I have gifted children? It would have been an interest for me. Why can't they all be little Mozarts?'

'We haven't got a piano,' Sylvia says.

'I'm away.' Going out, Colin stuffs his notebook into his pocket.

In the hall mirror he glimpses his own face, weakly handsome, frowning, abstracted. He loosens the knot of his tie. Despite what Florence said about him aging, he looks years younger than his wife. He tries the effect of a boyish lopsided grin. It reminds him of something; his father's hemiplegia perhaps. He erases it from his face and departs, banging the door behind him.

There were some eighteen people in the classroom, rather more female than male, rather more old than young. Teacher was rubbing the leftover algebra off the board, a plump lady in a cardigan, and chalking up the words WRITING FOR PLEASURE AND PROFIT. Excuse me, said Colin, stumbling through the desks and finding himself a seat to overflow. He looked around for Zelda Fitzgerald. She wasn't there.

'Perhaps if we all introduced ourselves,' Mrs Wells said. 'Perhaps if we all say a few words about the sort of writing we want to do. How we see ourselves.'

How we see ourselves, Colin thought in querulous alarm, how we see ourselves? I am a history teacher, a teacher of the benighted past to the benighted present, ill-recompensed for what I suffer and despairing of promotion. My feet are size eight and a half, and I belong to the generation of Angry Young Men, though I was never angry until it was too late, oh, very late, and even now I am only mildly irritated. I am not a vegetarian and contribute to no charities, on principle; I loathe beetroot, and the sexual revolution has passed me by. My taste in clothes is conservative but I get holes in my pockets and my small change falls through; I do not speak to my wife about this because she is an excellent mother and I am intimidated by her, also appalled by the paltry nature of this complaint or what might be construed by her as a complaint. The sort of writing I want to do is the sort that will force me to become a tax-exile.

He looked across the room and saw a woman, directly opposite him in the semi-circle into which they had lumbered the desks. He wondered why he had not looked up before. Habit, he told himself. Habit ends here.

'My name is Isabel Field,' she said. 'No, I have never tried to sell any work. I am not interested in writing commercially, I am interested in increasing my clarity of expression. I am a social worker.'

You are twenty-four or twenty-five, Colin thought, self-contained, reserved, sardonic. What struck him was that she had not hesitated; when she closed her mouth you knew she was not going to open it again until a fresh topic was raised. Her voice was accentless, or almost so. She had the fractured face of a Modigliani, clever yet obtuse; the long darting almond eyes and long supple neck. Her neat competent legs crossed when she sat down, crossed at the ankle and tucked under her chair. Her hands were long and lean, strong and beautiful, like the hands of the Lady with an Ermine.

The lady next to her said she was Mrs Higginbottom, would they please call her Sheila, and that she wanted to write for womens' magazines. Now that is a difficult market, said Mrs Wells with extreme vigour, a very difficult market indeed. The *Readers Digest*, a man said, those anecdotes, you know, page-fillers, Humour in Uniform, I could do a lot of those, because a lot of funny things happened to me while I was in the army. Mrs Wells seemed enthused. He was a man whose ears stuck out. Colin looked back at Isabel Field. He felt suddenly like a refugee, the past a memory of blazing ruins; the future, the long grey road and transit camp of the displaced heart.

Unanchored, Evelyn's mind moves backwards and forwards over the years. In the 1950s Muriel inhabited her body as though it were a machine. She had a powerful urge to bite, to tear with her teeth. For this reason, she kept her mouth covered with her hand, and swallowed her food without chewing. Reasoning that her teeth were seldom used, Evelyn did not try to take her to the dentist.

The first years were spent in cleaning Muriel, in reconciling herself to her existence. Evelyn wanted to be alone in the house; the house filled up, more than she had dreaded. After some time, Muriel began to appear sufficiently normal to be sent to school, but Evelyn was well aware that she was concealing her true nature. She spoke now more like other people, though she was still both clipped and sententious. At first she had said, 'Mother, Mother,' and Evelyn thought it was 'Murder' she had called out in the dark.

1950: a neighbour buys Muriel a jigsaw puzzle for Christmas, and she works it without fumbling on the parlour floor, blank side up. 1960: Muriel flings back at her statements once heard, a song from the radio, taunting her with the empty echo of her own speech. At the same time, the spare room becomes tenanted; the same mockery greets her on the stairs. Muriel has a passion for giving objects the wrong name, even when she knows the right one; it is a technique of bafflement she is practising. She glances only surreptitiously around her, moving her eyes, never her head; she can see, for self-preservation she must see, but she is not sure that she is supposed to look. Once she watched in wonder Evelyn's ritual with the milk-money. Now she has learned that coins pay for desires. She wonders about the changing face of the clock. Is it related to the lines on her mother's face, her increasing deafness and feebleness, the accumulation of dust upon their lives? Is it possible that every year is not the same, not just the same? Hurry, hurry, Evelyn always says: or you will not be on time . . . Yesterday, she says, today, tomorrow. Without causality there is no time, and there is no causality in Muriel's head. Evelyn's speech is just a noise, like the clatter of dustbin lids or the crack of bone, the incessant drip of the guttering. Events have no order, no structure, no purpose. Things happen because they must, because they can. Each moment belongs in infinity, each infinity cherishes its neighbour like turtle-doves on a bough. Muriel's heart is a mathematical place, a singularity from which, in time, everything will issue.

Mrs Wells had a flute-like voice; it would have been suitable for opening Parliament, and it seemed a pity that she would never get the opportunity.

'Rejection after rejection,' she was saying, 'until finally – '; and she would go on to read her class the story of the wealth and acclaim that had come to some struggling author overnight. But they were not much encouraged, for it was always some American of whom they had never heard, with a wildly improbable name. Colin had long ago ceased listening. Classrooms do not smell like classrooms any more, he thought, where is the scent of dried ink and bullying, where is my childhood?

'I also write fairy stories,' said the man whose ears stuck out. Mrs Wells stared at him glassily, at a loss.

And Autumn does not smell like Autumn, Colin thought; where is the woodsmoke and the russet apples packed in barrels, and what are russet apples anyway, a breed or only a colour? Where are the swallows twittering on the wires? What will the swallows do when we all communicate by telepathy? I have only seen one, this year, and it did not make a summer.

I will never be a writer, he thought, I will never learn it, just as last year I did not learn Russian, I will never do it, my mind runs to clichés like abandoned plots to seed.

'You have to give people what they recognise and understand,' Mrs Wells was saying sweetly.

Autumn is only the wet lamplight on the black wet road, soup out of Sylvia's packets, a splutter and a cough from the car engine at eight in the morning; kids whining and defaulting dragged by their scruffs from September through to Advent, transistor blah-blah, only two thousand shopping days to Christmas, blah-blah, God rest you merry, gentlemen, let nothing you dismay.

'Mushrooms,' said Mrs Moffat with pride. 'I have sent an article to *The Edible World* on the cultivation of mushrooms.'

My vegetable love will grow, thought Colin, vaster than Empires and more slow.

'Do read it to us,' Mrs Wells shrilled. 'Could you, would you, read it to us, and we might help you with helpful hints. But first we must have our little assignment, shall we? 'An Interesting Experience.' Mr Sidney?'

Colin grinned. 'I'm sorry, I haven't done my homework.'

'Oh, now, that's a pity, Mr Sidney.'

Her tone was light; if there was genuine grief, she kept it out of her voice. It is commendable, he thought, her restraint. A bare branch tapped and tapped against the window, dice in the evening's pot.

'I couldn't think of anything to write about.'

Mrs Wells was shocked into reproach. 'But Mr Sidney, there's *always* something to write about. That's the *whole point*.'

'I didn't think any of my experiences were interesting.'

'But there's a book in each of us, Mr Sidney.'

'Is there?' said Colin, engaged by this. 'I wonder if people would like to tell us what book there is in them? I should like mine to be *Les Liaisons Dangereuses* or *The Brothers Karamazov*, but more likely it is something like *Famous Five Join the Circus*.'

'I should like mine to be *Mansfield Park*,' said Isabel, without a smile.

'Now, Mr Sidney,' Mrs Wells said, 'you know I meant a book of our own, of our very own. We may think that we lead very ordinary lives, but believe me, it's this very ordinariness that is the stuff of great books of all time. Look at *Jane Eyre*.'

'I wouldn't call that ordinary,' Colin said. 'Having this madwoman up in the attic, biting people.'

'Stabbing,' Isabel said.

'Stabbing, biting . . . though come to think of it, it happens all the time in the classes I teach.'

'Well, there you are then,' Mrs Wells said. 'Miss Field, have you got an interesting experience?'

Colin turned in his chair, all attention. The Duke of Norfolk, he thought; not altogether inconsequentially, because it was the name of the pub to which he hoped to take Isabel Field.

The lounge of the public house was heaving with wet raincoats, smelling of damp fake-furs and warming plastic. Electric coals twinkled merrily; above the bar, coloured Christmas lights winked around the calendar, and a notice informed the public that spirits are served in measures of one-sixth of a gill. Colin read it avidly, and the notice which said he didn't have to be mad to work here but it helped. It was half-past nine, filling up. Colin manoeuvred for a corner table, and read the beermat as he pulled out Isabel's chair, thinking, nobody pulls out chairs in a pub, what do you think it is, the bloody Dorchester? He was very anxious about the impression he was making.

'It's the nearest,' he said apologetically, 'and it's quite nice really, you never get any rowdy people.'

'No horse-brasses. Good.'

'Plastic beams are my *bête noire*. What will you have to drink?'

She hesitated. 'Gin.'

'Righto.'

Colin began to push his way to the bar. Singularly failing, as always, to catch the barmaid's eye, he took time to look back at Isabel. Her eyes were cast down; perhaps she also read beermats. Her fingers were interlaced on the table in front of her in a formal pose, as if she were about to deliver a public statement. Patience on a monument, smiling at grief, Colin thought. This terrible habit of inappropriate quotation. How do you know she has a grief, perhaps she is just waiting for her drink, perhaps she doesn't like to stare around her. Absolutely the worst you can do, he thought, is to fail. Isolated in his gaze, she gave the effect of a study, monochrome, perhaps the unnoticed frame on the back wall of an exhibition, or one of those grainy smudged photographs of Russian streets, a woman looking indistinctly for a moment into the lens of a strange culture. Her clothes were always beige or charcoal or grey, or a peculiarly soft dead green which he had never seen on anyone else. But then he had never looked.

He set the glass down in front of her, gin and orange.

'Oh, no, no,' she said quickly, 'this wasn't what I meant.'

Colin's face creased with concern. 'I'm sorry, was it gin and tonic you wanted, you didn't – '

He began to get heavily to his feet. She arrested him with a quick flicking motion of her hand.

'This will be fine.' She picked up the glass and looked down into it, as if it contained a rare fish. 'I've never had one of these before,' she said.

She sipped the drink very quickly. She's nervous, he thought, not as collected as she likes to appear, she's a highly-strung young woman.

48

'You have to ask for what you want,' he said gently, as if instructing a child.

She smiled. 'Yes, I know.'

There was a pause.

'Sylvia always – Sylvia is my wife.'

'I didn't think you were married.'

'No? I don't look married?'

'You look unkempt.'

'She tries,' Colin said dismally. 'I'm just an untidy person. I'm sorry. I don't know why I brought my wife into the conversation.'

'There was no conversation for you to bring her into,' Isabel said. 'There seems to be one now.'

'I suppose now that – well, you won't want to . . . '

'What?'

'Have a drink.'

'Because you are married?'

'Yes.'

'Drinking gin is not really the same as committing adultery. Though I daresay it sometimes precedes it. I don't know. I have no experience.' She took a sip from her glass, her eyes fixed on his face. 'Would she mind?'

'I don't know,' Colin said. He honestly did not. He wracked his brains, but could get no further. It must be very remote from Sylvia's reckoning, that anyone would agree to have a drink with him. He wanted to say, why are you here, I am not good-looking, I have nothing you could possibly want.

'There's Mr Cartwright,' Isabel said. 'His ears stick out, don't they? I hope they're not all going to come in here. Mr Cartwright writes fairy stories.'

'What? Oh, yes,' Colin said. 'I thought he wrote Humour in Uniform.'

'And fairy stories. Didn't you listen?'

'No, I never listen.'

'He showed me one last week. I suppose he thought I might be sympathetic.'

Colin looked at her appraisingly. He would not have thought so, himself.

'Do you find it, you know, valuable, this class?' he asked her.

'No.'

'You don't?'

'It's not much our sort of thing, is it?'

Then she did see, she did feel, that there was some bond between them; Colin put the back of his hand to his forehead, as if he expected to find it warm. 'Then why do you come?' he said.

'I don't know. Why do you?'

'To get away from Sylvia.' He hunched forward. It had taken such a long time to grasp, such a short time to say. 'Last year I took Italian conversation and car maintenance and Poets of the First World War.'

'Ah, yes,' Isabel said.

'You see some connection?'

'No.'

'You sounded as if you saw some connection. As if it were significant.'

'There is no connection. That is what is significant.'

'I am a schoolteacher,' Colin said.

'Ah, then the general information is of use to you.'

'No, not really.' He felt defeated. 'I just do it, as I say, I want to get away from my wife.'

'What's wrong with her?'

'Nothing. She's a nice woman.'

'How many children have you got?'

'Three. Suzanne, she's eight, Alistair's nearly six, Karen's three.'

'Are you going to have any more?'

'Not if I can help it.'

'I was watching you,' she said. 'In the classroom. Trying to analyse you. You seem so discontented.'

'Do you like analysing people?'

'It passes the time.'

'Is that a main concern of yours?'

'Well, not really,' she said. 'It passes itself, without our assistance. It has the knack.'

'I'm in love with you,' Colin said.

'That's not true.'

'Yes, yes,' he insisted. 'Absolutely true. Do you believe in love at first sight?'

'That's academic,' Isabel said. 'This is not first sight.'

'But I have been in love with you, since the first week. Tell me, do you believe in it?'

'I don't think I believe in love at any sight,' she said grimly.

Colin's face fell. 'That's a terrible shame. A terrible admission. For a young woman.' He took thought. 'Another gin?'

'Please.'

'With tonic?'

'With tonic.'

'Look, you must feel my pulse,' he said. 'Go on, feel it. My pulse-rate's sky-high.'

'I don't know.' She ignored his hand. 'I don't know anything about pulse-rates.'

'Am I embarrassing you?'

'No.'

'I thought I might be embarrassing you.'

'Do I look embarrassed?'

'No, I must admit, you look quite calm. I had to say all this, I hope you understand why. I couldn't have lived with it for another week. To tell the truth, I can't stand seeing you only once a week. Will you meet me some other night?'

'Where?'

He was aghast. 'You will?'

She gave him a level stare. 'I didn't say whether I would or not, I said "Where?".'

'Wherever you like. I'll collect you. I'll pick you up. Where do you live?'

'I'll write down my address.'

'Have you got a pen?'

'Of course,' she said, 'I have a pen.' She took a small pad out of her bag, scribbled her address, and handed him the leaf. He put it in his wallet. His face showed disbelief.

'I live with my father,' she said.

'Do you? I didn't think . . . '

'Why not?'

'I imagined you having a flat somewhere. With other girls. You know. To be honest I'm glad. I couldn't see myself calling at a flat for you. I wouldn't like to, you know, present myself.'

'You don't think you're presentable?'

'What about your mother, is she . . . ?'

'Dead.'

'Sorry. Will you introduce me to your father?'

'I don't think you'd have much in common. He's old . . . he's retired. He was a bank manager. He has hobbies.'

'Oh yes?'

'Early railways. Numismatics. Military history.'

Colin smiled. 'I'll have to take some more evening classes.'

'I'd rather you didn't meet.'

'Would he disapprove of you . . . going out with me?'

'I don't know. I can't imagine what his opinion would be.'

'Aren't you close?'

'We lead our own lives.'

'Isn't it a bit dull, living at home?'

'No. It's not dull.' She leaned forward. 'So, Colin, am I right? Are you discontented?'

'Of course I am.'

'And do you think you will ever leave them?'

'Yes, I . . . ' He dropped his eyes, shifted his feet a little under the table. 'Yes, I think it quite possible that one day soon I won't find it possible to go on as I am.'

Colin drained his half-pint. He took out a clean folded handkerchief and dabbed his top lip with it. Already he was making giant strides.

Out in the conservatory. It is not really worthy of the name, just a glass lean-to at the back of the house, but Evelyn calls it the conservatory. There have never been plants in it. Clifford had not been much of a gardener. Get some flagstones down, had been Clifford's idea. Muriel could not tell flagstones from gravestones. She referred to them as such. Her morbid fancy has by now taken a thorough grip on Evelyn, who often imagines she is walking on the dead.

Out in the conservatory are Clifford's collections. Newspapers: the local *Reporter* for all the years they had lived at Buckingham Avenue. There was no topic which had interested him, no local good work or sport or sewerage scheme. He had merely laid them aside in the spare room, week after week. After his death Evelyn had left them for a while, and then, sensing that the room was needed, had dashed them in great bales down the stairs and humped them along the hallway and out through the back door. It is absurd to say, she tells Muriel, that we do not have newspapers. They are all there, with stopped clocks and defunct lightbulbs and a mousetrap, postcards from relatives escaped to Bournemouth, *Little Dorrit* with the back off, a cakestand, a china duck, a railway timetable from 1954. They yellow and moulder. In a lesser neighbourhood, there would be rats. Perhaps there are.

Muriel often comes to sit here. She thinks it as good and orderly as anywhere in the house. Sometimes she looks inside the decaying cardboard boxes which are piled almost to the roof. There is dust an inch thick in places, spiders' webs like veils from long-postponed weddings.

Isabel Field, standing on the Axons' front path, was growing irritable. Why is it, she thought, that I am sure there is someone in there? There was no movement behind the curtains, nothing to hear, and in fact the house had less life about it than most properties standing empty; yet she was sure that someone was there. How many letters? Three or four. What do they do, throw them away or leave them on the mat in the hall? It's their privilege, she supposes.

Most of the mildly handicapped, people like Miss Axon, live in the world with no one pestering them. She has more urgent cases, wretched and worn women keeping house for incontinent parents who have ceased to recognise them; the paranoid and the dangerously deluded and the terminally ill, the children in institutional cots staring without comprehension at the bars. With the very old and the very young, Isabel feels afraid. At the two poles of birth and death, she sniffs unbearable conjectures in the wind. She functions on the middle ground. By temperament and habit of mind, she is unsuited to her work.

I have of course, she thought, a right to be here. It was more with herself than with the Axons she was irritated. She stepped off the path and peered into the bay window of the front room. It was too dark to see very much, just the outline of a fireplace and an old-fashioned dining suite. The high lattice gate to the back was not bolted. It creaked; of course, it would creak. These are two women alone, they do not maintain their property. She stepped through dead leaves, along a blank brick wall. A low sky, a neglected garden; October in melancholy retreat towards November. Sharply she knocked at the side door. It was four in the afternoon. She could see her own breath on the air, and a distant sickle moon. She knocked again; nothing. She felt that someone was watching her, watching with interest; discounted it as absurd. The house was built on a slope, higher at the back than at the front, so that when she tried to peer in to the kitchen window it was too high for her, the bottom frame almost level with the top of her head.

There were steps down on to the overgrown lawn. She looked around for something to stand on – a bucket, perhaps. She jumped into the air to try to see into the kitchen, but she caught only a glimpse of a varnished cupboard door with a calendar pinned to it. If anyone is watching, she thought, I must look absurd. She wondered if she could get a grip on the windowsill and pull herself up for long enough to see if there was anyone in the kitchen. No, she thought, I draw the line at gymnastics, I am not trained for it. There must be another door, she thought, going into the kitchen or the hall from this sort of greenhouse. The panes were so filthy that she could hardly see inside. It seemed to be full of rubbish, boxes piled high. Something scurried away from her feet and she jumped aside. It was beginning to drizzle, and she realised suddenly that she had become very cold, and wanted a cup of tea. She pushed up her coat sleeve to look at her watch in the fading light: something past four. She walked back around the side of the house. It was like a place not occupied but still furnished, she thought, where some old person has recently passed away; and the relatives are going to come next weekend with a van, and take away what they call the decent stuff, and sell the good solid wardrobes for a couple of pounds each. There was a clean milkbottle with an envelope inside it. She bent down and touched it; coins jingled. Milk-money. She removed her hand quickly, feeling like a petty thief. She could not grow accustomed to the licence her profession gave her to enquire into the lives of other people. To look through their letterboxes, which she now did. It is beyond me, she thought, how anyone learns much by looking through letterboxes. The doormat said WELCOME, in green. There were no letters, no pile of circulars, no bills left to lie by a person broken-hipped or hypothermic. It was early in the year for hypothermia. And the daughter was quite young, wasn't she, and able-bodied, and reasonably capable? She had enough sense to get help, if anything was really wrong. The note in the milkbottle, left early, suggested people who had gone out and would be away for the evening; as if they might come back late, talkative and giddy, and forget to do it. It seemed an unlikely picture, but she supposed they might have friends, this odd mother and daughter who were familiar to her only from a buff-coloured file. The strangest people have friends, she thought, even me.

On the front path, she hovered again. One day, she thought, I shall always know what to do in these doubtful situations. When I am perfectly wise. When I am thirty years old. The rain began to fall harder. Deciding quickly, she turned and dashed back to the car, splashing the back of her tights. She was just going to miss the rush-hour traffic.

Up at her bedroom window, Florence turned away, to resume the living of her own life.

The new offices were open-plan. It was four thirty-eight when Isabel got in. The day was winding down. In the old offices, with their brown peeling doors, over-subscribed lavatories, dingy walls, you could shut yourself into the little cubbyhole that was designated to you and rub your hands over your own one-bar fire. They had merits, but they were not pleasant for the clients to visit.

'Tea?' she said unhopefully.

'We've had it.'

'Messages?'

'On your desk.'

She walked over the expanse of blue cord carpet. There had been a phone call from the Probation Service. The Housing Aid office reported their failure to find housing for someone. A child with leukaemia would have to go back to hospital. What concerns are these of mine, she thought tiredly. The Education Welfare office had been ringing. And Mr Sidney. This year social workers had become 'generic.' It was a new dispensation, for everybody to know everything about everything: and how to heal it.

'What's this?' she said to the secretary.

The woman looked up resentfully. 'Your messages.'

'This last one – Mr Sidney. Who is Mr Sidney?'

'A personal call, that was.'

Oh yes, Isabel thought. Colin. Who's going to leave home for me. She sat down at her desk and took the evening paper out of her bag. She read of a car-crash and a dog that had drowned. She did not want to go home; did not relish the evening ahead of her. But then she did not look forward, either, to the next working day. There is something radically wrong with my life, she thought, that I have fallen to such vicious amusements; and such stretches of emptiness between them.

It was almost seven when Isabel arrived home. The house was a brick-built bungalow, ten years old, of a solid and uninspired design. The lamps burned at each side of the wrought-iron gates, but Mr Field had not drawn the curtains. She put the car into the garage, and let herself in at the front door.

There were no lights on in the hall, and before she found the switch she caught her foot against something soft, lying beside the telephone table. She bent down and explored it with one hand. It was a plastic carrier bag, a small one full of laundry. A tablecloth – which had been clean, she thought – a few pairs of socks, one shirt. Token laundry, this. Damp blue powder clung to her fingertips. She flicked it off. Her heart began to beat faster. Anger and fear, she thought, fight, and flight. If only we could ever do either. She tried to calm herself, standing with one hand against the wall. Mr Field appeared at the top of the stairs.

'Is that you, Bella? You're very late.'

'Just as well, it seems to me.'

He cringed at her tone.

'Come down here,' she said.

'I'll make you a cup of tea. Oh Bella, please don't work yourself up.'

He came down and stood before her, blinking and contrite, a man of seventy.

'You've been drinking,' she said.

'Just a nip.'

She kicked out viciously at the bag of laundry. 'There's nothing wrong with the washing machine.'

'Bella, I have to have some life. Your mother left me.'

'The launderette. Why?'

'Meet someone.'

'Anybody in particular?'

'No,' he mumbled. 'But you can always find someone at the Washerama.'

Her mouth was dry. She could picture them, loose-mouthed women with bare blue legs, buttons hanging off their coats. It was in the autumn that you noticed them. Had they any homes to go to?

'I suppose you brought her back with you. Do you have to bring them here?'

'It's too cold for the park. Be human, Bella.'

'Oh, I feel sorry for you, I really do, having to get a bundle of washing together. I suppose otherwise the attendant turns you out, does she?'

'They watch you. They're mean old cows. But they can't stop people talking to each other, can they? Lonely people, Bella, like your father.'

'Oh, don't start with that pathetic tone. You nauseate me. What happened to Woolworth's café? That was favourite last year, wasn't it?'

He turned away, moving slowly towards the kitchen. 'I'll put the kettle on,' he said.

'You disgust me,' she shouted after him. 'Take the sheets off your bed and put them in the machine. I'm not going into your room.'

I always say that, she thought, but I shall have to go, and look at his clothes for lice. What can I do to stop him, whatever can I do? Unshed tears were choking her. She blundered into the living-room, snapped on the TV and slumped in front of it, staring without seeing, biting her lip till it bled.

'London Bridge is falling down,' Muriel sings, 'bawling round, trolling frown.' One word is as good as the next. Her mother tells her she is going to have a child. She is making plans to sing to it.

When is it going to be born, Muriel wants to know. Tonight? You stupid, stupid girl, Evelyn says to her. She glowers. You should know that, not me. Despairing, she reminds herself how little comprehension Muriel has ever shown of past or future. Look, she said, you count, nine months. Nine months from the day you . . . got it.

There are two things she can do. Take Muriel to a doctor, or go to the Welfare and tell them what has happened. Lay the blame at their door, where it belongs. If she had stayed in the house with me, Evelyn thinks, she would have come to no harm, or comparatively little. If she does either of these things, it will be in an extremity. She is afraid that Muriel will be taken away. 'Taken away,' she says. 'There are places for people like you. There are places for girls who have babies and no husbands.' She thinks of the uniformed guards taking Muriel away, to shave her head and beat her. It is something she has often imagined. But then she imagines closing the door, finding herself alone; alone with her companions. When Muriel follows her up the stairs at night, and she feels them creeping up, creeping up snapping from the bottom stair, she always plans that if they get too close she will put her hand on Muriel's chest and push her slithering down to them, fat bait, something to lick their lips over.

Sunday: Sylvia cooked roast beef (she does it brown, a full twenty-five minutes per pound plus twenty minutes), roast potatoes, carrots, frozen peas: rhubarb crumble, at which she is a dab hand, and custard.

CHAPTER 3

'Look,' Colin said, his hand half over the mouthpiece. 'I can't talk now. But why not Thursday?'

'Because Thursday is the writing class.'

'But you don't really want to go there.'

'How do you know that I don't?'

'You said you didn't find any profit in it.'

'No, but much pleasure.'

'Isabel, please – look, I'm in the staffroom, I can't talk.'

'Then what was the use of telephoning?'

'I wanted to fix something?'

'Well, then. But not Thursday.'

'It's just that it's such a good chance. Sylvia knows that I go out on Thursday.'

'Tell her you're going out another night.'

He was awed by the simple terms in which she saw his predicament. 'I – well, she might not just accept that.'

'That's your problem.'

'Well – which night then?'

'Monday.'

'People don't go out on a Monday. At the end of the week, that's when they go out.'

'For pleasure, but not for business. You wouldn't be going out for pleasure, would you Colin?'

'No, that's true. All right, I'll think of something to tell her. Can we go to a film, would you like that?'

'Yes.'

'All right then, I'll pick you up at half-past seven Monday, and we can have a drink first.'

'Fine,' she said. 'Goodbye.'

'Isabel – '

But he had heard the click. He knew she had gone, and still went on calling her name. He stood still. He realised that her plan was better. He could see her on Monday, and on Thursday too. After the class they could go to the Duke of Norfolk. He would see her two evenings instead of one, and it was Friday already.

Where had she been last night? He hadn't asked her. He could have raised the point, he could have said, ah, then why did you miss the class last night? But he hadn't questioned her on that one. He'd been too relieved to hear her voice. She always seemed to be out, or engaged with a client. He rushed to the phone between lessons, piles of exercise books slipping about under his arm, wedging the receiver under his chin, trying to juggle his cigarettes and his lighter for a quick drag before the next forty-minute period. Sometimes Luther King House was engaged, solid, for hours. All the weary morning he rang her, through to spam fritters and steamed fruit pudding, and into the afternoon. Once he dropped a whole pile of books, and his colleagues looked up from their marking and card games, and he felt they had noticed he was agitated and red in the face. When he heard her voice at last he could hardly believe his luck was in; it seemed to him a miracle that she walked on the same pavements in the same town, that the line distorted her voice, like anyone else's.

The tall and shady trees, the disconsolate sparrows huddling in the trees: these protected Evelyn and Muriel from observation. The oncoming winter stripped them of their shade, but because it was winter there was no need for Muriel to walk in the garden. By the end of October the plots were fenced by black arms held aloft, mourners from some more fervent culture; Brewer, Petty & Co nailed up their signboard on 3 Buckingham Avenue, and Evelyn's closest neighbours moved away. Sylvia remarked, when they next visited Florence, that the house would remain unsold until after Christmas; no one wants removals, she said, with Christmas upon us.

Evelyn gave Muriel some of her own old dresses. At five months,

61

even six, Muriel didn't show too much. She was tall, and ungainly at the best of times; her clothes had never been in the height of fashion. When in the end the dresses began to strain and pull in the middle, Evelyn went into the conservatory, and delved about among the boxes. She came out grey to the elbows with dust, lengths of fabric laid across her forearms.

She had found a pair of old blue curtains, very large. She hung them out on the line to get rid of the smell of must. When she brought them in they smelled of soil. Saxe-blue, she said, very nice. She took out a treadle sewing-machine and ran up a couple of garments for Muriel, two identical. She didn't need a pattern. She could wear them turn and turn about. She wanted for nothing, Evelyn said.

Cards from the Welfare dropped through the letterbox; apart from the household bills, there was no other post. Muriel collected a stack of the cards. She held them in her hands and shuffled them until they were greasy and turned up at the corners. Evelyn took them from her in the end and burned them.

'Do you want to go to the doctor?' Evelyn asked. 'Because if you do they'll take it away when it's born, and you'll have nothing to show for it.'

Muriel seemed to have lost interest in life. She sat a good deal of the time with her eyes closed, her fingers in her ears. Then her fingers would pinch her nostrils closed; when Evelyn had first seen this trick she had been distraught. 'What is the smell?' she had de- manded, trying to drag Muriel's hand away from her face. 'What is the smell?'

Soon she understood that Muriel was enjoying one of her strange holidays from the world. There was nothing she could do until the girl repacked the tattered baggage of her personality and came home. Sinking into immobility, Muriel would allow Evelyn to manoeuvre her around like a piece of furniture, putting her wherever convenient. I don't know how I am going to manage, Evelyn thought, if she is like this when the baby comes.

So Monday morning brought relief. Muriel was back. Her pale

eyes travelled around the house, without interest, but more freely than of late. 'You are being a good girl today,' Evelyn said kindly. Muriel got up and took herself upstairs to the lavatory.

Evelyn was in the kitchen when the knocking started up at the front door. Muriel heard it too. I know what is done, she thought, or what can be done, when that noise starts up. She remembered to rearrange her clothes, or to do as much rearrangement as was necessary under the enveloping blue dress. She watched her large feet going before her, placing themselves slightly sideways on each descending stair.

Evelyn snatched the pan off the stove. As she blundered down the hallway, she felt tiny malignant hands pull at her skirt and catch at her ankles. She could not, could not, make headway.

Her face contorted with effort and alarm. 'Muriel!' Muriel turned her head, gave her a blank look, her hand on the catch of the front door; then a slow, spreading smirk. The door swung open, framing mother and daughter, as if they had come to open it together in an expansive gesture of welcome.

A young woman stood on the doorstep.

'I don't think we've met,' she said. 'Isabel Field, Social Services.'

As she said this, she put one foot over the threshold. Presumptuous, Evelyn thought. For a moment she moved forward to block the doorway; stepped back just as the girl's eyes began to widen in surprise.

'Delighted,' Evelyn said. 'I can't think why we haven't met.'

Standing in the hall, the girl unwound a long woollen scarf from round her neck.

'I've written,' she said.

'Yes.'

'I've called before.'

'Really?'

'You've been out, perhaps.'

'Very likely.'

'So I've been unlucky.'

'Yes, indeed.'

'Are you well, Mrs Axon?'

'Quite well, thank you.'

'And is Muriel well?'

'Come through, Miss Field.'

Muriel sat and stared into the fireplace, pulling at a thread of her blue dress. She gave the visitor one glance devoid of all interest, then slumped down further into her chair.

'Hello, Muriel.' Isabel stood before her, but her client would not look up. She took a chair; leaning forward, a hand extended, she tried to engage Muriel's attention. Her voice was gentle, almost timid. She doesn't know how to go on, Evelyn thought.

'How are things, Muriel?'

'You'll find,' Evelyn said, 'that Muriel has no small talk. It's a big disadvantage to her, socially.'

'It's not really small talk, is it?' The girl glanced up at Evelyn. 'I am here on business, after all.'

'Yes, but there's no compulsion, is there? You don't have to come. She's not committed a crime.'

'No, no, of course not, but we are very concerned about Muriel. It's months since she's been to the Day Centre.'

'Well, she has a full life.'

'Really? That wasn't the picture we'd formed.'

'We?'

'Social Services. It's unfortunate that so many people have handled Muriel's case, but we do have records, you know.'

'Well, look for yourself. She's happy enough. She didn't like the class.'

'Didn't she?' Concern crossed the girl's face. She's all hot and strong when she talks to me, Evelyn thought, and gentle as a mouse with Muriel. But now she's wondering what to do.

'I didn't know that. She should have said something at the time. What didn't she like?'

'She doesn't care for being regimented. She likes a bit of independent action, Muriel.'

Again, Miss Field's attention flickered over her client. 'She seems so . . . so cut off. Is she often like this?'

'Now and again. She's a grown woman. She's got a tongue in her head.'

'I wish she'd use it.'

'How would you like it, Miss Field, if strangers came into your house enquiring into your circumstances? Suppose it were your own home?'

Now the girl blushed, a deep guilty red.

'Well, in a sense, Mrs Axon, I wouldn't like it at all. But I'm not trying to interfere, only to help Muriel. You see, looking at her there, hardly moving, her body all drooping, not speaking – well, it crosses my mind that she could be suffering from depression. Clinical depression. Of course, that would be a matter for your GP, in the first instance.'

'I'd take her to the doctor,' Evelyn said, 'if I thought it would help.'

'Yes, do take her, because if he thinks she is depressed, there are some excellent drugs. Then, if she felt better in a month or two, she might try the class again.'

'You think that's what's the matter, do you? Depression?'

'It could be.'

'You don't notice anything amiss with her physically?'

'Better let your doctor be the judge of that. I'll try to call next week, and you can tell me how you got on.' She looked around at Muriel again, again put out her hand. 'That's an unusual dress, Muriel. Where did you get that, then?'

Muriel closed her eyes, screwed them up, and grinned.

'She's got a sense of humour, hasn't she?' Miss Field said. She patted Muriel's wrist. And Evelyn's patience snapped.

'Sense of humour? Lovely dress?' The girl's head snapped back in shock at her ugly tone. 'I made it for her. I do adorn her, I deck her in all the modes. Yes, she's a wonderful personality, my daughter, not a beauty, but very striking. Isn't she, Miss Field?'

The girl straightened up. She was staring at Evelyn, her mouth slightly ajar.

'Perhaps she has a beau.' Evelyn laughed. 'Perhaps she slips out when I sleep in the afternoons, and meets him in the park. No wonder you get no answer when you knock, Muriel's on the razzle.'

The young woman turned, with a strange and frozen expression, and looked at Muriel. Stared, Evelyn might have said, as if she were seeing her for the first time. Muriel lifted her face, like an animal sniffing for water; she looked, her mother thought, particularly unintelligent and unappealing, just at that moment. Without a word, Miss Field scooped up her briefcase, and got herself most precipitately from the room. Evelyn followed her to the front door. The girl jerked it open, and took a deep breath of the leaf-mould air. 'I'll see you again,' she said, and fled down the path towards her car.

Evelyn watched her go with fleeting amusement, thinking that she would likely not be back; but they might send another one, there were plenty in reserve. Something had struck a chord. Her neck felt stiff, her eyes strained, with the effort of keeping her eyes averted from the middle of her daughter's body. She returned to the sitting-room.

'Thanks to me,' she said. 'Thanks to my tact, young lady, you aren't locked up by now. A month from now you won't be able to hide it.'

Muriel sat examining her hands. She always looked at them as if they belonged to someone else, and she was surprised to find them attached to her wrists.

'How many times have I told you about going to the door?'

Oh, once twice, thrice, Muriel replied uncaringly.

'You dare to cheek your mother!' Tears sprang into Evelyn's eyes. I am getting old, she thought, I am getting old and I do not deserve this. It is such a strain for me. Even the blue tits have learned to open the milkbottles; but Muriel has learned nothing at all.

Colin was surprised at how easy it was to tell lies to Sylvia. Her mind seemed to be elsewhere.

That night he drove up to Isabel's house at half past seven. He knew he was early, so he took the car slowly along the road, reversed into a driveway, and drove back. It was an unremarkable street on the outskirts of town, the kind of place where he would have been glad to live. The estate was too noisy, swarming with the kind of children he taught all day. His windows looked into other windows, and he resented the share of themselves with which his neighbours presented him. The gardens were heavy clay strips, waterlogged and cleared only recently of builder's rubble; the tiles were coming loose in the bathroom, and rain got in under the kitchen door. He wanted a house like the one in which he had grown'up; grey shrubberies and yellow-cream curtains of heavy net guarded each property. Ah, property, he thought, that is what they are, not merely houses but a statement of values. But surely, he thought in mild surprise, those are not the values I hold?

Colin stopped the car. He looked at his watch. His hand went for the door handle, and then withdrew. He sat hunched for a moment and slowly leaned forward, to let his head rest on the steering wheel. I am lonely, he thought, I am behaving very badly. As if I were free to do this.

Muriel had begun to imitate the visitor, crossing her legs at the ankle and tucking them under her chair, and absently smoothing her hair around the imaginary curve of a cheek. She wore the remote and abstracted air of the woman from the Welfare.

As punishment, she was being deprived of food. It annoyed Evelyn that she wasn't more affected by this. If you put food in front of her, she ate it; if not, she didn't miss it. By herself she would starve, Evelyn thought, or make herself very sick. She would bring a raw egg to the table, and set it down with every appearance of satisfaction; choose what was raw or half-cooked or stale, in preference to the good food her mother provided for her. The idea of mealtimes didn't seem to have got into her head. Is she human, Evelyn wondered that night; is she human or something else, and what is she likely to give birth to?

Colin brought their drinks, and put them down on the table.

'Not a very good film, was it?'

'We didn't really need to see a film. But if we just parked the car in a field and made love, you wouldn't think we had a proper relationship.'

Turning his chin very slightly, Colin looked covertly over his shoulder; and then the other way, out of the tail of his eye.

'Just . . . having a check round,' he said. 'I don't want to run into anybody.'

'You look shifty, doing that.' She seemed amused. 'You won't risk much, will you?'

'You don't love me,' Colin said heavily. He sat down and pulled up his chair to the table. 'You must be playing some sort of game with me.'

'I don't know what game that could possibly be.'

'Perhaps you're using me as a study. To extend your professional range.'

She laughed. 'You have a curious idea of my job then.'

'Isabel, before I knew you, what did you do at the end of the day?'

She stared. 'Substantially, what I still do now.'

'Did you have a boyfriend?'

'I didn't give anyone up for you, if that's what you mean. People with an active love-life aren't found at evening classes.'

'But there have been people?'

'You didn't think I was a virgin, did you?'

'I don't know anything about you. I don't know how it happened, the other night.'

'I have never understood this point of view, that only after so many meetings, so much money spent, so much conversation . . . I wanted it to happen, or I would have stopped you.'

'I know that. I wasn't apologising. I just want to know about you. It's natural, to want to know about the person you love. So you can picture them, when you're not together. I'd like to know what you do on the nights you're not with me.'

'I clean the house. And I put my feet up. My job's quite tiring.'

'Do you like your job? If you'd just tell me about your job, it would be something. When we're not together you have a way of seeming . . . nebulous.'

'You're possessive, Colin.'

'Because you're evasive.'

'Evasive?' She laughed without humour. 'Do you really want to know about my job? Today I met some people who are very evasive.'

'Yes, go on.'

I shouldn't talk about it, she thought. It's confidential; no names, but it's even possible he could know them. I shouldn't talk about it – oh, but I must, I must. Spit it out. Get the foul taste out of my mouth.

'These people – I've been chasing them for weeks. A mother and daughter. They'll never let me in. I cornered them today.'

'What's the matter with them?'

'Oh, the daughter's mildly retarded. She used to come to a Day Centre we run, but she doesn't want to come any more.' You handled it badly, said a voice inside her. You were brusque and unprofessional; and then you let the situation completely defeat you. Now tell him about it, set out the facts; so that in setting them out you will become sure of what they are. And only the facts; not some silly product of your imagination. 'When I saw the daughter I thought for a moment she must be pregnant. She was wearing the strangest clothes, a sort of blue tent. God knows where she found it.'

'Perhaps she *is* pregnant.'

'No, that's not possible. She never goes out, she has no opportunity. She's revolting, anyway. No one would want her.'

'You'd be surprised. The unlikeliest people find partners, I always think.'

Isabel shivered.

'What is it, are you cold?'

'No. I'd like another drink, maybe.'

He picked up their glasses and took them to the bar. Her eyes followed him. He may not be much, she thought, but he's sane, he's clear, he's outside all this; he has no truck with the filthy speculations I deal in.

'She gave me a shock,' she said, when he sat beside her again.

'Who? Oh, this girl. Sorry, go on.'

'She's not a girl really. A woman.'

'Are you worried about them?'

'We're not supposed to worry. Only to display professional concern. It's different. You mustn't identify with your client, or let her life touch yours. It's professional death, to get involved.'

'It must be hard to stay uninvolved, though. If you see people who are unhappy.'

She shrugged. 'It's not my fault that people are unhappy.'

'No, but isn't it rather your professional responsibility? Or am I pitching it too high?'

'Much too high. That's the trouble with social work, no one has fixed on what to expect of it. You can't be with people twenty-four hours of the day. If they're really going to beat their children to death, they'll find time to do it. And if you try to take the child away from them it gets into the newspapers, and you are shown to be a do-gooder and a tyrant. And you can't improve people's thoughts. You can't stop them creating private hells for themselves, if that's what they want to do.'

'Do you see eye-to-eye with your colleagues?'

'Not really. This miserable old woman today asked me how I would like it myself, some strange person coming into the house enquiring into things. I think, my reaction would be that things are bad enough without social workers.'

'I think perhaps you're in the wrong job, Isabel.'

'Probably.' She pushed her hair behind her ears. 'I sometimes think I don't care much for people. When I was a student I spent some time working with schizophrenic children. They frightened me. I used to think – I kept it to myself, of course – that there wasn't a lot that was human looking out from behind their eyes. Then I studied the people I met on the street. They had much the same expression.'

'We'll have to go,' he said. 'Where do you want to go to?'

It was a blunt demand, but he could not think of any way to soften it. It was not quite time yet; they might hang on for another ten or fifteen minutes. But that would solve nothing.

'Let me just get my coat.'

He helped her into it. 'Shall I take you home?'

'Do you want to get rid of me?'

'That's the last thing I want.'

'Let's drive then.'

'All right. Soon get the heater going, when we get out on the road.'

He opened the door and she slipped through it under his arm. The night buffeted past them like an animal avid for the hearth. They left the bright doorway for darkness and raw blue air. He felt her shiver against him, and took her arm. On the safe and public tarmac, splashed by yellow lights from the main road, he felt a fugitive wind on his cheek; the hollow-faced tossed bundles on to carts, eyes piercing for the camera. To be exiled, he had read, you need not leave home. Banishment is to the desert round of the familiar world, where small conversation is made and the weekly groceries are bought in good time. He had accepted this, as an intellectual conceit; now he felt the needles of loss. He tightened his grip above her elbow. 'Come on, it's chilly.' Their breath hung on the air. She slid into the passenger seat. 'If that van would move,' he said. They had to stop and wait. He edged gingerly out of the car park and on to the main road. 'Which way? Oh, Christ.' He slammed the wheel with his hands. He wanted to weep with frustration. 'This is ridiculous. Nowhere to go. Like kids. Kids do this.'

She reached out and put her hand over his. 'Colin, it's all right, calm down. Drive to where we went before, and if you prefer it we can just talk. Or, if you prefer it, take me straight home. Whatever you think best.'

She spoke very softly, very gently. He would always remember the tone of her voice and the tips of her fingers brushing his knuckles, inside the woollen gloves she had just pulled on. Later, when it was all over, he would think: at that point, if at no other, she must have loved me. Then, if at no other time.

'We'll go to where we went before.'

She pulled off her gloves again and unzipped her bag and fumbled for cigarettes. 'Shall I light one for you?'

'Yes please.'

He hardly ever smoked now but he wanted her to touch him again. He could not wait until they got to the field.

As winter set in, Colin waited every week in the street outside Isabel's house. It was not necessary for him to ring the doorbell. She never kept him waiting for more than a minute, and it gratified him to think that she must listen for the sound of the car.

'Take me to meet your father,' he said. 'He need not know that I'm married.'

'I'd rather not tell lies.'

'There's no need to lie. There's no need to say anything about it. You shut me out of your life,' he complained. 'When you aren't with me, do you ever give me a single thought?'

Her dark almond eyes flickered over him. Her face remained impassive, unimpressed. 'You have all the woman's lines, Colin. Have you noticed that?'

Once or twice he had glimpsed the elderly man in the doorway, wearing spectacles and a bulky handknitted cardigan. He would wave a hand limply and forgetfully to see his daughter off, and then withdraw into the house.

Then, between the great yellow orbs which flanked the gate, she would turn to him the paler luminous oval of her face; not smiling, not speaking, she would slip into the seat beside him and their evening would begin. These days she wore a belted beige trenchcoat pulled in at the waist, and a long brown woollen scarf. Her hands when she lit a cigarette were often blue and mottled with cold. I will buy her some sheepskin mittens, he thought: at Christmas.

They did not go much to the field now. They were afraid of the car sinking in the mud. They had taken to getting further away from town. Colin would drive to the motorway intersection, slot them between the lights of other cars, and put his foot down. For miles and miles ahead the wet black road gleamed under the orange lights. Wrapped in their numb silence, their eyes on the tail-lights ahead, headlights reflected in the rear-view mirror, they were locked into the process of the road; parts on its conveyor, diminished to its function.

He would pull in at the service halt. They sat on padded seats of turquoise plastic, facing each other over the litter of stained paper cups and scraps of cellophane ripped from sandwiches.

'It's so sordid,' she laughed. 'It's so properly sordid. Like a film.'

'I shall get a night from somewhere,' he said. 'I'll get some petrol in the car and we'll go – drive up to Manchester, get a decent meal and find a hotel. I'll come up with something. Just give me time.'

'Give me time,' she said mockingly. 'That's the anthem of the married man. Give me time while I make my excuses, give me time while I sort out my head. Just another week, just another decade, just till my wife understands. Be reasonable, give me time, just till my children grow up, give me time. And what do you suppose time will give to me?'

'Before the winter's out,' he said, 'things will be different. I told you that first night that I'd leave her. Give me – no, no, you're playing games. If I left her you'd laugh in my face.'

'You'll never leave her,' she said. A ginger-haired woman moved between the tables, whisking cigarette butts into a waste bag, her white face set in lines of ineradicable fatigue. She watched them with pale bitter eyes.

'She wants us to go,' Isabel said.

'Drink your tea. Then we'll go.'

'It's like treacle. It's the end of the pot. It always is at this time of night.'

She leaned forward and tears dripped into the cup and splashed on to the table. She got up suddenly, thrusting her chair back, and strode towards the door ahead of him, fastening her coat and looping her scarf around her neck. He was afraid of the clenched set of her mouth. The rain had stopped; he saw them hurrying, reflected in puddles, ghost-white flitting among the petrol pumps and headlights. She put her foot on a sodden mess of paper and slime and skidded to her knees. He ran behind her and picked her up. Holding her tightly by the waist he steered her towards the car. In her seat she unbuttoned her coat again and pulled up her skirt, rubbing at her grazed knees and picking at the shreds of her tights. She sobbed and sniffed, fumbling for a handkerchief. He reached across her and fastened the seatbelt in her lap, making the soft nonsensical sounds of comfort he used to his children.

'You must take me to your house. We can't go on like this – '

'I've told you, no.' Her voice shook. 'No, no, no.'

'What is it, love? What's upsetting you?'

She turned and looked at him, for a second, as if she had never seen him before. 'Whatever is wrong in my life,' she said, 'might have nothing to do with you.'

'But has it?' She turned her head away. 'Perhaps I've done you an injustice. Perhaps you do feel – '

'Oh yes, I feel,' she said harshly. 'I took a training course to educate me out of feeling. I'm not paid to feel. But still I do it.'

'Then it's your job that's getting on top of you.'

'I don't know.' She took a deep breath.

'And your Dad. Your home. Caring for him. Perhaps it's that.'

'I see you have your theories. Just leave off, Colin.'

'Leave off? Leave me alone, you mean.' He was angry. 'You want to have me around when it suits you, you want to talk about your work, you want to put the burden on to me. You burst into tears, then you say leave off.'

'I'm sorry if I upset you.' She lifted her face. 'See, I'm not crying now.'

'I worry about you.' He touched her hair tentatively. 'You're getting thin.' Suddenly he saw it. 'You need me, don't you?'

74

He did not ask, what for? She seemed vulnerable in her distress, naked; he rushed to cover her with willing assumptions.

'How shrewd,' she said.

'You need to pack in this job. You need a husband. You need a proper secure home.'

'And you're offering?'

'Isabel, give me something back. I'm human.'

'Sure.'

'You go on as if you hate me. As if there were some enemy in your life, and it's me.'

'It's not you, Colin.' She spoke slowly. 'I don't hate you. I'm afraid I don't.'

'Well . . . what is there to be afraid of?'

She began to laugh, a low-pitched and merciless chuckle. Or perhaps to cry? She is unpredictable, he thought; mad. Perhaps her period is coming on; I must keep a check. She pretends to be hard, to be casual, but everyone knows that women can't have casual affairs. She and I are equal now. But still – though the question was settled in his mind – her laughter made his skin crawl; as if there were some deep derangement in the situation that she meant to cherish alone.

'I hardly like to explore my own mind,' she said softly. 'I think I imagine things. I *hope* I imagine them. There are connections I make between events in my life, between people, and I hope they're not real connections. I tell myself it would be too much coincidence. But coincidence is what holds our lives together. That's why you always get it in books.'

'Do you have to be so cryptic?'

'It would be pleasant to be a victim: a victim of circumstance. If there were no patterns in our lives, we would have no responsibility. I would like to think that events were entirely random. It would be comfortable.'

'I can never see a pattern. Perhaps I can't see the wood for the trees. Stupid saying, that. I only . . . I didn't want to bandy platitudes. I only wondered if you loved me.'

75

'I'm afraid to ask myself what I feel.' She pressed her lips together; holding her damp handkerchief between her fingertips, she folded it into a tiny square. 'I distrust all my thoughts and all my emotions; how do I know I didn't get them out of books? I might even love you, but you can live in such a way that you get alienated from love, that you see its ghastly consequences all around you, and so I've tried to come to grips with it, I've tried to grapple with it in the back of your car. That's what people do, isn't it? They perform the actions and then they get the feelings?'

'Christ, I hope not.' Panic welled inside him. 'You say you might love me, but love could be too big a risk, so you're investigating, are you, at my expense? The town's just one big laboratory, and you keep me under a glass jar until it's time to take me out and experiment on my emotions again.'

'Human experiments are performed every day.' She sat back in her seat, her eyes closed. 'Forget it, Colin. Just forget it.'

He needed no prompting. He told himself he was her anchor in the normal world; he felt her tugging at him, out to uncharted waters. No one wants to go there. Resistance was his duty; his obtuseness was all he had to offer her, the leaden anchor of habit, the steadying weight of sad routine.

'Touch of the existential panic,' he said. 'I felt it too. There are some tissues in the glove compartment if you want to blow your nose.' Groping for the short end of his seatbelt, his hand touched hers, hanging loosely, as cold and stiff as the hand of a corpse. Like *The Duchess of Malfi*, he thought at once. He shuddered. 'We'd better get on the road. It's ten o'clock.'

The alarm shrilled. Sylvia's fingers groped for it. The noise continued to reverberate in Colin's head. He screwed his eyes shut.

He was distressed by his lack of control over his own dreams. It seemed monstrous that your own brain was capable, in the hours before dawn, of such divisive folly. He had dreamed so vividly of Isabel that he was afraid her spectre and after-image would parade about the bedroom for Sylvia to see. He had never seen her naked, but he imagined her long white limbs.

'Colin,' Sylvia said. Her voice was cautious, exploratory; the first limb of Monday morning reaching out to touch him in the dark. 'Colin, seven o'clock.'

'Mm.'

Sylvia sighed. She put her head back on the pillow and her rollers dug into her skull. She was going to the doctor's that morning to get the result of her pregnancy test. She was sure it would be positive. She was as regular as clockwork, she thought, you could set your watch by her menstrual flow. Furtively she slid a hand down over her blue nylon belly. I'll have to get myself a couple of patterns, she thought, and get the machine out, before the school holidays start. Sewing's all right but it makes a mess in ˌ ˌe house. 'Colin?'

'Yes, all right.' He massaged his closed eyelids with his fingers, sat up and swung his feet out of bed. 'Christ, it's dark,' he said. 'Why do we always get up in the dark? Year in, year out.'

Sylvia did not bother to say that life was arranged that way. Their morning routine did not include expostulation. A grunt, a twitch, sufficed for anything out of the ordinary. I'll get the kettle on grunt a boiled egg grunt the milk in grunt the fire on grunt and the children out of bed, and

'Why is it so bloody dark?' Colin bellowed. 'Why is life so lousy and uncomfortable?'

Sylvia felt unable to rise to the occasion. She did no more than glance at him out of the corner of her eye. It was the first time in their married life that he had asked such a question, and she could not think of a reason. She went into the bathroom, threw up neatly into the toilet bowl, pushed down the handle and wiped her eyes, which were misty from the effort. She poured disinfectant into the lavatory, flushed it again and rinsed out her mouth, scooping up the water in her hands. She was shivering when she got back into the bedroom, but Colin didn't notice. She reached for her dressing-gown. That makes sure of it, she thought. I'll put off telling him. I think I'd better.

Colin ate his egg in customary silence. His sense of grievance seemed to have subsided. He grunted once when he could not find his tie, then found it screwed up in the pocket of his jacket.

'I should take your overcoat,' Sylvia said.

'I'm late.'

'Suzanne, run and fetch your Dad's overcoat.'

'I'm late too,' Suzanne said. Her mouth was full of cornflakes. 'That's all you use me for, running up and down stairs. I bet I go upstairs ten times a day, getting things for you.'

'Twenty,' Alistair said. 'A hundred times. A billion.'

'Why don't you do it?' Suzanne said to her mother. 'You're lazy, that's why. You're old.'

'Christ,' Colin said. 'I'll bloody do without.'

He looked back at his children from the kitchen doorway, without hope. 'I'll be late, love,' he said to Sylvia. 'Not very late. I just thought I'd pop over to Florence.'

'All right.'

'Sylvia.'

She turned from the toast she was buttering for Alistair; slowly, as if she resented the extra effort.

'You look a bit peaky.'

'I'm all right.'

'About six o'clock then. Don't worry if it's a bit later.'

'I'll have your tea ready,' she said, and turned absently back.

The front door clicked behind him. He stood on the doorstep for a moment. The relief . . . the relief of being out of the house; the urge to confess was becoming almost unbearable. He took a deep breath of the foul air of the coming week, and began his matutinal wrestle with the damp-swollen garage door.

Muriel had taken to getting up early. Hearing the creak of the floorboards underfoot, Evelyn woke and lay stiff with alarm. Along the passage . . . 'Muriel? Muriel?' Evelyn called hoarsely, her voice weak with apprehension. Muriel's grinning head appeared around the door, dimly outlined in the half-light. Evelyn rolled her head around on the pillow, clutching up to her throat the old cardigan she wore at night for warmth. Her face had the look of thin old paper.

'Muriel?'

Why, she would brew her some tea, Muriel said. Brew her some coffee, brew her some milk.

'What are you doing up at this time? Are you sick?'

Muriel was not sick. She had never been sick at all during the course of her pregnancy. It had not incommoded her at all, except for the increased clumsiness of her swollen body. It was as if, Evelyn thought, the child was withdrawn and inert as its mother. A thing. A lump. Perhaps it was dead. Oh God. She struggled to sit up in momentary panic. A sharp pain shot through her shoulder. Let it not be dead. It was more than the house could contain. A ghost carrying a ghost.

'Muriel? Muriel?'

Muriel had gone downstairs. Why doesn't she put on the lights? How does it come about that she can see in the dark?

Muriel opened each door in turn. The shiny leather parlour shrouded in shadow. The cramped back room where they sat during the day. The furniture had not moved itself. There was no material change. Muriel could never feel sure about things like this. Paper might walk and wood might laugh; and how was it possible to know whether anything existed, when you were out of the room? Very well, she thought reasonably, *now* I am here, *now* the house is playing dead. Now I turn, I turn my head, I watch out of the corner of my eye. Now I go out . . . she slammed the door behind her then thrust it open again as quickly as she could, propelling herself back into the room. The tables and chairs, unmoved, smirked at her knowingly. She looked at them in a passion of enmity. Once she had been at their mercy, but now she was learning how to go about things. Now she was making progress every day.

In the kitchen drawer was a ball of string. A ball of string and a knife to cut. Back to the front parlour. With savage tightness she knotted the string to the back of one of the dining chairs, and looped it round the door handle. She passed it around the back again, and pulled, the rough fibres burning her fingers; round the handle, and back a third time, lifting the chair off its back legs. She went out into the hall and dragged the door shut behind her. An example to the rest.

And back to the kitchen. She opened a cupboard and took out her breakfast egg. She balanced it on her palm for a moment and then allowed it to roll off and shatter on the floor. The result was gratifying. Evelyn made such strange noises when she bent down to clean the floor. 'You're a useless lump,' she would squall. 'You never do a hand's turn.' Useless lump, used to a bump. Muriel patted her body confidently. She thought she would go out to play.

It was very cold in the lean-to, but the cold was something that had never bothered Muriel. Over the last few weeks, when Evelyn had sternly forbidden her to go out of the house, she had taken to spending more and more time there, delving more deeply into the rotten cardboard boxes, shaking out the rusted tins and heaving aside planks of wood to see what was underneath. The recent wet weather had made it a musty, fungal place, with a private and unpleasant smell. Water was getting under the doors and soaking into Clifford's collection of newspapers.

There seemed no likely end to the pleasures of the boxes. Here were images, for instance of people in strange clothes; furry little brown-and-white images, creased and smudged. And keys, for doors, a great bunch of them tied together. Locking doors, now there was a thing to do. And this fine garment.

An overcoat, Muriel thought. She could walk out in it. Promenade. She made a verse. An overcoat, across the moat, a man to dote, costs but a groat. It touched some chord in her heart, brushed some faint memory. She held up the coat and shook it out. It was thick and heavy, its dark wool mildewed but intact. Muriel wrinkled her nose at its ancient and complex smells. At first she wondered whether it had been left there by one of the corpses under the stones outside the door of the lean-to. Then her eye caught some writing. Writing in a coat? Who would want to write in a coat? She sniggered.

She carried the coat over to the light to make sure. Yes, there was a kind of tape sewn into it, yellow and frayed, and faint grey letters on the tape. This coat had a name. Or its owner had a name. It would be pleasant to find out who was under the stones. Evidently corpses wrote in their clothes; evidently they had a strong sense of private property.

She spelled it out for herself. CLIFFORD F. AXON. Here was another matter. She smiled gently, and began to scrape with her fingernails at the mould which speckled the collar.

Colin had the third period free. It helped, this small oasis so soon after the dire start of the working week.

Frank O'Dwyer, his Head of Department, was coming out of the staffroom.

'Any change for the phone, Frank?' Change had become his obsession, lately.

'You may be the lucky one.'

They stood opposite each other digging into their pockets, like gunslingers in difficulty.

'What's the magic of this telephone?' Frank enquired. 'You spend half your working day on it.'

'I want to ring my sister.'

O'Dwyer produced a handful of loose change and decanted it into Colin's palm.

'Did you run me off those copies?'

'5B's exam? Yes ... only twenty-five. Will that do? Bloody machine's knackered again.'

'It always picks its time,' Frank said. 'Twenty-five will suffice, they look over each other's shoulders anyway, miserable little sods. Once we get the exams over it puts itself right during the night, do you notice? If it went to Lourdes, it would be called a miracle.'

Colin grinned weakly. He wanted to get away, but it was not possible to have a short conversation with O'Dwyer. He was a large lanky, charming man, with heavy glasses which slipped down his nose and needed continual readjustment. His breath smelled faintly of the nip of whisky which he took to get himself started each day. Ten years ago, even five, people had said he was much too good to be a schoolmaster; ought to be lecturing, ought Frank, ought to have his doctorate. They had stopped talking in those terms, but Frank had kept his pretensions; only his clothes mirrored his state, the neckties starved narrow with dearth of variety, disappointed. jackets in sagging tweed. Colin saw himself; the regalia of stagnation, the shroud of opportunity, rags of receding hope.

'We ought to get together, Colin. You must come to dinner.'

'Surely,' Colin said. 'We will. After the exams?'

Now Colin sat with a pile of exercise books before him. Form 1C. The Vikings. He tried to gather strength to open them.

'Smith of English? Who said that thing, "Work fascinates me: I can sit and look at it for hours"?'

'It came off a matchbox, I imagine. I don't know. Ask Smith of Woodwork.'

If Florence did not understand . . . if Florence was not sympathetic . . . then when the Christmas holidays came, and all the schools closed, and all evening classes were over (and Sylvia knew they were) . . . then, when he could no longer mumble about Parents' Evenings as he sidled out in the mornings (and hope that she would not somehow find out) . . . then when his small ingenuity was defeated, how and when and where was he going to see Isabel?

Smith of English made a sound expressive of pain.

'*Animal Farm*,' he said.

Colin looked up. 'Pardon?'

'All right, listen. This is 3A. This is the O-Level stream, this. "George Orwell wrote *Animal Farm* in 1867."'

'They have those cribs, you know, those little books. They just copy down any date that takes their fancy. 1867 will be *Das Kapital*, I should think.'

'Mm,' Smith said. 'How about this next one then? "George Orwell wrote *Animal Farm* in 1857".' He raised an eyebrow. 'Indian Mutiny?'

But Florence, thought Colin; tell Florence? 'Excuse me,' he said. He fished in his pocket and went over to the phone.

'Colin's ringing his turf accountant again,' Smith said.

'Luther King House. Social Services.'

'I'd like to speak to Miss Field, please.'

'Just one moment. Putting you through.'

Click.

'Yes?'

A small sensation in Colin's chest rose and lodged itself in his throat. Grief.

'Yes?'

That deadly secretarial voice, that hope-crusher, that frustrated old maid; some slab-toothed old hag with thin knees pressed together and her glasses on a little gold chain, some Medusa in an Orlon cardigan.

'I wanted Miss Field,' he whispered.

'Miss Field is not in the office at present.'

'When will she be back?'

'I'm afraid I couldn't say.'

'Can't you ask? Someone in your office should know where she's gone and when she'll be back.'

A slight intake of breath told him that offence had been given and taken.

'Miss Field is a busy Social Worker with a full caseload and I think it most unlikely that her colleagues would be aware of all her intended movements in the course of the day. In any case it is not our practice to divulge what visits a caseworker is making, as we do not breach the confidence of our clients.' She paused, to let this sink in. 'If this is an emergency, I can pass you on.'

'No, could you just find out – '

'I can pass you on to another caseworker.'

'Thank you, I only want to speak to Miss Field.'

'Shall I pass you on?'

'No.'

83

'Would you care to leave your name?'

'That's all right.'

'Would you care to leave your name?'

'Thank you, no, that's all right.'

'Would you care to leave a message?'

'No message.'

'Shall I tell Miss Field that this is a personal call?'

'No.'

'Are you by any chance the caller who was trying to contact Miss Field last Friday?'

'Not me.'

She had finished. She had exhausted her repertoire of frustration and snub, and she was finished now. He put the phone down. Where is she? Just out, that's all. She will not tell him enough about her work for him to be able to envisage it; as if her clients' paltry secrets were of any interest to him, as if his life could possibly touch theirs at any point. She is seeing people, or at that childrens' home she goes to. She was out on Friday. Three times he had called on Friday, and had gone into the weekend hollow and lost. Now he had put the phone down on the secretary cow and antagonised her. Now she would say Isabel was out when she was in. Now she would say Miss Field cannot accept personal calls during office hours. What is your name, rank or number, whether married divorced single, number of children in box provided, state professional qualifications, whether subject to epilepsy or visual defects, whether certified sane or insane, state whether dead or alive and name a referee. (Isabel ring me.) I don't want to make a great performance of it, it's not a lot to ask, no messages, no names, no packdrill, whatever that expression means. (Ring me. I need to hear your voice.) The bell. Lesson Four.

Give me this God and I'll take myself off and give you some peace. I'll not be back asking favours year after year. There's only one thing I want. I won't ask you to bring my blood pressure down. When I get cancer I'll not even squeak. You'll never hear me say I'm hard done by. Come God, I'll praise you; isn't that what you like? Form 3A, the American Revolution. Is it so much to ask, is it so bloody much?

How she laughed and said, you have all the women's lines. Man's love is of man's life a thing apart/T'is woman's whole existence. Thank you, Lord Byron, mind how you go. Have a nice day.

CHAPTER 4

Evelyn had to take her time now. Coming downstairs, with her bad knees, was more painful than going up. She kept her head down, bowed over her hand tight on the banister rail. I'll just get a bit of breakfast, she thought, and then I'll have to get to the shops. I'll lock Muriel in the back room. She's not to be trusted.

What a lucky thing, to have a solid old-fashioned house with locks on the inside doors.

She stopped on the second step from the bottom. Muriel was standing by the front door.

'Muriel?'

She raised her eyes to the dark shape that swung gently above Muriel's head. Its folds were dense in the half-light. Clifford had come back, and hung his coat on the hallstand.

Isabel left the office in a hurry. She had been reading the file on Axon, Muriel Alexandra, when the Hollies Day Centre had called to say did she know anything about Anderson, Louisa Jane? Was she still staying with her daughter in Kidderminster, because it was her morning, and she hadn't turned up. Miss Anderson was seventy-six, she lived alone, and the weather was cold. The temperature had dropped several degrees overnight. She had never missed a day before, the Centre said, she looked forward to the hot meal and the sociability. She was in good health but – 'I have a file,' Isabel said. She rummaged in her desk drawer for the A–Z.

'All right, that will take me ten or fifteen minutes and I'll call you. She's not answering the phone? No, I see. Well, she won't if she's still in Kidderminster. If she's okay I'll drop her into you and if she's not I'll sort things out. Leave it with me.'

Miss Anderson was a vague lady. She had an application in for Sheltered Housing. She had two years to wait. Social Services had got her a telephone but she kept it off the hook, because she was harassed by obscene callers. This might be true or it might be a delusion. She had told the police, and they had made a note of her and taken her home in a car. She would not go to Kidderminster permanently because her daughter's husband was a Communist. This might be true or it might be a delusion.

When Isabel reached her car she realised she had Muriel Axon's file under her arm, gathered up with her street map and her note of Miss Anderson's address. I shouldn't keep reading it, she thought, it only scares me, it only makes me sick. I should go there, but I won't. If anything went wrong at Buckingham Avenue someone would call for help. It was a responsible middle-class neighbourhood. The file shouldn't go out of the office; but she didn't want to delay herself by taking it back. She tossed it into the back seat.

Probably Miss Anderson was still away. But she hurried, in rising apprehension at what she might find. As a trainee she had visited a geriatric hospital, and it had shocked her profoundly. She blew her horn at a caped and dripping cyclist who meandered into her path, and swore at him under her breath.

'Whatever have you done to your face, Missus?'

'I had a fall,' Evelyn said. 'On the stairs.'

'You want to watch yourself,' the meter man said. 'Given it a fair old bash, eh? Whatever will your young man say?'

The gas meter was in the kitchen. It was a nuisance. She followed the man. 'You don't get any natural light coming in, with all that stained glass,' he said. 'Like a bloody funeral parlour. Haven't you got a light in this passage?'

'This hall,' Evelyn said. 'The bulb has gone.'

'Well, you don't want to go climbing up there. You could come a right cropper. You want to get your friend to do it.'

'Friend? What friend?'

She stood over the man, watching his bent back as he flashed his torch into the little dark cupboard. He twisted round, squatting, and looked up at her.

'Well, you've got somebody stopping with you, haven't you?'

'What?'

'There's somebody looking out of the bedroom window.'

Muriel? Muriel was locked in the back parlour.

'Are you all right, Missus? You've gone white.'

One of the less substantial tenants of the upper floor then, one of those who taunted and gibbered from behind the locked door of the spare room; one of the lepers, one of the grinders of dry bones.

'Have you got any brandy in the house? You want to have a drop, and then put your feet up. You can't always tell with a crack on the head. You ought to go to evening surgery.'

'Do your job,' Evelyn said. 'Read the meter and then get out.'

'All right, Missus, all right.'

The man turned away, flashed his torch again, made a note and straightened up. 'Say no more,' he said. She followed him back down the hall. At the front door he turned back to her, relenting. 'Look, Missus, if you've got a spare bulb I'll put it in for you. It's not right, living in the dark at your age.'

'I haven't got one. I never keep them. I shall manage for myself. Good afternoon.'

'I'm sure,' said the man. 'Get your fancy man to fix it for you, eh? Sorry I spoke.'

She stood in the doorway to watch him down the path, to make sure that he was really gone. Curiosity about her arrangements was something she could not stomach. The man disappeared behind the bushes of the Sidney house. She craned her neck. Suddenly she felt a terrific blow in the small of her back. She pitched forward, off the doorstep. One arm flailed in the air. With difficulty she regained her balance. She stood gasping, winded. The door clicked behind her. She was locked out.

It had taken Isabel two minutes to establish that Miss Anderson was not going to answer the door, and just another minute to raise her next-door neighbour.

'She's stopping with her daughter,' the woman said. 'She'll be back on Thursday. Are you from that place she goes to?'

'Well, I'm from Social Services. The Day Centre asked me to call. When she didn't turn up this morning they were a bit worried. In case she'd had a fall or anything, you know.'

The woman tutted. 'She should have let you know. Fetching you out on a morning like this. Old people are inconsiderate, I think, don't you?'

'It's all right. I'm used to it. Going out, I mean.'

'Well, you needn't bother again,' the woman said. 'I keep an eye on her, you see. If she doesn't take her milk in I go round. I'd get the doctor to her if there was any need.'

'That's extremely kind of you. Look, here's a card with the number of the Social Services Department, if you ever need it. You can give us a ring.'

'Okay,' the woman said. 'My name's Mrs Johnson. Would you like a cup of tea, love?'

Isabel would: but I'd better be off, she thought.

'Wouldn't be surprised if we have fog coming down.'

'Goodbye, Mrs Johnson, and thank you very much.'

As she drove downhill towards the city centre, the promised fog began to gather. The traffic slowed to a crawl. I wish I had taken five minutes for that cup of tea, she thought. But she was impatient of lonely women. There must be something wrong with the heater. Her feet were frozen, and the Axons were still on her mind. And what in God's name was that? A shape loomed across the windscreen, the same bloody cyclist, she could swear . . . she stabbed at the brake and heard a sickening crunch from behind her. Her seatbelt bounced her back unhurt, her pulse racing. She closed her eyes. She was not at all surprised. She sat still, trying to calm herself, until a face appeared at the window mouthing was she all right Miss? The cyclist was unhurt. It was not a day for drama. Isabel and the man who had run into the back of her stood on the pavement and exchanged names and addresses. She inspected the damage, running her hand tenderly over the fractured paintwork. Considering the low speed of the other vehicle, it was a surprising mess. Her head ached insistently and she felt guilty. Earlier in the day, at least, her driving had been careless and impatient; her mind had been wandering, and most accidents, she told herself, are not entirely accidental. My humour drew the cyclist on; on a good day, I would have been elsewhere.

She drove very slowly and carefully to a public callbox, and rang the office. Someone has run into the back of me, I shall put the car into the garage now and come back by bus.

The garage couldn't see their way to tackling it much before the weekend. But it's only Monday, she said helpfully. Very true, the man said, but it was more than Monday, wasn't it, it was the time of year. But it's not a big job, she said, surely you can fit it in. Miss, said the man, wasn't she aware that this was the holiday season? What holiday? You don't mean that people have started their Christmas holidays already? She must understand, said the man, that this was a notoriously tricky few weeks, she would probably not credit, even if he were to tell her, the difficulties the festive season could cause. She could if she liked to try Thatcher's Motors at the top of the hill by the lights, but he personally was willing to bet any money that she would be wasting her time. Far be it from him to do Thatcher's out of trade, and if she wanted to waste her time he supposed she was entitled, it being a free country, but he could assure her that they would quote her ten days, and would they say the same about the time of year? They most certainly would. Could he solve her problem, solve it he would. She could then again go to some cowboy who would do a botched job. Of course she could if she liked, he supposed it was her money, and that it was a free country. Cowboys were not subject to festive difficulties but what would you get? A botched job. He personally had seen some right messes. Still, it was her choice, entirely. If she wanted to leave it with him, he would see what he could do, and could he say fairer than that? Now, he would tell her what, if it had been a windscreen, he could probably, making no promises but probably, have let her have it by Thursday. It's not, she said, so what's the point? She had it there, he said. She had put her finger on it. He was taking it as what he supposed she might care to call a sort of illustration. The fact was, it was not a windscreen. It was Bodywork.

At the end of this conversation the feeling of heavy unreality inside her skull was much increased. She waited a long time for a bus, and as it crept along in the still thickening fog her mind emptied of her problems and professional duties and became blank and grey. When she arrived at the office she found she couldn't get warm. People said she Might Have 'Flu Coming On. She put her head in her hands and rubbed her eyes. Her friend Jane said that they should go to the pub and get her a double Scotch and some cottage pie. All that, the Senior said glibly, the common cold, 'flu, hay-fever, it's a form of suppressed weeping, you know. It was only when she got back from lunch, and felt no better, that she remembered that she had left Muriel Axon's file on the back seat of the car. She telephoned the garage, but of course there was no answer.

I've driven up out of it, Colin thought, turning into Florence's drive. The first part of the journey had been nerve-wracking. The dismal city centre jangled with noise, lights flickered in strange places, distances were unjudgeable. Faces distorted with apprehension flashed momentary and half-lit behind glass, locked into their metal shells, alien machines with mad demands.

'I can hardly believe it,' Colin said. 'It's clear up here and it's not even raining. You should see it down the hill. It's a nightmare. The hospitals will be full before tonight's out.' He struggled out of his jacket and Florence took it from him. 'Hot,' he explained. 'Tension. They won't slow down. How they can do it beats me.'

'Is that all you wear? Haven't you a decent overcoat?'

'Yes. I forget it. I always wear my pullover.'

'You must take care of yourself,' Florence said. 'I heard about the fog. It says on the wireless it's all along the motorway as well. I just phoned Sylvia, to make sure the children had got home from school all right. I thought you'd want to know.'

'Bless you, Florence. That was thoughtful.'

'I've made some tea. It's all ready for you.'

A sense of *déjà vu* took hold of him as he stood in the hall, and would not let him go. Perhaps it was the dislocation of the fog, and his confused state of mind. It could have been his mother waiting, himself a boy in a cap and blazer, algebra homework lying heavy on his stomach. In the hallway Florence had changed nothing, nothing had ever been changed as long as he could remember; the dust was moved, that was all, and came floating back, speckled, settling, spinning in the spring sunlight and drifting on the smoke of autumn garden fires. But the past had not been like that. It was negligence, not sentiment, that kept things in their place year after year. This was the paradox and danger of time-travel, altering the past to suit. His mother had never met him in the hall and settled him with something to eat. She would be lying on her bed with pins in her hair, or still doing the morning's jobs (like cleaning the toilet), or reading a novel in which a governess was abducted into a harem. And Florence was older at forty than his mother would ever have chosen to be, solid and set in her barren maternity.

'What is it?' Florence said. She poured the tea and pushed a plate towards him.

'Ah, I was just thinking of Mum.'

'Mum? You never called her that. We never called her Mum.'

'No. It's just a funny feeling, to come home, home from school, come in here. Being a man . . . in your own house . . . such incessant demands. I don't feel always that I can meet them, nowadays.'

'We all get these fits of inadequacy,' Florence said.

'Is that what they are?'

'You feel you're not doing what you should be doing.' She spooned some sugar into her tea. 'You feel, surely there's more to life than this. But there isn't, and it passes off. It passes off.'

'That's disappointment. That's different.'

'Not really. Milk? Because you feel, if you measured up, if you measured up at all to any kind of standard, then you would have something more in your life. You'd have made something more.'

'Yes. You usually know what I'm thinking, Florence. You usually have a good idea of what's on my mind.'

'Do I?' She bit into a sandwich and put it back on her plate. 'It seems strange though to hear you talk about Mother like that. I never thought of her as — well, as a great comfort. Nor as a source of security. Perhaps because you were the son it was different for you. You know, when she became ill I felt so guilty. I didn't like her much, I felt I ought to have done more.'

'No one could have done more,' Colin said firmly. 'You had her at home for as long as anyone possibly could.'

'She wasn't really a lot of trouble.'

'She was terrifying, Florence.'

'Yes.'

'You couldn't be expected to sacrifice your life to that.'

'No?' she said ruefully. She glanced away. 'I can't think what else I was expected to do.'

'You have no cause to feel guilty, none at all.'

'It was funny — ' she paused with the tea-strainer in her hand. 'I could manage her better when she was ill. It wasn't really — I suppose it wasn't like dealing with a person at all. It was before that she used to annoy me, her legs being so thin, and that lipstick she used to put on, all her silly little coquettish ways. She seemed to stick, somehow, she wouldn't get old decently . . . and then look what happened. Will you have some of these meat paste?'

'We talk about her as if she were dead.'

'I sometimes wish she were. I often wish it. I think and think . . . that morning when I went over to Cousin Eileen's, and I came back, she'd been out, there was her bag in the hall, four months after Father's death — whatever happened, Colin? She was normal in the morning.'

'They said her brain was damaged. You know that.'

'But why?' she persisted. 'Why should it be damaged? She didn't go anywhere. She didn't bang her head.'

'I don't think they meant . . . I think they meant, some sort of seizure . . . I don't know. I never got to the bottom of it. You know what doctors are.'

'Anyway, I feel she *is* dead really. Can I fill your cup up? I hate going to see her. We'll have to go, I suppose, Christmas. It's a pointless business, isn't it? She doesn't know who we are. She doesn't know whether it's Christmas or not.'

They paused, considering in separate minds the same picture: their first visit, when they had noticed that the dark rinse she used on her hair was growing out, and a thin seam of tallow showed at the roots. And the bored medical voice: 'I want you to put right out of your mind any fantasies you may have concerning straitjackets and padded cells. Happily we have available to us nowadays some excellent tranquillising drugs which are just as effective, but far more pleasant.'

'Pleasant?' Colin had said. 'Pleasant? You mean pleasant for you? Look, what you mean is, you can keep her quiet but you can't cure her?'

The doctor had smiled patiently. 'We would hope to see some improvement.'

'But what's she got? What disease is it?'

The doctor became even more bored. 'As far as we can ascertain, your mother has what we call delusions of nihilism. She believes that she no longer exists.'

It was too much to take in. Now her hair had grown out a soiled yellow-white. It was combed carefully by a nurse over the tiny skull, and secured by a great black hairgrip. Florence was shocked by it every time. She would whisper to Colin in indignation, as they left the ward, 'She would never have been seen with her hair like that.'

'You can't know,' Colin said finally. 'You can't imagine it. Let's face it, even with normal people . . . I say you know what's going on in my mind, but that's not really true, you can't. They say only connect but how can you? They say no man is an island but – '

'Be more cheerful, Colin,' his sister said. 'Have some date and walnut cake.'

'I can't. I'm in trouble.'

Less than islands, he thought, jagged bits of rock without names, and an ocean of lies and deceit and egotism.

'What sort of trouble?'

'Oh, nothing . . . a personal thing.' He stood condemned out of his own mouth. How could he ask Florence to concern herself? He'd told her to let alone the problems of her neighbours. To live her own life. How was he any different?

'Colin,' she said deliberately, 'I looked after Mother. I was prepared to go on doing it. I chose to be depended upon, not to depend.'

'And circumstances came and kicked even that from under you.'

'I only mean that I will do what I can for you. Is it Sylvia?'

'What else could it be? It's Sylvia.'

'Are you very unhappy?'

'I have been thinking about leaving her.'

'Well . . . ' Florence said. She put her cup down. 'The children, Colin.'

'Yes, I know.'

'Well, you would have to think it out very carefully.'

'I don't think I should have bothered you about this. The thing is that I thought I had my mind in order, but I see that I haven't. I'm not ready to talk about it yet.'

'It would be a terrible mistake to act in haste.'

'Of course.' Colin stood up. 'I'll be off, Florence.'

'Can't you tell me what's bothering you?'

'I'd like to. Sometime. Not just yet.' She watched his face as he heaved his jacket on. 'By the way, I saw your neighbour, Mrs Axon. She was in the garden. She waved to me.'

'In the garden? She'll catch her death. I never see the daughter these days. What was she doing?'

'Doing? Well, maybe – I don't know, but she looked all right. Look, Florence, I'll see you over the weekend, if that's okay.'

She followed him to the door. 'Colin, if you left her, I suppose you'd come back to me?'

He turned his head away, unable to answer. 'Sometime Saturday then,' he said. As he drove around the corner he saw that Mrs Axon was still in her garden. Silly old bat, he thought. His stomach felt like lead. Next week was the last week of term, and he had no plans at all.

Evelyn rapped sharply on the door, two or three times. Of course, it was useless. She rubbed her back where the blow had caught her, and began to walk around the house.

The door of the lean-to was bolted. She could break the glass and put her hand through, at least it would give her some shelter. She could get into the kitchen if the door was not locked. She tried to remember. Then, peering in, she noticed that Muriel had been moving some of the boxes and had piled them up behind the lean-to door. She doubted if she could budge them.

She went to the window of the back sitting-room. It was too high to look into but perhaps she could find something to stand on and signal to Muriel what had happened. What was this? The curtains were drawn. She banged furiously on the glass. There was no response. Muriel was in there, she knew, because she herself had turned the key on her. And here she had the key in the pocket of her cardigan. Break the glass, put the key through to Muriel; no, attract Muriel's attention, and get her to open the window, and then . . . but she could never climb through. Not unless Muriel exerted herself to help her, and she had never been known to do that. Then, attract Muriel's attention, get her to open the window, pass her the key, tell her to release herself and go down the hall and open the front door. Simple.

Could they have done Muriel some damage? If they could hit her in the back and push her out of the house, there was no saying what they might have planned. Surely they had not come for the child already. She thought bitterly, they have only to wait.

Turning away, she shambled to the front of the house again. No doubt Muriel had simply drawn the curtains and fallen asleep. She was prone to do that. Florence Sidney's brother was driving past. He waved to her. She raised a hand, the smile painful on her face.

Colin had not seen Isabel for a week. When he telephoned her home, her father answered.

'Are you one of Bella's friends?' he asked.

He said that she was in bed with 'flu. Colin saw his chance to break the deadlock.

'May I call?' he asked. 'To cheer her up?'

'Oh, no,' Mr Field said. 'I believe it could be infectious, you know. No, I don't think that would be advisable, not at all.'

A few days later Colin spoke to her. He had to leave the house to make these calls. She sounded strained and weak; her throat was still sore, she explained.

'But I can meet you if you can pick me up. My car – no, you didn't know, did you? I had a bit of an accident, that day it was foggy. Somebody ran into the back of me. I haven't collected it from the garage yet.'

'You were all right, weren't you?'

'Yes, fine, it was only a brush, but that's the day I started this cold.'

'Listen, Isabel, I can't meet you. I could maybe get over during the day but I can't take you out.'

'Oh – why is that?' Her voice cracked.

'Because it's the holidays. Can't you see? Didn't you think about it? I haven't got any excuses.'

'You could have warned me.'

'I thought you would realise. I'm so sorry. I do want to see you very much. The only thing I could do would be to come during the day.'

'No, Colin, you're not to come here.'

'Well, that's that then. Can I phone you? That's all right, isn't it?'

'Yes, but look, when will I see you?'

'When term starts.'

'But I can't go through to January without seeing you.'

'You'll have to. You must.'

'When will it be?'

'January 12th, but it will take me a few days – '

She began to cry. 'Listen, Colin, haven't you got any friends you could pretend to go and see? Anybody you usually see at Christmas?'

'I can't think of anyone. I have no friends of my own, you see, I have only places where Sylvia goes with me.'

'But there must be something you do on your own.'

'Only evening classes. But they're over now.'

'Yes. Well . . . Colin, please.'

'Look, I'll try, I'll really try, but I can't think how I'm going to manage it.'

'Well, try, see if you can – I really want to see you. We're going to have to discuss things, we'll have to decide.'

For the first time he heard the note of pressure in her voice. It was a tone he had heard before. Where? He thought with surprise, in my own mouth.

'Yes, we must. Though I don't know . . . I honestly don't know what we're going to do. Look, Isabel, I'll have to go, the children are waiting for me.'

'You've got them with you?'

'Yes, they're outside the phone box. I brought them out to buy them some sweets. I'll have to go.'

She laughed shakily. 'What we are reduced to,' she said. 'Good-bye.'

He heard the line buzz. She's upset, he thought. It's her illness. 'Flu leaves you like that. He stepped out of the kiosk and took a gulp of air. He felt desperately harassed.

'Who were you phoning, Dad?' Alistair asked. His mouth was sticky with sweets.

'Just a man.'

'What was his name, Dad?'

'Frank.'

'That's not a name.'

'Yes, it is, Alistair,' Suzanne said remotely. She took her brother's hand. He immediately suspected her of an ulterior motive.

'Well what was his other name, Dad?'

'Frank O'Dwyer.'

'Who's he, Dad?'

'Just a man, Alistair, somebody at work.'

'You don't go to work. You go to school.' A pause. 'Why didn't you phone him when you were at home, Dad?'

'Because the phone wasn't working at home.'

'It was,' Suzanne said. Colin took her hand and halted her at the kerb. She removed her hand from his.

'I can walk by myself, thank you very much,' she said.

'Do your road drill,' Colin said wearily.

'What?'

'Look right, look left, look right again, if the road is clear begin to cross. Don't you know that? Haven't they told you at school? Alistair, look, don't run, come here. Haven't you been told not to run across the road?'

'What would it matter, if there's nothing coming?' Suzanne said. 'And if there was, you'd be better running, then it wouldn't have time to hit you.'

'Suzanne, don't argue.'

'The phone *was* working. Mummy phoned up Aunty Peggy.'

There was a time, he thought, when I had comparative peace of mind. I was dull, yes, but I didn't spend all my days in frantic plotting and my nights lying awake worrying about when the plots would come home to roost; there was a time when I didn't have to use my children as an excuse and get tied up in knots like this.

'I've finished my sweeties,' Alistair said. 'Can I have some more?'

'You'll be sick,' Suzanne warned him.

'I hope you saved some for Karen.'

'What?'

'Have you eaten Karen's? Oh, blast.'

'She'll cry,' Suzanne said.

'Come on then, we'll go back and get her some. Come on.'

'You greedy pig,' Suzanne said to her brother.

'I'll kick you,' he said.

'See if you can.'

'Will you stop this?' Colin hauled his son away. 'Come on now. Hurry up.'

He swept them along the pavement, clutching one by either hand, quelling their struggles. One day, he thought, when it has all come out about Isabel, and it is over, and they are grown up, they will look back and remember that day I took them out to buy sweets, remember my uncharacteristic good nature: and how I went into a callbox, and how I lied to them: and they will begin to piece it all together and make sense out of it. Oh yes, they will say, he was phoning *her*, he must have been. He was using us to get out of the house – he was never so nice at other times – and didn't he tell clumsy lies? How disgusting it all is.

When they got home, Suzanne said, 'Is the phone working, Mum?'

'Yes, why?'

'Dad said it wasn't.'

'Look, Suzanne,' Colin said, 'anybody can make a mistake.'

'What mistake?' Sylvia said.

'He went into a phone box and phoned somebody. Just now, when we were out.'

Sylvia looked at him questioningly.

'I rang Frank O'Dwyer, it was just something I had on my mind, about plans for next term. I thought it might go out of my head if I didn't do it right away.'

'Oh,' Sylvia said. She wasn't greatly interested; to Colin it sounded extremely feeble, but it was the best he could do on the spur of the moment.

'Why did you say the phone was out of order?' Suzanne asked. 'You told a fib.'

'Get off my back, Suzanne,' Colin said. 'You're getting very cheeky.' He picked up the newspaper.

'Did you get those Swiss rolls?' Sylvia asked him.

'Sorry. Forgot.'

'I asked you, Colin,' she said mildly.

'Then I'll go back.' He put the paper down.

'He wants to phone again,' Suzanne said. 'I'll go with him, shall I, and see if he does?'

Oh God, he thought, is it worth it? This is only the Christmas holidays. It is only two weeks and a half. What will happen when the summer comes?

Evelyn had made herself a cup of tea. It had been an ordeal. When she had found that the front door was open after all, she had stood hesitating on the step. Once, she would not have been able to nerve herself to go in.

'I'm tired of your tricks,' she said out loud, and pushed the door open carefully. The hall was empty.

Muriel got up sleepily at the sound of the key turning in her prison door. She rubbed her eyes. Evelyn could see the dent in the cushion where her head had rested. She went over to the window and pulled back the curtains, but night was coming down and she saw that there was no point in it.

'I was locked out,' she said to Muriel. 'Didn't you hear me knocking on the window?' She sighed and went into the kitchen.

Muriel followed her. Evelyn talked, to keep the silence away. Muriel had an elaborate air of not listening: humming to herself, twiddling her fingers in front of her eyes.

Now, that overcoat, Evelyn said. Nothing was made nowadays as well as it used to be; neither coats nor mothballs. Of course, she had put it carefully in the wardrobe, not knowing when it might be needed. After all, it had been practically new. At some time she must have transferred it to the old chest in the lean-to. And over the years she had forgotten it. Who would have thought it would have kept so nice? Seeing it hanging up had given her such a turn.

Evelyn's tone was easy, conversational. She was anxious to make it clear that she did not hold the business against her daughter. In matters of this kind, Muriel was as innocent as the day is long.

Evelyn put a cup of tea down before Muriel. Muriel began to devote all her attention to it, gazing into its depths avidly.

How long now? Evelyn thought. She had made no preparations,

as yet. Clearly, she would have to take responsibility. She would have to do it all. She tried to remember Muriel's birth, whether there had been difficulties, whether it had been painful. It was all so long ago now.

In the days after their marriage, the house had been very tidy. She had polished and swept all day. Clifford came and went. He went out to business. He was a handsome, taciturn man, a fastidious eater, a vegetarian. He shaved twice a day. She did not really know him well, not well at all.

She had made an appointment with the doctor, an elderly and sallow man.

'Well, I suppose you know your condition,' he had said. 'It is sufficiently evident.'

She had gathered her courage, clearing her throat softly. 'How does this come about?' she asked.

The doctor had looked up at her. 'My dear lady.' He chuckled without a semblance of humour. 'My dear lady.'

She had told Clifford the same night. He was not pleased. But he said that no doubt the child could be trained to be not much inconvenience. After all, he had never imagined that he would be a dog-owner, but the Airedale was very well-behaved.

Unfortunately, soon after Muriel was born, the Airedale chewed up a rug and Clifford took it away to the vet's. Muriel lay quietly in her cot. Clifford's temper was short, but she gave no cause for complaint.

A brief sharp pain interrupted Evelyn's thoughts; now she remembered. She had been left alone to scream, on a high white bed. The landscape of her pain had been her high, knotted, purple stomach. The parasite was straining to be away. A woman with a clamped mouth had stuck her head around the door, and asked her to please have some consideration.

And dangling from the doctor's hands, upside down and blood-smeared, like someone horribly executed: Muriel Alexandra, a lovely daughter.

She looked at Muriel in pity, turning at once to exasperation.

'Now what is that you have there?'

She pulled the bit of card out of Muriel's hand. It was tatty, crumpled, thumbed; a reminder from the Welfare. Dates and times. The Day Centre. Miss Field has called.

'How long have you had this?'

No answer.

Evelyn ripped it through once. I'll burn it, she said. If you have any more, give them to me at once and I'll burn them all.

Muriel raised her head and gave her a direct look, engaging her eyes. It was something she did so seldom that Evelyn was shot through with alarm. She understood that she was being threatened.

'Why should they bother about you?' she said. 'Why should they come looking for you? What are you worth, to anybody?'

Muriel subsided. She tapped her fingernail rhythmically against the side of her cup. Strange, Evelyn thought, but it was some time now since she had wondered how her daughter had come by the baby.

'You can drive nature out with a pitchfork,' she said, 'but she gets back in.'

Muriel got up and opened the cutlery drawer, jerking it as she always did, as she always did to irritate her mother. She took out a fork and fingered it speculatively.

'Put it down,' Evelyn said. 'You'll prick yourself. Don't go touching my things.'

Muriel threw down the fork with a clatter, and slammed shut the drawer. She seized the dishcloth and wrung it between her hands, dripping greasy water on to her feet. She flung it at the table and moved across the room, tapping the chairbacks with her knuckles and slapping the palm of her hand against the cupboard doors.

'Stop it, stop it.' Evelyn got up, pushing her chair back, convulsed with anger. 'Everything in this house is mine.'

She doubled her fist and struck out at Muriel, pounding at her shoulders and arms and ribs. Muriel stood, stoic. The blows bounced back from her plump solid body. Evelyn whined and gasped. Weariness stopped her. She stood glaring at her daughter, her arms limp by her sides. Suddenly, Muriel smiled. The grin split her face and lit up her eyes. She was delighted, she said softly. Delighted to be here. Welcoming you all. A short programme of song and laughter. For your entertainment. Tonight.

Three days before Christmas, Colin said to Sylvia, 'Frank O'Dwyer phoned up.'

'Oh yes?'

'I thought I might just run over there. There are a few things he wants to get straightened out, about next term.'

Sylvia gave him an odd look, he thought. 'Can't it wait till after Christmas?'

'Well, yes, but you know how it is. The holidays are over before you know where you are.' He paused, watching the effect of this; none discernible. Sylvia was peeling potatoes. 'I think he might want a bit of company as well. Poor old Frank,' he added sentimentally.

Sylvia filleted out an eye with the sharp end of the peeler. 'All right,' she said.

'Only you wouldn't want to come. It would mean getting somebody in to babysit, and we'd only be talking shop.'

'I've a lot to do,' Sylvia said, and added warningly, 'Christmas is no holiday for me, you know.'

The following night Colin sat with Isabel in a chilly country pub twelve miles out of town. It was one of the unregenerated kind, with stone floors and a picturesque but quite inadequate open fire. A limp paperchain or two hung over the bar as a nod to festivity, but the customers were quiet and the landlord surly. Isabel looked up and watched Colin as he walked across the room with her tepid gin and his own pint of flat warm beer. Frankly he wondered how he was going to be able to manage these expeditions; the money for drinks, and the extra petrol. He always had an overdraft by the end of January. Every year.

'No ice,' he said jerking his head back towards the bar.

'It's all right here,' Isabel said. 'It's quiet.'

'I could hardly believe Sylvia didn't know I was up to something.'

'Up to something? You make me sound like a practical joke.' She lit a cigarette. 'Colin, I wanted to see you because I've got some decisions to make. I'm thinking of leaving my job.'

'Well . . . I didn't think you were happy.'

'Happiness seems a bit ambitious. I'm not sure I can see my way to that.'

'You're not thinking of going away, are you?'

She watched his face, for the dawn of any hope. How have I come to trust him so little, she wonders, how has all my life become so soured?

'I've been offered a post in a new set-up – a therapeutic community, we call it. Must I blush for my jargon? It's only a few miles away. But they'd like me to live in.'

'And you don't want to leave your father?'

'I don't feel that I can.'

'It's bad luck on you to have no brothers and sisters, and a father who's so elderly. I suppose he can't get about as he used to.'

Isabel opened her bag and took out her handkerchief. Inside the bag were her father's spectacles. He could not manage without them. After some thought, she had hit on this method of confining him to the house. 'This place,' she said, 'it's a new approach, small numbers, a good staffing ratio. It's for children who are mentally ill.'

Colin noticed the blue circles under her eyes, the tightness around her mouth. 'I should think that would be intensely depressing. What have children got to make them mentally ill? Are they born that way?'

'Are you asking me for information?' she said. 'Or is it a debating point?'

'For information. You'd be surprised what I don't know. Explain to me.'

'Some babies don't eat, they don't cry. Nobody knows why.'

'It can hardly be society. It must be their genes. Genes are not much in fashion, I think. It must be their mothers.'

'Some of the mothers don't seem to make relationships with the children. They don't treat them as people, just as objects. They let them lie for hours and don't react when they cry. The children feel that nothing they do can influence the world. They can't control it. And they give up trying.'

'Like me,' Colin said. 'I can't control the world. I'm like that. I have it.'

'It's not a disease, it's a state of being. The constant frustration of one's efforts to adapt the world, and the resignation of the attempt.'

'It's common.' He sighed. 'Look at the Labour Party.'

'Oh, Colin, it isn't a bit the same. The frustrations we meet every day are of a different order. Sometimes the mothers are quite normal, and then we can't account for it. When they get a bit older the children just sit, or they lie, and they gaze into the distance, you know, or just play with their fingers. They seem not to want to live. They seem afraid of it. Afraid of everything.'

'Nobody can do anything about anything,' Colin said. 'They are right, the rest of us are wrong. Deluded. Why should we victimise them? Poor little sods.'

'But it's a practical problem. They have to be fed. Kept alive. The whole world seems to them completely destructive.' She paused. 'Maybe it is. I see your point. They have the nuclear weapons inside their heads. The megadeath.'

'Why don't they give up then? Just give up and die?'

'Some do.'

'And the others?'

'We presume that they once felt some security or goodness. At the breast. They are fighting to get back to it.'

'But you can't get everything from the breast.'

'No. You can't get very much at all.' She looked up at him. 'Could we possibly, do you think, be more cheerful?'

'It *is* Christmas,' he said automatically. 'Look, Isabel, I don't think you should rush into a decision. On the one hand, would you be any more satisfied with that sort of work? On the other hand, perhaps your father should stand on his own feet. Plenty of people that age manage for themselves. He might live another twenty years, and then what? You'd be a prisoner.'

Isabel put her bag down at her feet, and edged it under the table.

'Don't put it down there, love, you might forget it.'

'Women never forget their handbags. They're womb symbols. You wouldn't forget your womb, would you? I bet Sylvia never does.'

'You've not been well, you know. You look very run down. Put everything off for a month or two.'

'Well, I can't seem to cope, that's true enough. I do some stupid things. I lost a file. At least, I put it in the back of my car, and then it went into the garage, and when it came back the file wasn't there.'

'Nobody would want it, would they?'

'It would be of no use or interest to anyone. That's why it's so annoying.'

'Have you told them, at the office?'

'Not yet. I shouldn't have taken it out. I only did it by accident. We did lose a few things when we moved from Wilberforce House, but I think they turned up. I don't know what the procedure is.'

'Well, there must be some way round it. Have you phoned the garage?'

'Oh yes,' she said tiredly. 'But they're all really stupid people. I never did come to grips with that case, somehow. I could almost think I lost the file on purpose.'

'I think you make too much of people's subconscious motivations, Isabel. You're always looking to complicate things.'

'I dare say you're right. I dare say this particular case hasn't half the complications I've seen in it. Somebody else would handle it more rationally.'

'Has it upset you? Do you want to talk about it?'

'I shouldn't talk about my clients. No, it's not an upsetting case, compared to some. It's just been very trying and distasteful. The file can never be put together again. It goes back too many years, too many people have been involved.'

'They'll have to make a fresh start.'

'I don't think anyone's ever made a fresh start. Except Lazarus.'

Colin went to the bar. She sat with her eyes downcast as he carried their glasses back again. She was pale, and she had a cough; she seemed to have lost more weight. She was nervous, less competent.

'Is all this ... quite what you wanted to ask me about?' Colin said as he sat down. 'You sounded so urgent on the phone.'

'No, of course it wasn't. I wanted to talk about us. I think it's time we made some decisions, Colin.'

'We've had this conversation before.'

'I want to live with you.'

And now it is she who pleads. The passing weeks have worked a little miracle. She didn't touch the glass he had put in front of her.

'So you are asking me,' he spoke very deliberately, 'to break with Sylvia in the near future?'

'What's the far future? Do you want to wait until Karen is twenty-one?'

'You know there's nothing left between me and Sylvia. It's the children. That's all.'

'You still sleep with her, I'm sure.'

'Yes. Well, I do.'

'So there is something there.'

'Something.' But no one who has been married, he thought, would presume it to be affection. 'The point is, I have to think very carefully. Their whole future hangs on this. I have to make the proper arrangements.'

'But deep down, Colin, you don't think *any* arrangements are proper.'

'I'm not saying that. I'm not saying I won't leave her.' He struggled for a judicious tone, something measured. 'But can't you see, Isabel? I feel torn.'

She reached for her coat from the chair beside her, reached for her bag under the table. 'Ah, this tired old scene,' she said. 'I should have known. How is it possible to be of moderate intelligence and reasonable education, and not know? I've read the Problem Pages. I ought to know. Come on, Colin, let's be going. I can't sit here and run through the lines that society has written for me. They've outlawed wire nooses and gin traps, but they can't legislate against this.'

They sat in silence; then, leaving their drinks half-finished, got up and walked stiffly out to the car.

Earlier that day, Florence Sidney had taken a conspicuous initiative. Her morning had begun badly. She had telephoned Sylvia to discuss arrangements, only to be told curtly that everything was under control and that she had nothing to do about Christmas dinner except turn up and eat it. Sylvia contrived to make her feel a fumbling amateur at family festivity, a selfish, disorganised, childless woman. Whereas the truth was, Florence thought bitterly . . . she looked down at her small, cool, pastry-making hands, and went into the kitchen to make two dozen mince pies.

At eleven thirty she stood at the Axons' front door with a plateful of the pies in her hand, warm and fragrant. From the hall she heard Evelyn Axon's voice raised in apparent anger; but she had already knocked. There was a sort of scuffling, a few seconds silence, and then the door opened on Evelyn's strained face.

'Yes? What is it you want?'

Florence stepped backwards. Evelyn's tone was coldly hostile. Without a word, Florence smiled miserably, and lifted the napkin to show the pies.

'I see,' Evelyn said, sneering.

'I thought – Merry Christmas.' Florence held out the plate; then suddenly, determination seized her. She stepped forward briskly, up the step and over the threshold, and Evelyn dropped back before her, caught off guard.

'May I come in?'

'You're in already, aren't you?'

'I hoped I could wish Muriel a Merry Christmas.'

'I dare say.'

'Is Muriel ill? It seems quite a time since I saw her out and about.'

Evelyn looked at Florence and saw nothing yielding about her; heard nothing apologetic, just the hard note of the professional enquirer. She heard a rustling from above, from the top of the stairs. Was Muriel preparing to come down? If this woman cast half an eye —

'You had better come in and sit down. This way.'

The front room was the safest, she thought, the least informative about their life and possessions. She rested her hand on the door-knob, and turned back to see Florence looking about her. 'How is your mother, Miss Sidney?' she said. Florence jumped and followed her.

The door was stuck. Evelyn gasped. Someone was at the other side of it. She heard a clunk, a scraping — the wood of the door knocked against something hard and resistant. Quickly, she turned with her back to the door.

'Is it stuck? Here, let me.'

'No. Get away.' She pushed Florence hard in the ribs. Florence dropped back, and two of the pies shot off her plate and plopped moistly on to the hall floor.

'Well, really. I was only trying to help.'

'You will hardly help yourself by going in there,' Evelyn said.

'I wasn't trying to help myself,' Florence said. 'It is of no interest to me. I was trying to help you.'

Evelyn's eyes narrowed. 'Have you any notion of what you may be doing, trying to force your way into locked rooms?'

'But it isn't locked. What are you talking about?'

'You have no idea what may be behind that door,' Evelyn said. 'Neither, for that matter, have I. Something is holding it shut, and it is certainly not damp.'

'This is absolutely ridiculous,' Florence said with passion.

'Ridiculous? I am glad you can take so light a view of it. Go into the back room.'

'Now look, Mrs Axon, I simply came to bring you some mince pies. I have no particular desire to go into your front room. Or your back room. I think possibly the best thing I can do is just give you the pies and go.'

'No,' Evelyn said. She pointed to the door of the back room. 'We are going to celebrate Christmas.'

Florence walked in ahead of her.

'I am going to give you a drink,' Evelyn said from the hall. 'Sit down and stay where you are.'

Florence looked around her. She had never been in the Axons' house. Her mother, she knew, had sometimes visited. The most remarkable thing was the quality of furniture, each heavy and unpolished piece pushed up against the next, jostling for space on a mud-coloured carpet; surely, Florence thought, carpets are not woven in any such shade. The upholstery of the suite was greasy and worn, the wallpaper yellow with age. What a way to live, Florence thought; creating a slum, here in this neighbourhood. What was the need for it? She tried to place the smell. Cats? No. Well, perhaps she was too fastidious. Not everyone had the same tastes in decor. And there was nothing too frightful, just some pervading air – Florence bit her lip.

Evelyn returned carrying a small tumbler of something pale. She stood opposite Florence, holding the glass. Florence noted with distaste that it was greasy.

'Aren't you joining me?'

'No.'

Florence reached out for the glass and swallowed it quickly, anxious to have it over with.

'Merry Christmas,' Evelyn said. 'At the same time, I must tell you that I regard you as an odious and interfering woman.'

Florence spluttered. 'I am sorry,' she said. 'I can't drink whisky. I didn't realise that it was neat whisky.'

'How unfortunate,' Evelyn said. 'I went to a great deal of trouble to find it for you. It is some years since anyone wanted it.'

Florence stood up. 'I am sorry to have put you to so much inconvenience. Perhaps you will give Muriel my best wishes for Christmas and the New Year.'

'Certainly,' Evelyn said. 'This way.'

'Yes, I know the way,' Florence said faintly. She gestured down at the plate containing the ten remaining pies, which she had placed on the arm of her chair.

'Not really,' Evelyn said.

Florence picked the plate up and walked out into the hall. 'You seem to think I have intruded on your privacy. I sincerely apologise.'

'One lives and learns,' Evelyn said blandly. 'Muriel is putting on weight, you know.'

'About that door. Obviously something is wrong with the frame. You ought to get a man in.'

Evelyn sniggered. 'Oh, we have that. We have had a man in.' She watched Florence down the path.

Thoroughly unnerved, Florence walked into her own tidy kitchen and filled the kettle. She stared for a moment at the mince pies on their plate, then with an abrupt movement picked it up and slid them into the wastebin.

CHAPTER 5

Christmas morning.

'Just shut the door on them,' Sylvia said. It was six a.m. She was huddled into her quilted dressing-gown. The children shrieked and howled from Suzanne's bedroom. 'I'll go down and brew some tea,' Sylvia said. 'There's no point in going back to bed.' And on this as on almost every other day, a grey fatigue shook her; another baby, what for, when the three were too much for her, but if only she could think sensibly about this, think logically, if only she could run all the strands of her thinking together for just half an hour. She never seemed to have half an hour, that was the trouble. In the cold kitchen she bit into a corner of dry toast; all she could face, these last couple of weeks. The electric light was brilliant and hard, like an operating theatre; her laminate surfaces gleamed empty and scrubbed, ready for the severance of 1974 from 1975. Condensation ran down the windows. Already the fights had begun upstairs; she could hear Alistair working himself into one of his fits. When he was younger, he used to go blue with temper and stop breathing. She moved about the kitchen, aimlessly dazed with bowls and spoons and teapots. She pulled back the curtains on to the blue-black morning; a streetlight burned fuzzily on the opposite side of the road, the great artificial moon which shone each night on to her marital bed. Already in the neighbours' houses lights were clicking on, the children rampaging downstairs shredding wrapping paper and mauling cats, shaking the ornaments from the Christmas trees. She put her hand against the radiator. It would soon be as warm as they could afford. She had always wanted a cosy house, low and cream, with plump flowered cushions; now she was as cosy as a fish under ice. Another year almost gone, the house no nearer paid for: the piling up of the interests on the debts.

Colin stood by the small window on the landing at the top of the stairs, looking out, with a damp towel from the bathroom in his hand. Some people, unbelievable as it seemed, lived in such a way that they had their own towels. A door opened and Karen lurched towards him, her face streaked with tears and dirty – how could it be dirty? – already. Grasped in either hand she had by the wrist identical dolls, fatly flaxen, improbably frilled.

'Come on now, pet,' he said, but she avoided him with a warning growl and swayed downstairs. Suzanne came out, glowering, her face heated.

'Florence has brought me a rotten sewing machine,' she said. 'I never get anything decent.'

'What's the matter with Karen?' Colin asked mildly.

'She's a crybaby. Stupid kids. I'm fed up pretending about Father Christmas. Daft stupid kids.'

'I didn't know you'd been enlightened,' Colin said. 'Could you just manage to pretend, for your brother and sister? Just for this year, at least. It would spoil it for them, you see.'

'Spoil it for you,' Suzanne said, acutely.

'You're eight years old,' Colin said, with ferocity; the accumulation of pinpricks. She stared at him and laughed, and went downstairs.

Sylvia was doing an explanation, when he arrived in the kitchen. She held out the two dolls and looked helplessly from one to the other.

'Besides, I'll make them new dresses,' she said. 'Then they'll be different.'

'When? Today?'

'Well, soon, lovey, but not just today, because your Aunty Florence is coming. Besides, isn't it nice, what they are, you see, they're identical twins.' Karen had stopped crying, but her mouth drooped dangerously; Suzanne was openly sneering. 'I'll make them on the machine,' Sylvia promised. 'Special little dresses.'

'Just as long as I'm not expected to do it,' Suzanne said. 'I'll get filthy Alistair for his breakfast. Get his pigswill out.'

'Come here,' Sylvia said to her husband. They backed off into the corner by the fridge. Her voice was dangerous. 'Florence. I bloody told her. I bloody told her what I'd got for Karen but she won't be told.'

'I can't help it. She didn't do it on purpose, did she? Look, just leave it, just leave them to fight it out amongst themselves.'

'A finely practical attitude,' Sylvia said. 'Do you want the house wrecked? Alistair, if you don't stop messing about in that sugar basin I'm going to come over there and slap you, Christmas or no Christmas.'

Colin moved and took her by the arm. A corner of the vegetable rack caught him painfully on the shin.

'This is what I stay for,' he said. 'They're your children, you wanted them. Can't you manage better than this? Do you realise this is what I stay for?'

'Stay?' Sylvia gaped. 'And where are you planning to go? What are you talking about? Who else in the name of God would want you?' Her mouth quivered like Karen's, in disbelief, and suddenly tears plopped out of her pale blue eyes and ran down on to her housecoat, Christmas or no Christmas, the first in years.

At mid-morning, Colin slipped away. He went up to the bedroom, and from his briefcase drew out Isabel's present. He had missed the opportunity to hand over her mittens. They would have to be a late gift; when would he be able to deliver them? Term started on January 12th, and then, perhaps, there would be excuses: Parents' Evenings, visits to Frank O'Dwyer, extra-curricular drama. Even sports, as the nights grew lighter; but how to sustain it, through another winter?

It was a flat parcel, in red paper; a record. He pulled the paper off. 'Marches of Souza.' In the field, maudlin after physical pleasure, he had spoken of suicide and his plans for evading it. For the season, it was a bitter joke.

Because it cannot be sustained, he thought. Last time they met, the strain was telling on her. These days she forgot things, lost her files, she jumped when she was spoken to. He saw her corroded spirit in her eyes, watched her twist her fingers together, frail, timid, flawed. She was not the woman she had been in September.

He thought of Sylvia weeping in the kitchen, her face cruelly blotched. His marriage had not disappointed him; his grief was that it had turned out exactly as he had expected. The past can't be changed, but you should be able to change the present. My present isn't under my control, he thought, it doesn't seem mine to dispose of.

He slipped the record back into his briefcase; then, on second thoughts, retrieved it. He carried it downstairs and intruded it into the pile on the radiogram. Sylvia would never know.

Until well into the morning Evelyn did not remember it was Christmas Day. She knew it was near, of course, because of the festive irruption of Florence, and because of the signs she had seen in the shops a few days ago when she went to buy food. She had not made plans to mark the festival. They were not religious.

Some time ago, two cards had fallen through the letterbox. At least, they were lying on the hall floor, as if they could have come through the letterbox. One was Florence Sidney's, she knew by the writing. She sent one every year, as one of her impertinences. Gingerly, she held up the other one and peered at the address. It was to Muriel. From the father? Possibly. Who else did Muriel know? Evelyn did not succumb to curiosity. She carried the two envelopes into the lean-to and thrust them both into a pile of damp newspapers.

Far back in her memory was a picture of another Christmas Day, at her family's house in Shropshire. She stood by the window of the morning room, the long french window, an overgrown girl of thirteen. She was wearing the party dress that had been bought for her when she was ten. It was too short now, and her great bony knees and wrists seemed like the exposed parts of some terrifying machine. Outside the glass the wind whirled the sleet into eddies. Goose pimples prickled her bare arms, and she shuddered at the thought of the festivities. They were to be meagre this year. Father had died of influenza. Water had got on his lungs, they said. She listened at doors. Blaise had been careless; the policies were not in order. Matters were outstanding, they said. Matters matters matters. A woman from Craven Arms had come up to the front door; bold as brass she had said outright that she had two children by Blaise and had been promised all sorts. She demanded compensation. In other ways, too, Blaise had been careless.

Mother was to be brought downstairs for Christmas dinner. Mother was an invalid and never left her room, but she would do so on this occasion because it was understood that this was the last winter in their own house. They were to be sold up, said voices in the air.

Evelyn rubbed her arms, clamping them across her thin chest. The garden had gone to seed; snow drifted in the hollows and a single blackbird scavenged in the weeds, pecking without hope at the iron-hard ground.

Remembering that Christmas, hands now slack in her lap, Evelyn felt no inclination to busy herself for Muriel's sake. An accustomed weight lay around her heart. In February the house was sold. She left with one box-trunk for her Aunt Norah, in Liverpool. She cried as the taxi took her down the drive, not because her childhood had been happy, but because crying passed the time.

Aunt Norah had a tall black house, a city house with many staircases. Half a mile away skinny children played in the streets. On certain days a smell drifted up from the docks, of rubber and salt and decaying fruit. At Aunt Norah's she cried every night. She stood by her bedroom window looking down at the pavement far below, tempted by the wicked railings of the street frontage. When she opened the window, a preparatory step, the night howled about her ears. She closed it again quickly, hearing her quick breathing in the dark, and watching the faint crack of light that crept under her door from the passage. She felt as if she were suffocating. But she was not more unhappy than she had been before.

Her mother, smelling of urine, was now confined to a nursing home. Evelyn visited her four times a year. Latterly, she screamed if she was touched. When she finally died, Evelyn was seventeen.

Aunt Norah now gave her notice that she must make her own way. She had performed her duty to her sister and had, indeed, met the hospital bills for the past six months. There was no more money from any source, and every mouthful of bread Evelyn ate had been put there by the charity of her Aunt and her Uncle Reggie. Every mouthful of bread.

Three weeks after this ultimatum came Clifford Axon. He was a senior shipping clerk who worked for Uncle Reggie. He had decided recently that his life would be better regulated if he had a wife to oversee his domestic arrangements and provide him with a few small comforts. Explaining this, he had proposed to as many as four young ladies, and they had all turned him down on the spot. His misfortune was the subject of general merriment in Uncle Reggie's Chambers. Uncle Reggie bet Clifford five pounds that he knew a girl who would be willing to marry him at once, on first meeting.

'Is she ugly?' Axon asked.

'Ugly? You'd not say so. Plain, perhaps, but what would you?'

He did not say, faintly peculiar, but poured himself a glass of whisky, a little pale fire on a foggy afternoon, a toast to the Gaiety Girl.

Evelyn accepted. After the wedding, Axon, who did not care for the jibes of his colleagues, left the firm and went into an insurance office, and was moved away from Liverpool. Afterwards, Uncle Reggie was vaguely sorry. He suspected Axon of indulging in sexual deviations. But it was too late to do anything about that.

When Evelyn thought of her childhood, it seemed to have taken place in another century.

When the meal was over the children went upstairs, screaming and bawling, to play with their toys. The sound of their disputes punctured the air at intervals, like machine-gun fire.

Sylvia yawned, and reached out for the congealing dishes with their remains of pudding. She began to scrape the leftovers into one dish.

'Florence doesn't think you ought to scrape the plates at the table,' she commented. 'She carries them out two at a time. It's hard on the feet.'

'I'll do it, if you like,' Florence said weakly. After the heavy meal, Sylvia's activities were making her nauseous.

'That's all right,' Sylvia said. 'You can sit still, if you'll allow me to suit myself at my own table.'

'I didn't say anything,' Florence protested.

'No, but you looked plenty.' Sylvia reached across for a sprout which one of the children had rolled on to the table cloth, chopped it into the general mess, and stood up to carry the pile of dishes away.

'I'll help you,' Colin said. He made movements to show that in time, after preparation, he would push back his chair and rise to his feet. He felt gross and sated. He eyed the last inch of red wine. Self-indulgence was tripping through his bloodvessels, tiptoe on warning feet.

'Get the presents,' Sylvia said. 'We might as well have them in peace while the kiddies are out of the way.'

She went into the kitchen, and Colin took the presents from the sideboard. Sylvia had refused to have a proper tree, on account of the pine needles, the sweeping up they entailed, the danger to children's feet and their habit of appearing embedded in upholstery, to next September and beyond. Every year she set out her argument, passionless, step by step, and every year Colin refused to put the presents under her Tesco artefact with its stiff tinsel branches.

'This tree,' he said to Florence. He shook his head. 'I like a tree. A proper one.'

'It's not worth quarrelling over,' Florence said. 'They only came in with Prince Albert.'

'Nonsense,' Colin said. 'It's a pagan custom.'

'I didn't know you were a pagan,' Sylvia said, returning. 'I thought you were an agnostic.' She sat down and wiped her hands on her paper napkin, and looked expectant. Impelled to goodwill, Colin placed two parcels before her, and doled out the same to Florence.

'Well,' Colin said. 'Another drink, anybody? Such largesse. I always think this is the nicest moment. I mean giving, of course, as well as receiving.'

'It's a pity you weren't a vicar,' Sylvia said.

'If I were a vicar, Sylvia, we should have even less money than we do, and certainly none to spare for presents.'

'Really, do you have to go on like this?' Florence muttered. They composed their faces to amiability. From upstairs came Alistair's long-drawn and hideous wail; his sisters were pinching him and calling him pig. There was a loud, almost shocking rending of paper, as Sylvia pulled out of its wrapping the bottle of scent Colin gave her every year.

'A new one,' she said. 'You've bought a new kind.' She opened the box, prised it out, unscrewed the cap and began to dab the scent on her wrists.

'Steady,' Colin said. 'Don't waste it all.'

'This was imaginative of you, Colin,' Florence said.

'I thought, oh, you know, try a change.' He looked modest.

'I don't think I was praising you,' Florence said. 'I think I was being sarcastic, really. Have you actually bought her the same each year?'

Sylvia held her wrist to her nose and inhaled deeply, closing her eyes. They snapped open, and a flicker of surprise crossed her face.

'Well?' Colin demanded. He was eager to get on with his own parcels.

Sylvia hesitated, and proffered her wrist.

'Very nice,' Colin said. 'Very nice indeed.'

'Let it warm up on your skin, Sylvia,' Florence suggested. 'That might make all the difference.'

'I hope so,' Sylvia said.

'It wasn't cheap,' Colin said. 'It wasn't bloody cheap, if that's what you're thinking.' He thrust his chair back, glowering.

'I know,' Sylvia said quietly. 'I know the prices of perfumes.' Because I walk around the shops and covet them, she might have added. 'It's my skin. It doesn't suit it.'

'Well, surely it cannot be intended to smell like that,' Florence said. 'They must take into account that people have different skins. One would think so.'

'I don't think they took mine into account,' Sylvia said.

'Look, I'm sorry. I'll get you something else. How was I to know? Oh, Sylvia, for God's sake don't start crying again. It *is* Christmas.'

Sylvia took out a handkerchief smeared with gravy. She applied it to her heated face and smudges of mascara and tan foundation adhered to it as she patted her skin vigorously.

'I'm sorry. It's not your fault.' She whimpered and sniffed. 'Just ... it's only once a year ... and I've been working hard to get the dinner and make everything nice, and I don't feel myself – ' With a neat and surprising movement she slipped under the table. Florence gave a cry of alarm, and half-rose from her place. 'It's all right, I'm only picking up these peas from under Karen's chair before they get trodden in the carpet. Stay where you are.'

She sniffed loudly again, hidden under the cloth. Relieved at the return to normality, Colin handed Florence her book token. Sylvia had given him a blue shirt with a matching blue and white tie, pinned together under their cellophane wrapper. He thought this a very neat idea, because he always had trouble matching shirts to ties, and had to call on Sylvia to do it for him. She would be out of patience, because she was trying to get the children fed with their breakfasts, and she would snap at him, and fling his clothes across the room; but if he chose for himself she would mock at him at the breakfast table, and ridicule his efforts. His first thought was how much simpler life would be with this innovation; then immediately he saw something sinister in it. Was Sylvia preparing him for life alone? Did she know something, and had her words been more, that morning, than a vicious stab in the dark? He saw himself alone, crushed by alimony and abandoned by Isabel, spending his Christmas in a dirty bedsitting-room, with a bottle of milk on the table, and the cheapest kind of card, from each of his children, scrawled hastily and collapsed in the draught from the cracked window. A tin of fruit and a walk about the street; such a complete and vivid picture of his future desolation came to him that tears of self-pity welled up into his eyes. Sylvia did not notice. She was staring at Florence's gift to her, twelve plain cream linen tablenapkins, requiring to be washed, starched and ironed.

'Blimey,' Sylvia said. 'Real serviettes, Florence. I always have paper ones, you know, when there's company, otherwise I don't bother with any.'

'Ah well,' Florence conceded pleasantly. 'Of course you're not newly-weds now. When you are putting your household together these gay little informalities are excused you, but as we get older, and established, it is not always becoming to be casual.'

'Why didn't you put a message in them?' Sylvia asked. 'Just to make the point? A little motto, like you get in the crackers?'

'We never had linen at home,' Colin said.

Florence caught his eye. She looked betrayed. 'No?'

'No.'

'Your memory is at fault, Colin.'

' 'Tisn't.'

'I think it is.'

'We had paper.'

'Oh,' said Florence drily, 'if you are right, I must have learned it out of books.'

Sylvia had been extravagant. She had bought Florence a cookery book, lavishly illustrated, called *Entertaining for Two: Menus for Candlelit Evenings*. Her second present showed how long she thought these evenings were likely to last, for it was a candlewick dressing-gown, of a spinach shade and a formidable stiffness.

'And this is your other one from me, Colin.'

It was a Five-Year Diary, with a lock and key.

This time he saw the implication immediately. She felt he had secrets. She knew he had. She was laughing at him, asking him to place them between covers of leatherette. It was hardly the world's most secure object; she could have bought another identical, with the same key. He was damned if he would write anything in this book. He turned it over admiringly in his hands.

'How did you think of this?' he asked her. 'Very useful. I never miss not having a diary till about April, and then I really need one, and there aren't any in the shops.'

'I don't think you're meant to put your engagements in it,' Sylvia said. 'It's not that kind. You're supposed to put down what you do, so that you have something to look back on.'

'That's right,' Florence said. 'You will be able to look back at the date and see at a glance that this day four years ago, you were at the dentist. For example.'

'I hope more will happen than the dentist,' Colin said. 'I hope there will be more than that to record. You know,' he said, with a strained chuckle, 'there's a saying that only virgins and generals keep diaries.'

This epigram left the company listless. Renewed howls erupted from upstairs. Virgins and generals, he thought; and I need the sentiments of the former and the strategic sense of the latter. Or perhaps it is the other way round.

At ten o'clock, Colin drove Florence home. There was too little drink in the house for him to be the worse for it, and he was under the necessity of saving some of it to get him through the rest of the holiday.

As Florence got out of the car, her presents balanced in her arms, she said. 'I wonder what sort of day the Axons have had. I do feel guilty about them, in a way.'

Colin wished she would shut the car door. He was getting frozen.

'Goodnight, Colin. Thank Sylvia for me.'

'Don't mention it, Florence. Goodnight. Merry Christmas.'

She slammed the door and started towards the gate. Colin watched her until she was safely inside her front door, and turned the car for home. He thought of Isabel, not of the Axons. He stopped at a telephone box. There was a delay before she answered and her voice sounded chilly, remote and strained.

'Oh yes. Merry Christmas,' she said. 'Yes. Goodnight.'

He imagined he heard her father's questions in the background.

He hoped he did; that she would not be so curt for no reason. Better if he had not made the call; if he had only dreamed of doing it.

The house was silent when he let himself in, with the foreboding silence of places struck by disaster and bound to be struck again; criminal neighbourhoods, earthquake zones, the more popular battlefields of Europe. The children had been downstairs and the floor of the living-room was littered with their cast-off toys – plastic hand-grenades, broken railway tracks, battered dolls with torn frocks and twisted necks.

Sylvia had gone up to bed, exhausted by the day. He followed her. She was in her nightdress, sitting on the bed, a torn Christmas wrapper lying beside her. Grotesquely, she waved to him with both hands, like a performing bear. She had found Isabel's sheepskin mittens.

'You were going to surprise me,' she said coyly. 'I wondered what on earth they were.'

'Do they fit?'

'Oh yes, they fit anybody. Lovely. I've always wanted some of these.'

What depth of the lover's imagination are here plumbed? he asked himself. How are they formed and educated, men who give a mistress sheepskin mittens, all one size?

'Why didn't you get some, then?' he asked her.

'Well . . . I didn't like to.'

'I see you managed to get them to bed.'

'Alistair had a bit of a do. Screaming. He broke his sub-machine-gun. They quietened down, though. They've worn themselves out. Poor little pets,' she added fondly.

Colin did not comment. His thoughts on his children, heated by alcohol, were unseasonal. Sylvia could not have chosen a less opportune moment, but it seemed to her that nobody could be angry with fecundity on Christmas Day.

'Colin, there's something I've got to tell you.' She watched him take off his tie, roll it up around his hand, thrust it into a drawer. 'I've started another baby.'

He stared at her, his neck stretched and his chin tilted up, so that he could release the stiff top button of his shirt. For a moment she thought he had simply not heard her. His eyes closed momentarily, and his mouth opened, as if he were being slowly choked. The button slipped through its buttonhole; his hand, trembling a little, stayed in mid-air.

Sylvia held up her sheepskin paws defensively.

'I've started another baby.' He turned his back on her and walked to the window. He wanted to stare out into the night. He understood why, in books, people did this, but he pictured them in rooms worth striding across, gazing out on to blasted heathlands silvered by the moon. He laid his hand on the rampant ready-made daisies, on their lilac and pink, and tried to scoop them aside.

'Mind my curtain hooks, love,' Sylvia said.

The estate was shutting down for the night. The screaming children were tranquillised and the tipsy wives flicked off the fluorescent lights and climbed the stairs. Mountains of turkey giblets passed before their dreaming eyes. What will next year bring?

So either, Colin thought, I must tell her now, I must tell her now and pack a bag and go to Florence's . . . he felt her behind him, waiting. At the same time, a great weariness crept up and engulfed him. He felt the weight of the winter, of the short sterile days and early dark. Already, his affair was passing into the realms of fantasy. He, a history teacher, a married man; he did not have affairs. He was not attractive to women, he went to evening classes, no one would look at him. Duty with her steel teeth gestured to him from beyond the windowpane, obscenely inviting him to the realms of the just.

'Take your mittens off,' he said. 'You look silly.'

Unwillingly, she extricated her hands, which now looked stupidly small and inadequate. She put the mittens on the bed, stroking them with one finger.

'Say you're pleased,' she asked flatly. 'I know you're not, but just say you are.'

'Why?'

'Because its the only way to go on.'

'Oh, you say that. But we do go on. Pleased or not pleased.'

'It is your baby.'

'I didn't for a moment suppose it belonged to anybody else.'

'I mean, you are responsible for it. It's part of you as well as me. Draw the curtains. You're letting the heat out.'

Colin turned away from the window. He could think of nothing to say. He sat beside her on the bed and patted her knee with small mechanical taps. Still his throat felt constricted, almost bruised. His face twisted in a horrid parody of emotional generosity. A clock struck. Boxing Day.

Evelyn felt so tired. Her arm ached, there was a pain in her chest, her legs felt too heavy to move. She sat by the electric fire and stared at her feet, puffy inside her old bedroom slippers. 'You'll have to get the dinner today,' she said to Muriel.

Muriel was in no mood for cooking. She was busy making her rhymes. The farmer's wife, the blind clock mice, Jack and Jill and time to kill.

'You've got it wrong,' Evelyn said. Fatigue and hunger pinched her into savagery. 'You've got it all hopelessly mixed up. Sometimes I think you're a mental case.'

Colin drove Isabel to the field where he had first made love to her, and pulled the car off the road. There seemed no danger of the wheels sticking in the hard frosty ground. He pulled out a small bottle of brandy and handed it to her.

'We don't usually have this,' she said. She took it from him, tipped back her head and swallowed a little. 'I'll be warm in a minute. It's a good idea. We couldn't do what we used to do. It's too cold to uncover an inch of flesh.'

'Sylvia's pregnant,' he told her. Faintly, the headlights of cars crept along the main road, like lost souls. She passed him back the bottle without comment. 'So you see,' he said, 'you must understand, I can't leave her now.'

'I expect you're glad,' she said.

'Glad? Glad? Why should I be glad?'

'Off the hook, Colin. You've felt it, these past few weeks. Or at least, back on the old familiar hook. Don't people get used to the pain?'

'I expect you mean there's no chance of us carrying on.'

'Carrying on?' She laughed. 'That's what people used to say, they've been carrying on together. Weekend bags and seaside hotels and tipsy hilarity. Well, now they're not carrying on. Let's go, Colin, just save the explanations and preserve some dignity and let it go.'

'You sound bitter,' he said dully.

'Do I? Give me a chance. Time hasn't had a chance yet to do its legendary healing work, but the sooner time gets on with it, the better it will be. How long does it take?' She spoke rapidly, the syllables tripping after each other into a dim future. 'One year? Two? Three?'

'I don't know. I don't know, if it comes to that.'

Triteness was in his mouth like a foul taste long incubated; but what can you expect from the tired old situations, except the tired old phrases? 'I can't imagine the future without you.'

'You can't imagine it with me, though.'

'You know I had very little to offer you.'

'And what you had, you weren't prepared to give.'

'Isabel – '

'Memory will make you a cosy selection. In time you'll forget the motorway and the field and the humiliating telephone calls. You can give yourself better lines, make yourself more potent.'

'That's cheap. Isn't it, cheap?'

'Yes. Ah, what's the point? We knew at the beginning it would end up like this. We knew but we did it – I did anyway – because there are some mistakes you have to make.'

They sat in the damp darkness of the car, no sound but their steady breathing, almost hoarse, like people who had exerted themselves and were not used to it. He was conscious of their last moments trickling away.

'Give me a cigarette,' she said. He lit it for her. 'I want to tell you something. A little story.'

'Bearing on us?'

'No, it has nothing to do with us at all. I tell it to anyone I think might be able to tell me what it means.' She took the cigarette from her lips and smoke curled out of them, out of her body. For a minute he thought he was seeing torments, the damned in hell, smouldering viscera and dripping flesh. He blinked. 'It's a true story,' she said. 'I read it in a book when I was a student.' He tried to ease himself back in the driver's seat, but he did not feel at ease. He took out a cigarette and then pushed it back into the packet.

'Are you running out?' she asked.

'No. I think I might give up.'

'Well, it will save expense. You are making changes in your life. Isn't it going to be too much for you, all at once?'

'Tell me the story.'

'All right. It was in the war, the last war. There were two people, Jews, in Poland. The man was a weaver. He saw this woman whom he wanted to marry. But she – she wouldn't have him. Everybody thought it was ridiculous, quite unsuitable. They had nothing in common, they were from different backgrounds, different classes. But he was very persistent.'

'This was before the War?'

'Yes, this was before the War. But when the invasion came the man knew what was going to happen. He had a friend who was a farmer, he wasn't Jewish but he was prepared to help him. Under the floor of his friend's farmhouse he made a hole in the ground. He got a handloom, and a lot of wool, as much as he could lay his hands on. Then when the Germans started rounding up the Jews he went to this sort of dug-out and shut himself in and began to weave the wool.'

'Yes?'

'And he asked the woman again, would she live with him? She refused. At first she said she would rather be dead. But soon most of her family had been killed or taken away on the cattle-wagons.

She was on her own and there was nowhere to hide. He couldn't come out of the hole now, but he kept sending messages to her, and in the end she was so frightened, with everyone else gone, that she agreed. She went to join him under the farmhouse floor. But she said she would never marry him, she wouldn't have sex with him.'

'But that's asking the impossible,' Colin said. 'In that confined space.'

'Look, will you just shut up, Colin?' He turned, startled. Her cheeks were hollow, her eyes alight. She snapped another cigarette into her mouth and her anger blazed and flickered in the lighter flame. It began to rain, harder and harder, thundering on the metal roof. 'Will you just keep quiet and let me tell you the story?'

'I'm sorry.' He thought, how long will this take, will it turn to mud, is the car going to start sinking? What will Sylvia say about the mud on the wheels?

'When the man had made some cloth the farmer sold it, and this kept them going, all three of them. But this hole was so small they couldn't stretch out. Every night they had to take the loom down before they could sleep, and set it up again every morning. The wool was around them all the time, they slept in it and breathed in it, it must have almost suffocated them, I think. Imagine their dreams.'

'I can't imagine. Why don't you just tell me the facts?'

'The facts only? But these must have been the facts. This little hole, no air, no light, the clay and the fleece all around them. Sometimes I think I am not sure of the facts.'

'What's the point then?'

'The facts were in dispute anyway. Do you think they told the same version afterwards? Long, long after, the story came to light. Who couldn't imagine? You wouldn't be human if you didn't try.'

'Yes. Go on.'

'The hole was under a trapdoor inside the farmhouse. The floor of the farmhouse was made of earth. Soldiers came a few times, but they didn't find it.'

'How was it ventilated?'

'I don't know. Barely, it must have been. They couldn't cook down there.'

'What did they eat?'

'Raw vegetables.'

'God,' Colin said. He turned his face away and looked out at the rain. 'I'd better move the car.'

'Yes, you'd better.'

'I'm sorry to interrupt you.'

'It'll keep.'

'Where shall we go?'

'Just drive me home.'

'Do I have to?'

'I think that would be best.' She stared at the stub of her cigarette, greedily, and wound down the window to hurl the glowing end out into the night. She put on her seat belt.

'Will you finish the story?'

'For a year they didn't have sex, and then they did. They say – he, the man, said – that she had lost her will to live by then. At least he had the work, weaving, putting up the loom and taking it down. She had nothing except the earth and the wool, and thinking over the past and hating him. All this time, you have to remember, she hated him. But she says differently, that he threatened to drive her out of the hole if she wouldn't have sex with him.'

'He could have raped her. Who could she have complained to?'

'Perhaps. Perhaps he did. After another year they had a child. It was a girl.'

'But how could they?' He was aghast. 'How could they, in that hole?'

'You fool,' she said bitterly. 'Now do you see why she didn't want to have sex? Do you think she could pop out and go to the chemist's for something? Sometimes . . . very occasionally . . . they went up into the world and walked about. Only at night. Not very often. They wanted, you understand, to scream at each other, just scream, but the farmer said he'd throw them out if they didn't keep absolutely quiet.'

'But the baby must have cried, mustn't she?'

'They put their hands over her mouth. For a year and a half. For a year and a half, the mother had milk, but then it gave out. The baby had to eat the raw vegetables. But you see then, the mother couldn't kill herself, could she, she couldn't walk out of the hole. She had the baby.'

They were on the main road now, driving through town. An odd figure under an umbrella scurried away from their sight. A gang of boys huddled under the yellow lights of a shopping centre.

'Shall we stop for a drink?' He looked sideways at her. 'Anywhere. It doesn't matter now if we're seen. Anywhere you like.'

'Better go home, I think. Shall I finish the story?'

He sighed. 'Yes, go on. It's a terrible story. I don't like to think about things like that.'

'None of us likes to think of other people's hells. We avoid it if we can.'

'But you're paid to do it, aren't you?'

'Yes, but even so. You see there was food of a kind, shelter, and it was warm — at least it was warm. That's how they survived. And nobody found them, they did survive. The Russians came. They were sent to a Displaced Persons Camp. I think, later, they went to America, and the couple split up. I don't know. The end of the story isn't important.'

'But what about the child?'

'Well that's what's most horrible. She was like a wild animal. When she was brought out of the hole she screamed and clawed and attacked people. At other times, she was completely mute. As if they still had their hands over her face.'

'But they'd had to do it. I suppose. Or her existence would have destroyed them all. But later — what became of her?'

'Oh, she went from one institution to another. No one could keep her. I told you, she was like a wild animal.' She paused. 'What is the point?'

'The point?'

'Of the story.'

'I don't know,' Colin said. 'I wish you hadn't told it to me. It's one of the most horrible things I've ever heard.'

Isabel looked at him appraisingly. 'Would it have been more bearable if the child had grown up in some other way?'

'Normal?'

'Yes, normal.'

'I suppose so.'

'At that time, when they were buried in the hole, the people above them were much worse than animals. Animals have no cruelty, we always defame them. At least, whatever became of the child, she had no opportunity to become cruel.'

'But you can't speculate . . . you don't know about these people. To survive like that you would have to be a different breed.'

'I think they must have been terrible people, to breed such monstrosity out of desire for life. But not different.' She turned her head. 'Do you see how he made her suffer, by loving her? When she had the child she could not even walk out and go to Treblinka. Now I know all about it . . . the stifling power of love.'

They had reached her front gate. Colin stopped the car. He was afraid to look at her, knowing that he had failed to find any meaning in the story, to give anything at all back to her.

'I didn't know such issues preoccupied you,' he said. 'Have you found some moral in it to apply to me?'

'I hadn't thought of it in that light, but now that you speak of it – '

'Isabel, kiss me, don't just go.'

She unclipped the seatbelt, swung open the door, and paused halfway out of the car.

'Now that you speak of it, when you are so spiritually stifled, what kind of life can you hope to give birth to?' The door clicked behind her. 'I'll miss you, Colin. You think I won't, but I will.' She walked around the back of the car and bent her face to his window. 'When you are fifty you will be able to tell people what a gay dog you were. What an untrammelled life. And look at the heap of ashes you live on, and blame Sylvia.' He stretched out a hand but she pulled away almost playfully, and with a little smile turned and walked in at the gate. She was playing all the time, Colin said to himself. Hunched in his seat, he sat for fifteen minutes watching the front of the house; lights going on, upstairs curtains drawn, light finally switched off. She has slipped through my fingers, he thought. He drove home.

Muriel looked pale. Suspecting her to be undernourished, Evelyn got her coat on, picked up her purse and her basket, and set off for the butcher's shop on the Parade. When she got to the door she saw that there was quite a queue waiting to be served. Her first thought was to pretend she had not wanted anything and walk away down the street. But she hesitated for a moment, and heard a voice behind her:

'Liver looks nice. Hello there, Mrs Axon. I thought I saw you passing.'

She would have to go in now. After all, nobody looks into a butcher's window for idle amusement, they would think she didn't have the money, they might talk about her. Evelyn turned her head stiffly. Josie Deakin from number four, a woman of forty-five in her brown leather knee-boots and pixie-hood. She heaved up to Evelyn, bustling with her shopping bags, edging her into the shop doorway.

'Nasty weather, Mrs A,' Josie said cheerfully.

Mrs A? Evelyn thought. As if she were the subject of an experiment.

'Seasonable,' she replied.

'How are you keeping then?'

'Very well, thank you.'

'And Muriel?'

'Very well.' Some residue of social unction oiled her tongue. 'And you, Mrs Deakin?'

'Can't complain.' Mrs Deakin took off her woollen gloves and rubbed her hands together. 'Haven't seen Muriel about for a bit. Too cold for her, is it?'

'Yes. Too cold.'

'I used to see her last summer, striding along, you know, not a care in the world, and very nice she looked in that pink angora cardigan. You do keep her lovely, Mrs A. I said to Dennis, Mrs Axon keeps Muriel lovely, to look at her you'd never know. Well, I said to Dennis, if people only knew. I bet Muriel's got more about her than people give her credit for.'

'And what did Dennis say?' Evelyn enquired.

'Well . . . I expect he said, I agree with you. I don't remember exactly what he said but he certainly agreed with me. To tell you the truth, Mrs Axon, it is a coincidence me running into you today like this.' She craned her neck to look at the counter. 'Oh, aren't they slow in this shop! The thing is, do you still do seances? Only Uncle Bill's passed on, end of September, liver complaint, he'd had it for years – and Auntie Agnes – she's my father's sister, you remember our Ag – she's mislaid one of the policies.'

'And so she wants to get in touch with him?'

'Well, I know you do that sort of thing.'

'I'm afraid I don't any more.'

Evelyn was careful to keep all colour out of her tone, all emotion off her face. And no doubt, she thought, this about Dennis Deakin thinking Muriel attractive, it was something and nothing, a passing fancy. She imagined Mr Deakin coming softly down the path in his bedroom slippers, putting his hand on Muriel's arm, guiding her down the garden to the shed; the smell of grass cuttings, compost, the lawnmower oil, and Muriel's dumpling thighs exposed in the broad sunlit afternoon. No, he could not be the father, flies undone amongst the diving swallows, Ena Harkness rotting softly towards midsummer. Deakin's beds were orderly ones.

'Oh, don't you do them now? Ag will be that disappointed.' Mrs Deakin bobbed up on her toes. 'Don't put that roast ham away, I want six ounces,' she called out in a piercing voice. 'Well, I mean, it's no good letting them wrap it up and put it away again, is it? Only I mentioned you, you see, I'd a feeling you'd given seances at one time, and I asked Florence Sidney, and she said she'd a feeling you did as well.'

'I've given it up.'

'That's a shame. Only you ought to be more sociable, Mrs Axon. Florence was saying she never sees you. Couldn't you just do one for Ag? You might enjoy it. Take you out of yourself.'

'Thank you, but I really have given it up.'

'Only can you recommend anybody? Mrs Dobson in Argyll Street has a ouija board.'

'Has she? She must be careful that she doesn't get more than she bargained for.'

'How do you mean, Mrs Axon?'

'Oh . . . ' Evelyn sighed. Could she really be bothered to explain, on the chance of saving Mrs Dobson, whom she did not know, and who probably deserved what she invited? 'Oh, people get in . . . things get in . . . the house gets overcrowded.'

'She says she does limit it to six people. Because their rooms aren't big, you know, and that's all she can get round the table.' The queue shuffled forward a bit. 'I mean, it's only harmless fun,' Mrs Deakin said.

When Evelyn got to the head of the queue she asked for steak, two large pieces. She would have been appalled at the price if she had stopped to think about it, but in the event she thrust some crumpled notes into the man's hand, leaving him to hand one back to her and then sort out her change; she snatched it from him, thrust the parcel into her bag, and made for the door without a word. The man shook his head comically, and made little circular motions with his forefinger. The queue went tut-tut, at this insult to a paying customer, and crackled their stiff raincoats. Mrs Deakin said, 'You can't expect that lady to waste her time chatting with tradesmen. She's a very well-regarded Spiritualist.'

Evelyn arrived home, and put down the parcel of meat on the kitchen table. The brown blood was seeping through the wrapping. She heard a rustling noise from the lean-to, and went to investigate it. When she returned, having found nothing, the meat was gone. A trail of dark drops led towards the kitchen door and out into the hall. Bending painfully, she peered at the floor. On the parquet of the hall she lost the trail, but there was another splash, on the staircarpet, halfway up.

Evelyn sat down on the bottom step, and rocked herself back and forth like a child. Such appetites, she thought, such vile appetites for raw and bloody meat. Were their jaws at work, behind the spare-room door? And if she went up there would she hear them, salivating and sucking, smacking unpicturable lips? Baby flesh would tear like butter.

They do not have claws, Evelyn told herself, they do not have claws or jaws, they do not have faces at all. But one thing was for sure, she would not dare to stand in their way. Muriel might, if she liked; self-sacrifice is a mother's prerogative, and Muriel would be a mother soon enough.

Since Christmas, Muriel had become more and more lethargic. Her ankles swelled. She took no interest in anything.

'I have to think of everything myself,' Evelyn complained. She worried quite often about what she would do if Muriel got into difficulties. 'You ought to be all right,' she reassured her. 'You're a strong type of woman. There's nothing wrong with you, Muriel. Not physically anyway.'

Conscious of the responsibility facing her, she went to the public library to borrow some books. She chose first aid books, which told you how to deliver babies in an emergency. The library had changed a good deal, she noticed. The old wooden desks had gone, and the newspapers in racks. There were low vinyl seats that an elderly person could not get in and out of comfortably. There were modern pictures on the wall, sunbursts of yellow and orange, and a part marked 'Children's Play Area'. Children did not play in it, but ran about, loud and healthy. Fluttering notices on a cork board advertised yoga classes and Community Welfare Programmes, play-groups and Councillor's Surgeries. People talked quite unashamedly, in ordinary voices; there had been only an odd subdued whisper in the past, in the old days when Clifford used to step down to get a detective story, and she used to ask for a nice mystery from Miss Williams on the desk.

Evelyn shuffled up to the counter, cradling her books. 'Where's Miss Williams?' she asked, as she put them down.

'Who?' A fat girl looked up at her, a fat girl in a fluffy pink cardigan, very like the one that Muriel used to wear.

'Miss Williams. The Librarian.'

'We don't have a Miss Williams here.'

'Has she left?'

'I don't know. I don't remember any Miss Williams. Frances!' she called. 'Frances, have you got a minute?'

'Shhh,' Evelyn said.

'What's the matter?' The girl was irritated. 'You asked me a question, didn't you? I'm trying to find out, aren't I?'

Frances glanced up from the books she was stacking on to a trolley. 'There's been no one of that name while I've been here. Miss Williams? No, I don't think so.'

'Never mind,' Evelyn said. She put her tickets down by her books. 'What are these?'

'Oh, really,' Evelyn said, 'don't be so foolish.'

The girl picked the tickets up and held them by one corner, as if they were contaminated. 'These expired thirty years ago,' she said. She looked at Evelyn, a strange sideways look, as if she were considering calling for help. 'You'd better fill in a form,' she said at last. 'Are you a ratepayer?'

'Where did you get that cardigan?' Evelyn demanded.

'What?' The girl's head jerked back, her eyebrows raised, her leaky ballpoint pen poised in the air. Evelyn turned her back and made for the door.

'Just a minute – ' the girl said, but she didn't come after her. Somebody laughed. Evelyn found herself back on the street.

She walked down to the town centre, to the Central Library. They had the same books, the ones she wanted. She just put them under her arm and walked out, past the desk, nodding to herself. Nobody saw her go, nobody tried to stop her. It was easier that way.

It was a cold, misty day. The town was full of people tramping to the January sales. The buildings seemed distant and insubstantial, walls of air and smoke. Nobody looked at her, stumping along in her old grey coat. Nobody looks at an old woman to see if her clothes are fashionable; old women have a set of fashions all their own. The crowds clutched their parcels and their slippery plastic bags, heading for home, weary and overheated from the department stores. Evelyn stopped on a street corner, by the entrance to a great cavern brilliantly stacked with scented soap and woollen hats. She felt a kind of safety and peace that she had not known in years, or that perhaps she had never known; but it touched her with a warm finger of nostalgia. Treading in the footsteps of the crowd, no demon would know her. She would get herself a parcel, jostle in a bus-queue, she would never, never go home. Impulsively, she turned to go into the store, and a young woman collided with her, a pale woman with dark almond eyes that seemed familiar from somewhere.

'I beg your pardon,' Evelyn said; but the girl did not look at her, simply closed her arms about her burdens, gathered them to her chest with an irritated twitch of her lips, and hurried on, her eyes downcast. City manners, Evelyn thought, the vast indifference of the heated crowds. She shrugged inwardly. Courtesy had gone, gone with Miss Williams, no one remembered that it had ever existed. But then another thought struck her. Had the girl seen her at all? Was there anything to be seen? In sudden panic, she started to walk, seeking her reflection in the plate glass windows. She saw other women goosestepping with their stout legs, the glow of their faces almost warming the glass, their big check coats and their big boots; and then, faint and flickering, a wraith of herself, her melting face with its hollow eyes, her hatchet nose like the nose of a corpse. She began to hurry, faster and faster, trundling up the hill to Lauderdale Road, panting, trying to outpace the fate she had seen for herself.

CHAPTER 6

The week before half-term, Frank O'Dwyer made good his long-standing promise, and invited Colin and Sylvia to a dinner party. Sylvia would normally have worried about what to wear, but in the circumstances had no choice but one of the all-purpose floral smocks she had kept from one pregnancy to the next. Colin thought, I should have noticed that she had not got rid of them, after Karen. If he looked in Sylvia's wardrobe more often, he might be able to divine her intentions.

Sylvia had been to the hairdressers. Her pale hair, heavily lac-quered, was fluffed up like a ball of cotton wool. With her pink face, and her cheerful frock of red and green leaves and sprigs, she looked like a badly-constructed Christmas decoration that someone had forgotten to put away. It occurred to Colin now that he had never told anyone his wife was expecting. Would they congratulate him, and then mock him behind his back, or would they pretend not to notice?

Since September he had rehearsed imaginary conversations in which he told his colleagues about the break-up of his marriage and about his new relationship with a young professional woman with no ties. This way and that he put it to them, in his head. These monologues had become a habit, and a ghostly parallel to his real speech. Sometimes he interjected his listeners' exclamations of amazement, incredulity and envy; sometimes he elaborately countered difficulties they raised. Now these conversations would never be held, but they were hard to give up all the same. He let them run, little hallucinations to accompany his pain.

He woke up in the mornings, and Isabel was his first thought. For this reason, he tried to delay the moment of waking. 'You're ever so dozy these days, Colin,' his wife said. 'We'll have to make an effort to get to bed earlier.' The sick pain of loss jolted through him before he had opened his eyes. He saw images of himself staggering through the days, grey-faced, with fatuities on his lips. Daily he took the matter in hand, promised self-discipline, tried to shut her out of his mind. His thoughts fled back to her as the dieting obese think of food, an abstract orgy of longing and inner greed, one thought for the pain and one for the world, systole for living and diastole for Isabel.

The telephone was ringing. It was the night of the dinner party, wet and black. Seven p.m.

'59428.'

'Mrs Sidney?'

'This is Mr Sidney.'

'It's Tracey here.'

'Sorry?'

'I said it's Tracey. I'm supposed to be babysitting for you.'

'Oh yes, hello Tracey,' Colin said with an excess of bonhomie. 'When are you coming along then?'

'I'm not coming, that's what I'm phoning for, sorry.'

'Oh but Tracey, now – '

'Me mam says I've got to stop in because me Grandad's coming.'

'But surely, Tracey – look, would you have a word with Mrs Sidney?'

'No point, is there?'

'Could I have a word with your mother, do you think?'

'She's gone down our Doreen's shop for a lettuce.'

'When will she be back?'

'Dunno.'

'Look, Tracey, are you sure you can't come?' Colin took his schoolteacher's tone, full of aching reasonableness. 'You see, it's letting us down rather badly. This was an important evening for us, and it's too short notice to get anyone else, so it does put us in difficulties. Now you did promise, Tracey. Did you explain that to your mother?'

'No point.'

'Surely she'd understand that a promise is a promise.'

'I don't think so.'

'Anyway, Tracey, look at it this way, you want your pocket money, don't you?'

'Well, it's only one fifty, isn't it, and if Grandad sees me he gives me a fiver.'

'Oh, I see,' Colin said. 'Well, I'm afraid I'm not prepared to engage in an auction for your presence, Tracey, that wouldn't be right at all. So we'll just have to manage without you.'

'Tough life, innit?' Tracey said. 'Bye.'

Colin bellowed up the stairs, and Sylvia came out of the bedroom in her bra and half-slip. She had powdered her face and lips very white, preparatory to painting them back in again, and she smelled of Coty's *L'Aimant*, which was not this year's Christmas present.

'What's up? Who was it?'

'It was some half-witted child called Tracey who it seems you've engaged as babysitter. She's not coming.'

'Oh, no!'

'Her grandfather's coming over, and will probably give her a fiver, so she's not going to put herself out for one fifty.'

'Oh, dammit,' Sylvia said venomously. She began to scramble down the stairs, her stockinged feet large and flat. 'Give me the phone.'

'Don't you offer her any more money,' Colin said. 'It's blackmail. We can't have that.'

Colin went into the bedroom, and contemplated the clean shirt laid out on the bed. He heard Sylvia's voice raised in expostulation. Shortly she came back into the bedroom, slamming the door.

'She won't come. Honestly. It's not often, is it, it's not often, that I get a night out? You wouldn't think one night was too much to ask.'

'Well, it's no good taking it out on me,' Colin said.

'I'm not taking it out on you. What on earth are we going to do?'

'I don't know, but honestly, Sylvia, that girl sounded half-witted. When I picked up the phone she said, "Is that Mrs Sidney?" '

'How could she be expected to know who picked the phone up?'

'Because I spoke, didn't I, I said "59428", I don't just pick the phone up and breathe into it, for Christ's sake.'

'I don't know what you're getting yourself worked up for.'

'I'm getting myself worked up because we're due at Frank's in forty-five minutes, and we haven't got a babysitter, because you make arrangements with some half-witted child that doesn't turn up. Do you really think it's safe, leaving them with somebody as clueless as that? How old is she?'

'She sounded pretty sharp to me.' Sylvia said. 'She's fourteen. I know her mother. Anyway, they're not going to be left with her, are they, so what are you talking about?'

'We'll have to ring Florence,' Colin said.

'Florence never babysits for us. She doesn't know how to manage them.'

'Are they as bad as that? What do they need, qualified nannies or policemen?'

'There's no need to get nasty. It's not the kiddies' fault, Colin.'

'Have you got a better suggestion?'

'Ask her if she'll have them for the night, then. Go on. Phone her.'

'You phone her,' Colin said. 'You got us into this mess.'

'I'd like to know why it's always my problem to fix up a babysitter. You always leave it to me and then you criticise. It's you that wants to go to this dinner, not me.'

'All right,' Colin said, 'all right. Then I'll just phone up Frank and say we can't make it, shall I? Frank goes to a lot of trouble over his dinner parties. He's very interested in cooking and he goes to a lot of trouble, trying to select the right guests.'

'And I go to trouble every night of the week. You don't think about that.'

'Don't be so bloody ridiculous, Sylvia. Are we going or aren't we?'

'Well, if I phone Florence, you'll have to go down and get them their sausage and beans. Children have to be fed as well, you know.'

'I'll phone,' Colin said. 'You see to them.' He stumped off downstairs. He took deep breaths. Self-command, he thought, control, order; he realised, amazed, that this upset had dismissed Isabel from his mind for at least fifteen minutes. But he could not arrange to live in a permanent row. 'They can bring their sleeping bags, tell her,' Sylvia shouted after him. Here was material for reworking, for weeks and weeks of quarrels. Colin could hear the children shouting each other down above the noise of the TV set. I'd be most adept at feeding lions, he thought, or giving rabbits to pythons.

Florence sounded doubtful, mildly shocked. 'But the beds aren't aired, Colin. It's such short notice.'

'Sylvia says they can bring sleeping bags.'

'Well, that doesn't sound very suitable to me, but I do admit it might be the lesser evil.' Oh, cut it out, Colin thought, yes or no? 'They can't sleep in beds that aren't aired,' Florence said.

'Okay, but if we bring the sleeping bags, and listen Florence, they've been fed, and I'll be over for them first thing tomorrow.'

He put the phone down, relieved. He would have felt such a fool, making his excuses to Frank; Frank seemed to have smart intellectual friends who would not have problems like babysitters, and he would probably not understand. He had been looking forward to this evening, relying on it to take his mind off Isabel. He would rise above his situation tonight, he would be witty and carefree and relaxed, and not, he vowed, not have too much to drink, so that Sylvia gave him warning glances in front of everybody and nagged him all the way home about the breathalyser.

All he had to do was change his shirt. He ran a comb through his hair and was ready by a quarter to eight, standing expectantly in the hall. Sylvia had painted her eyelids with a luminous stripe of sky-blue, and her eyes beneath, rather bloodshot, appeared angrier than ever. Fuming quietly to herself, muttering under her breath, she dumped bundles and baskets in the hall, marshalling the children with little pushes and taps on the backs of their skulls.

'What are you standing there looking so useless for?' she demanded. His brief ebullience vanishing, Colin took her by the arm, steering her into the kitchen for a little private row.

'I do wish,' he hissed at her, 'I do wish that you could manage not to talk to me like that in front of the children. How do you expect them to have any respect for me? What are they going to think about me, if you speak to me like that?'

Sylvia glared at him. Then she dropped her eyes and disengaged her arm from his grasp. 'What does it matter?' she said tiredly. She swerved past him and back into the hall.

'You undermine me,' he shouted after her. 'You've got enough stuff there for an Antarctic expedition. One night, they're going for, woman, not a bloody month.'

The children were complaining at being dragged away from the TV. They had been looking forward to bullying their babysitter and getting the better of her, and forcing her to let them stay up long past their usual bedtime. Florence was an unknown quantity; she alternated with them between doting and frigidity, and she had no TV set. Packed into the back of the car, they became instantly fractious. They flailed their legs and jostled for room, jabbing each other with their elbows. Karen began to sniffle, and Suzanne took out a pencil she had about her person and dug it into her brother's leg.

'For God's sake, will you stop it?' Sylvia twisted round in her seat to deliver slaps left and right.

'How can I drive?' Colin demanded. 'How can I concentrate on the traffic? There'll be an accident. You'll cause an accident if you go on like this.'

'Oh, Dad, Dad, Dad,' Alistair wailed. 'She's made a big grey hole in my knee. It'll go septic, Dad. I'll have to stay off school.'

At the traffic lights Sylvia lurched over the back of her seat and snatched the pencil from Suzanne. She wound down her window and hurled it out. It struck the windscreen of the car drawn up next to them with a noise like a gunshot and rolled with an astonishingly loud clatter down the bonnet.

'My God,' Colin said. People in other cars were staring. Scarlet with embarrassment and breaking out in a sweat, he accelerated away from the green light.

He drew up in Florence's driveway, under the dark shapes of the dripping trees, and took out his new clean handkerchief to mop his forehead. 'Well, we've made it.'

Sylvia swivelled her legs out of the car. 'These damn mouldy leaves,' she said. 'My evening shoes will be ruined.'

Florence appeared immediately, looking apprehensive. She must have been watching from the front room, standing in the dark. Sylvia propelled the children towards the house and Colin followed, his arms loaded with their baggage. A sleeping bag escaped from his grasp and unrolled itself like a serpent on the wet path. He dragged it after him, hoping no one would notice. Sylvia was saying, 'They've been fed, they're to get straight to bed, they don't want anything.'

'But what if they do?' Florence said. 'I mean, what will I give them, and in the morning –'

'Look, you don't need to give them their breakfast even, we'll come for them,' Sylvia said.

'I'm not unwilling to give them their breakfast,' Florence insisted. 'It's not that, don't think that, Sylvia, but I don't know what they're used to, for instance if they have fresh bread or stale.'

'Stale bread? What would they have stale bread for?'

'Yuk,' Suzanne offered. 'I'm not eating stale bread.'

'Well,' Florence said, 'when we were children we never had fresh bread. Children didn't have it. It's bad for them. They can't digest it.'

'Go on.'

'It's no joke, Sylvia. You ought to be careful what you give them.'

'Sylvia, it's gone half-past eight,' Colin said. 'We're late.' Florence turned to him, looking stubborn.

'Perhaps you can convince her, Colin, as she doesn't take any notice of what I say.'

'Florence, if we had stale bread when we were children I expect it was because mother was too lazy and disorganised to have any fresh in the house.' He turned to Sylvia. 'She got fussy as she got older, you know, but when we were kids it was a different story.'

'I think that's very disloyal, Colin.' Two red spots appeared on Florence's cheeks. 'I don't know how you dare. She was an excellent mother, and there was nothing wrong with the way we were brought up.'

'I've not got time to discuss it.' Colin hauled his cuff up again and tapped the face of his watch. 'Sylvia –'

'You've not answered my question,' Florence said stubbornly. 'About the bread.'

'Bread?' Colin's self-control fled now with a great yell into his sister's face. 'Bread? They chew nails, this lot. You could feed them nitroglycerine and ground glass and they'd bloody digest it.'

Sylvia pulled at his arm, and Alistair, red-faced, wormed among the overnight bags and took Florence by her skirt.

'Aunty Florence, I've got a septic hole in my knee.'

'What, my pet?'

Standing on one leg, Alistair pointed to his wound. 'You'll have to get your glasses,' he said.

Florence bent over his raised knee and looked up with a face full of alarm.

'It's all black, Sylvia. Whatever's happened?'

'Take no notice of him, it's nothing.'

'But it's black.'

'It's from a pencil. It'll wash off.'

'I'd better get my first-aid kit,' Florence said. 'I don't think you ought to leave me with him like this.'

'I've told you, it's nothing. Alistair, I'm going now, and if I hear from your Auntie that you've been playing her up there'll be trouble.'

'Oh all right, you go,' Alistair said. 'I expect I'll be up all night crying with the pain, that's all.'

Suzanne sat down on the stairs and clasped her arms round her abdomen, rocking with simulated mirth; standing amid the baggage, Karen began to scream.

'We're off,' Sylvia yelled above the noise. 'Thanks a lot, Florence, and we'll see you tomorrow.'

'But you can't leave me with them like this. He might be ill. What if – '

Sylvia bolted out of the front door, Colin was already in the car. Alistair's voice followed her, 'I expect my leg will be cut off and you'll have to push me round in a wheelchair,' and Karen's wails and Suzanne's snorts of laughter. Mud splashed the back of her tights. She slammed the car door.

'It's quarter to nine.' Colin said.

'How far is it?'

'Half a mile as the crow flies, that's all.'

'As the crow flies? Does that mean you don't know the way? Oh, what a bloody business it all is. My evening's ruined before it starts.'

Colin edged the car out of Lauderdale Road.

'And Colin, remember you've to get up early in the morning to fetch the kids, and before that you've got to get us both home tonight.'

'When do I get drunk, Sylvia? Come on, when have you ever seen me drunk?'

'You drink too much if you get the chance. You always do, and you know it.'

'And how often do I get the chance? Come on, Sylvia, when did you last see me reeling round the estate smashing people's windows and singing "I belong to Glasgow", and throwing up on the pavement? When was the last time, eh, when?'

Sylvia lapsed into moody silence. 'They'll settle down,' she said, after a while. 'They'll settle, won't they?'

'I hope so. Florence isn't used to them.'

'I mean, it's not just them, all kids are like that. There's many worse. Florence doesn't know. Colin, this is a long half-mile.'

Colin saw that he was in a cul-de-sac. He slowed the car to a crawl.

'Are we there?'

'No, we're not. Look out, will you, and see if you can see Balmoral Road.'

It was the very edge of Florence's respectable district, bigger houses well back from the road, flat-land encroaching, street names buried in dripping hedges.

'Andover Crescent,' Sylvia said.

'That's no help. Well, okay, I'll just drive along it.'

'Hadn't you better go back?'

'If it's a crescent, it's bound to go round, isn't it, use your common sense. I wish you'd learn to drive, Sylvia, then I could have a drink sometimes without you nagging me.'

'Nobody's going to get a drink at this rate. I thought you knew where Frank's was.'

'If I knew, we'd be there, wouldn't we? Do you think I'm doing this for pleasure?'

'There's no need to get sarcastic. At least three times in the past two months you've been over to Frank's.'

Fear shot through him, joining the anger churning his intestines. 'Not from this direction. I know it from our house but not from this direction. All these streets look the same. And in the dark, too.'

They drove around for another ten minutes, and then Colin stopped the car at a phonebox. Inhaling the smell of stale urine, he leafed through the directory, a draught from a broken pane blowing piercingly down the back of his neck. The 'O' section had been torn out jaggedly, cutting him off at O'Connor. He dashed back to the car.

'You're getting soaked,' Sylvia said reproachfully. She was scrabbling through her handbag looking for change. 'Haven't you got Frank's number in your wallet?'

'I'll find another box.' Colin drove on. 'Here, I might have, take it out and have a look through.'

They had by now reached the main road and Sylvia searched through his wallet under the generous light, unimpeded by trees. 'Well, I can't see Frank's number. I don't think you've got it. Here, what's this? Social Services. What do you want the number of the Social Services for?'

'For school,' Colin said promptly. Sweat started out again on the back of his neck. 'We have to carry it. For emergencies.'

'What emergencies? I thought you got ambulances for emergencies.'

'Are you looking for a phonebox?'

'Here, stop here, I think that's one. It's not got a light. Here, pull up.'

'At least we know where we are now.'

Colin grabbed the directory and hurled himself back into his seat, peering at the listings by the dim light of the interior bulb. The door was half-open and rain spattered in. Sylvia shivered.

'Here's Frank. Give me that 10p.'

He dialled the number and was relieved to hear the ringing tone. It rang and rang. When he was on the point of giving up, the receiver was lifted and an unfamiliar voice answered. He heard it calling out for Frank.

'Here, Frank, here's some extraordinary chap called Sidney who's got lost.'

Frank came to the phone. 'Hello? Colin?'

Colin expected him to sound irritable, but he was quite jovial, perhaps alarmingly so. Must be a good party, Colin thought, good conversation, lots to drink. His spirits briefly rallied. The directions fixed in his mind, he jumped back into the car.

'Right, got it this time. Be there in under five minutes.'

'I'm cold, Colin. Freezing.'

'Cheer up. *En avant*.'

'Is that a foreign expression?'

'Yes. Course it is.'

'I hope you won't be using foreign expressions tonight, making a fool of yourself. And remember, about the drinking.'

Colin struggled for words for a moment, and found none. He slammed on the brakes and brought the car to rest outside Frank's house. Some long-sealed capsule of rage seemed to explode inside his skull, so that the rest of the night passed for him in a sort of haze, odd incidents and scraps of conversation rising jaggedly above the tide of his wrath; so that next day, when he was forced to think it all over, he could not pin any sequence to events, or say if they were real at all.

It was nine-thirty. Frank answered the door. He looked vacant, rather slack-jawed.

'Hello,' Sylvia said. Frank took her hand and kissed it. Startled, she pulled it away and rubbed it on her coat sleeve, then took off her coat and handed it to Frank as if he were a cloakroom attendant. Looking him over, she saw that he was wearing white shoes. She raised her eyebrows meaningfully.

Frank had a large Victorian house, a bit dilapidated but gracious in its proportions; he had a few good pictures, and quantities of junk-shop and repro furniture intermingled with a few antiques. He leaned to the idea that books furnish a room, and frequented jumble sales in search of leather bindings; he was not as interested in the contents of his finds as he knew he ought to be. The overall effect was harmonious, a little dusty, genteel. He had bought the house before prices shot up, with his savings and a small legacy, and financed his task by letting off bedrooms to students from the Teacher Training College. Colin imagined they paid a high price in humiliation, for Frank loved to patronise the young. I must take a good look around, he thought, I'm supposed to have been here quite often.

Frank did not seem to know what to do with Sylvia's coat. 'This way,' he said.

They followed him into a large, high-ceilinged room, where the other guests sat with drinks in their hands. In a tiny pause in the conversation, heads turned; turned back, and the talk resumed, a touch rumbustious, grating, over-loud; collars loosened and faces glowing. They're in full swing, Colin thought, we really are terribly late. Perhaps it would have been better to cut our losses and not come at all. He began to stammer out fresh apologies, but Frank brushed them aside.

'This is my colleague, Colin Sidney,' Frank said to the room at large. 'This is his charming wife, Sylvia, whom we all immediately notice is expecting another little Sidney, and this is Sylvia's wet coat.'

'Why does he want us to call him Sidney?' one of the guests said. 'Why can't he use his real name?'

'Don't be facetious, Edmund,' Frank said. 'Have you seen my drawing-room since it's been redecorated, Colin?'

'Oh well, we'll call him what he wants,' the other man grumbled. 'But either we should all go under our real names, or we should all have pseudonyms.'

'What?' Colin stared at him for a moment, and returned his attention to Frank's question. 'Of course I have, of course I've seen it,' he said heartily.

'I didn't think you had. I've moved the idiot box into the morning room, not that I ever watch the thing except for the odd documentary, and the telephone's through there in the junk room. They couldn't seem to understand that I wanted it through there.'

'Why not?' the grumbling man said. 'Most telephone conversation is junk. The art of letter writing is dead.'

'Colin, have you met – I'm sure you must know Edmund Toye?'

'I'm afraid not. How do you do?'

'Now that is a question.' Edmund Toye was a yellow-faced man, with a goatee and a snide pseudo-aristocratic expression; not unlike Cardinal Richelieu in some respects, but very unlike him in others. 'Now that is a piece of what you might call conversational junk. I mean, you say how am I, but if I were to tell you about my spondylitis, you would be very put out. My dear lady,' he said to Sylvia. '*Enchanté.*' Sylvia removed her hand hastily, fearing he might kiss it. 'Now is that more meaningful, or not, Sidney? I wonder.'

'Edmund,' a woman said in a sweetly warning tone. She presented them in turn with her hand. 'I am Charmian Toye.'

'Pleased to meet you,' Sylvia said.

'Now that is what I call an overstatement,' Toye said. 'Or a piece of hypocrisy. At best, she might be indifferent, certainly she has no reason to be pleased, and in fact she is simply trying to impress us with her grasp of the social niceties.'

'Well, well,' Charmian said. 'We may just get along stormingly together, and she may be awfully pleased in the end, so you see, Edmund, she is only anticipating. Anyway, it's a perfectly innocuous statement. Or so I should have thought. It may pass without comment.'

'It may, but of course,' said Edmund, 'it has not.'

Momentarily, Colin was alarmed. Who were these people with the odd names, and had they been drinking? Well, yes, obviously, but had they been drinking too much, or did they always talk like this? He was glad to see that one of his colleagues from school was present – Stewart Colman, who taught English – but although he was at least sanely named he was not a reassuring dinner companion. He seized Colin's hand now and pumped it earnestly, wisely adding no spoken greeting. There was a peculiar glint in his eye, Colin thought. He was a wiry man with very black hair. During his last summer vacation he had grown a beard, which to his grief and astonishment had sprouted the vibrant shade of bitter thick-cut marmalade. Having braved ridicule on the first day of term, he would not court more by shaving it off. His wife Gail was a big-boned woman of thirty-five, contrastingly sober in hue, who followed him around like an apology.

'Well, you seem to be saving lots of time by recognising the Colmans,' Frank said. 'Though I must say, Colin, you do appear a trifle distrait.'

'I'm just sorry we were so late. I can't apologise enough.' He paused, wary in case this turn of phrase should excite Edmund Toye's derision. 'We must have held up dinner.'

'Oh, we hadn't thought of dinner,' Frank said. 'We're doing some serious drinking. Let me provide for you. Whisky, I suppose, and for you, Sylvia? Gin all right? Gin's all right for Sylvia. Anything in it, Sylvia? Splash of something? Orange? Good Lord, I didn't think anyone over the age of sixteen drank gin and orange. Never mind, my dear, you shall have whatever you desire, I'm no snob.' Frank whirled about, Sylvia's coat in his arm like a comatose dancing partner.

'Here is Brian Frostick, and this is Elvie, whom we immediately notice is Brian's very newly married wife.'

Frostick was gaunt and pallid, and intimated that he was a solicitor; his wife Elvie, no more than twenty to his forty, was brown and short, with cropped hair and sturdy bare shoulders rising from the flounces of a vivid scarlet dress. Her handshake was bone-crunching.

'Well, why don't you sit?' Frank demanded. 'I'll dispose of Sylvia's outerwear and give you drinkies in a trice, when I think how to manage it.' He wandered from the room.

'Frank's well away,' Frostick said. He sniggered.

'I say,' said Edmund Toye sharply, 'don't sit there.'

Sylvia stopped, her backside in mid-air, then reached behind her to retrieve a violin, which Frank had placed carelessly on a chair in an effort to raise the cultural tone. She held on to it, looking about her helplessly. Soon, Colin thought, she would become angry.

'Oh, do,' Toye said with a gesture. 'By all means, if you feel moved. I dare say Frank can provide a selection of sheet music. You do play, I suppose?'

'You suppose wrong,' Sylvia said. Her voice was flat. 'I just want to know what to do with it.'

'My dear lady,' Toye said. Colin took the violin from Sylvia and edged up a very tarnished silver candelabra to place it on a sidetable. Mrs Toye was patting the chaise-longue beside her. She was a tiny woman, buttoned-up and rather cross, with a small pointed face and an air of extreme self-possession.

'What a pity, Sylvia,' Frostick said. 'What a pity, I really thought you would give us a recital. What a merry little Zingara you looked, in your festive red and green.'

'What's a Zingara?' Elvie asked.

'A type of gypsy, I believe,' Edmund Toye said. 'Speaking of the Romany people, does anyone, I wonder, read George Borrow nowadays?'

At that moment Frank arrived with the drinks. Gail Colman leaned forward and asked Sylvia pleasantly, 'When are you due?'

'July.'

'Oh, the ladies are going to talk about their confinements.' Frank seemed delighted. He pressed a glass into Sylvia's hand. 'Do harrow us, freeze our blood.'

'Well, I know nothing about it,' Elvie said, in the manner of one delivering a crushing snub. 'I only left school last year.'

'Thanks,' Sylvia said. 'Cheers, everybody.' She sipped her gin. 'Oh, it's very strong,' she said. 'Do you have children, Mrs Toye?'

'I have six.'

Colin turned and regarded the neat little woman with open astonishment.

'My goodness,' Sylvia said. 'I expect they keep you busy.'

'They don't keep me busy,' Mrs Toye said, a shade reproachfully, 'they keep me occupied.'

Sylvia was silent for a moment; all were silent. 'Well, Charmaine,' she said at last, 'I'm not going to cut any figure beside you. This is my fourth I'm expecting, and I'm quite sure it'll be my last.'

'Oh, not Charmaine.' Mrs Toye closed her eyes. 'Not as in the popular song.' She sang softly, ' "I wonder why you keep me waiting, Charmaine, my Charmaine." ' Her eyes snapped open again. 'Charmian, as in Iras and, A and C. "Give me my robe put on my crown I have immortal longings in me." If you find it easier, do call me Mrs Toye.'

' "Withered is the garland of the war, the soldier's pole is fallen," ' Toye remarked. 'That of course is a more than faintly ludicrous line. Really, I sometimes wonder if Shakespeare had any sense of the sexually ridiculous.'

Toye had by now taken up his stance before the fireplace, and was toasting his meagre buttocks before the electric logs. 'Do go on with what you were saying,' he ordered Frostick. 'About the *so* fascinating Road Traffic Acts.'

Stewart Colman leaned forward confidentially. 'Between you and me,' he told Colin in a hoarse whisper, 'these dinners are a bit pretentious. Frank's a bit pretentious. I don't know what they're talking about half the time. Truth be known, I don't think they know themselves. Intellectually speaking, it's a case of fur coat and no knickers.'

Unexpectedly moved by this image, Colin looked at Colman gratefully. He wondered when dinner would appear; he was feeling very hungry. Sylvia edged towards the end of the chaise-longue, away from Charmian, and touched his hand.

'Colin, are they all mad,' she muttered, 'or have they had too much to drink? That woman singing . . . '

'I don't know. Keep your voice down. Try to take no notice.'

'Can't we go?'

'Not till after dinner. Have a drink of your gin, and then you'll feel more into things.'

'Can we go right after the meal?'

'Yes, I don't think they'll miss us.'

A gust of Elvie's piercing chatter blew across them.

'I don't think they'd miss us if we went now,' Sylvia said.

Frank was moving amongst them, circling the room with a bottle of Gordon's in one hand and a bottle of Johnnie Walker in the other. He poured a liberal measure of the gin into Charmian Toye's glass, a quintuple by Colin's estimate. Colin could not help but total it up and add in the cost of the whisky Frank slopped into his own glass. Ashamed of himself, he looked at his watch, as a diversion. It was ten thirty.

'By the way,' Frank said, giving himself a final dash of Scotch, 'I've invited Yarker to join us for dessert. I didn't think we wanted Yarker for the whole evening, and yet did think that at some point Yarker would be necessary.'

'Does he know when to come?' Elvie asked.

'Yarker always knows the moment,' Frank said. 'You should know that, Elvie.'

'Christ, yes,' Frostick said, with a smile that showed his gums.

'Do you remember when he put Charmian's knickers on his head and pelted everybody with sardines? Yarker's good value.'

Colin's heart was sinking fast. The present company he could possibly cope with, but this threat of physical extravagances seemed unbearable. Would it be worse in anticipation, or worse in reality? People said that things were never as good as you hoped or as bad as you feared, but then, he thought with a pang, there had been Isabel, and on the other hand there had been the time he had his wisdom tooth out.

'By the way,' Frostick said, 'when's the food, Frank?'

'Oh, stop fussing. Where's your glass?'

It was another three-quarters of an hour before they were seated at Frank's elaborately laid table. Sylvia and Colin were at opposite ends, but Elvie and her husband had been seated together, because, Mrs Toye advised mysteriously, 'it was not yet a year.' By now it had become clear to Colin that the Toyes and the Frosticks were at home in the house, because the men had become ruder to Frank, and had started to help themselves to drinks. It seemed also that the two couples knew each other well, even intimately. Colin felt a sense of sinister exclusion. He had hoped to be seated with Gail Colman, but he had Charmian instead. He thought that with this seating plan the evening had reached its nadir, but he did not know then what would occur over the saltimbocca.

Muriel had decided to go to bed. When she was halfway upstairs, a sharp pain brought her to a dead stop, as if someone had slammed a door in her face. She put a hand to her back and stood where she was, her large feet wedged a little sideways and her hand slapped down on the banister rail, flatly where it had fallen. After a time, when the pain ebbed, she turned gingerly and sat down on the step. She waited, not aware of what she was waiting for, not trying to think about it. Lately the affairs of her body had taken a turn for the worse; here was a turn for the worser. Evelyn had just gone on being the same, except snide and looking sideways and jeering about her misfortunes, and doing a performance she called worrying about the future.

When the pain came back, Muriel leaned forward and dug her fingers into her thighs. The vast bulk before her seemed to pulsate dully, throbbing and jumping like a machine. There was no guarantee that she would not always have to stay like this, her head down, a dry grunt coming from her throat. But after a minute or two the spasm slackened and released her. She took a deep breath, ran her hands along her legs and stroked her knees. This was a change in her state. This was a process, she thought. There would be something at the end of it.

It was so long since Colin had eaten that he felt slightly nauseated. Frank was an accomplished cook, and he had taken a great deal of trouble. It was obvious that the meal had not been waiting. Did that mean, Colin asked himself, that his lateness had made no difference at all? If he had sat there with the rest of them, consuming Frank's generous drinks since eight o'clock, he would have been in no state to drive home; and they had hardly started on the wine that was to accompany their meal. He looked apprehensively around the ring of faces. They looked little different from when he first came in, but different they must be, edging by degrees towards inebriation; he hoped there would be no scenes.

'Insalata di funghi e frutta di mare,' Frank announced. He tripped slightly, bearing the plates in, but retrieved himself. His glasses were completely steamed up from the heat in the kitchen. But he did not seem to notice. 'No squid, of course,' he said gloomily.

'Ah well, Frank,' Mrs Toye said. 'Squid is next to impossible, especially those tender little sea creatures which the Italians, so poetically I always feel, call sea-strawberries.' Mrs Toye now sat back with a languid air, as if, because of the absence of squid, she could expect to find no further pleasure in the evening.

Colin looked down at his plate, and down the table at Sylvia. She wouldn't eat raw mushrooms, that was for sure. Oh well, she could blame her pregnancy for anything she couldn't manage.

'Sidney. I'm speaking to you,' Edmund Toye said. 'I say, I understand you are also a schoolmaster.'

'Yes, that's right. I teach history.'

'Well, you say history, but I wonder what you think history is. Probably a question we would need considerable time to go into. "It is a sign of the gods' especial detestation of a man, when they drive him to the profession of schoolmaster." Now which of the ancient writers, I wonder, said that?' Toye did not wait for a reply, but pressed on keenly, thrusting a forkful of salad into his mouth. 'Tell me now, what is your preferred form of creativity? Frank of course has written some delightful poetry. As an actor he is extremely skilful. His painting I feel is artificial. Intellectualised.' A stray thought claimed Colin's wandering attention and involuntarily he raised his eyes to the deep blue ceiling above the Regency Stripe. Didn't he remember Frank complaining about the cost of undercoat? No, Toye didn't mean that, evidently he didn't mean that.

'Frank,' he was saying, 'have you told Colin about your novel?'

'My novel,' Frank said, beaming. 'You want to hear about my novel, Colin?'

'That would be very nice,' Colin said. 'I had no idea.'

'Well it's just a germ as yet, you understand.' Frank took off his glasses and polished them vigorously. 'It's all rather circumstantial . . . as a matter of fact, I had a stroke of luck. Do you remember that bad fog we had, when my car got a bump, and was in the garage?' Frank paused, took a sip of wine, then a gulp. 'Robust,' he said. 'Here, Colin, let me top you up.' Colin pushed his glass towards Frank. Out of the corner of his eye he checked on Sylvia. She didn't seem to be making too much of a fool of herself. There was an untouched glass of white wine by her plate, and he knew she had only had two gins.

'Well, the odd thing was,' Frank began.

'Perhaps for brevity I should take the story up,' Toye cut in. When he got his car back, it came complete with the most extraordinary document. Obviously belonged to somebody else with a car in for repairs, and the garage men had taken it out and then put it back in the wrong car. At least, that's the explanation we came up with.'

Colin felt uneasy. 'What exactly was it?'

'Oh, a most extraordinary thing,' Toye said. 'A kind of case file which a set of wretched social workers had been keeping over the years. Really, you cannot imagine the low level of literacy among those people.'

'The entries,' Charmian Toye said slowly, 'have given us much innocent pleasure.'

'But look,' Colin's heart was hammering in his throat. 'Look, Frank, you must give it back at once. It's the property of the Social Services Department.'

'Oh, knickers to that,' Frank said. His grin was distinctly lopsided, and his eyes behind his spectacles seemed to slip out of focus. 'Finders keepers. It's all about two dotty women. It's a gift. Grist to the mill. I'm going to turn it into a novel.'

'Frank could never,' Toye said, 'have invented such grotesquerie by himself.'

'For goodness sake,' Colin said. He was aware that his voice was very loud, and that the Frosticks, man and wife, had turned to stare at him. 'Frank, think now, this is confidential information you're talking about.'

'Then someone should have taken better care of it. Here, Frostick, open another three bottles, will you, I'm talking. You can't imagine the lives some people lead. I might turn it into a sort of allegory, you see, about the state of our society.'

'But regardless of how it came to be lost ... some poor social worker ... the consequences could be very serious.'

'Poor social worker be damned,' Frostick said. 'I'm not sure that they're not the villains of the piece. Interfering do-gooders. Caring Society. Huh.' Frostick showed yellow teeth in contempt, and took to grappling with the corkscrew.

'Come on now, Frank, you've got to give these papers back.' Colin's tone was pleading.

'Not a chance. I've already written Chapter One. Stranger than fiction. It's inspired me.' He waved an arm. 'It's all through there, in the study, waiting for me to get back to it tomorrow morning.'

'Really, Frank,' Colin said, 'you can't do this. You've lost touch with reality.'

'He has if he thinks he'll do anything tomorrow morning,' Elvie said. 'Except vomit.'

'But these are real people. You can't make their lives public property.' He turned around on Toye. 'You've no right to abet him in this. You know it's wrong, probably illegal.' Toye stroked his beard, and regarded him sardonically.

'I'll change their names,' Frank said sulkily. 'I wish I'd never told you, Colin. You're spoiling it.'

'Yes, and I'm right to spoil it. This could have serious consequences, and not just for you. Some client – these clients – may be suffering because the file's missing. And someone's job may well be in jeopardy, if things go wrong. Even losing the file is bad enough, but it was obviously pure accident – and some poor young woman – or man,' he added hastily, 'won't be able to do their job properly without it.' He leaned forward, his face reddening. 'Give it back, Frank, hand it in, for God's sake.'

Frank sprawled back in his chair. 'Client,' he murmured. 'He knows all the jargon.'

Frostick leaned over Colin and refilled his glass. 'Calm down,' he said.

'Yes, calm down, Sidney,' said Toye. 'You're spoiling the party.'

'I don't give a damn about the party.' Colin crashed his fist down on the table. 'Give that file to me.'

There was a silence. From the other end of the table Sylvia implored him. 'Please, Colin, what does it matter to you?'

'It does matter, because – I happen to know – Oh, Christ.'

'Know what?' Elvie said.

'Frank's heart's set on it,' Charmian added sentimentally.

'Never mind,' Colin growled. He dabbed his mouth with his napkin, as if there were blood on his lip. He would, indeed, have liked to lean over the table and punch Frank as hard as he could manage. Frank was what he had always suspected. He was a blind, antisocial egotist, and not fit to have charge of the young. He should have known it was useless to appeal to any residue of morality left in Frank. And no other kind of appeal was open to him, without giving himself away. Was there any possibility that he was mistaken? No, not a chance. That was Isabel's file, and Isabel's error that Frank was hoping to blazon to the world. And of course, Frank would succeed in his project. Frank and the Frosticks and Edmund and Charmian between them could write any number of books. He glared at Elvie Frostick, now glowing like a bulb above her lampshade of a dress. Elvie probably took shorthand.

Colin reached for his glass, drained it. He put it back on the table, and quite suddenly, instantly, he was drunk. Around him the conversation resumed, louder, crueller; he heard it in snatches, above his own thoughts, clattering after logic like some unoiled and primitive engine.

A door was creaking. In time, in time, Evelyn's figure appeared below her at the foot of the stairs, her hand fumbling for the lightswitch that still worked. She snapped it down, and as light burst over Muriel, a frenzy of pain burst out in her body, an unstemmable riot of pain, hers and hers alone.

Evelyn mounted the stairs. 'Get up, get up,' she said. 'Do as I tell you. You have to. I'm responsible. I'm in charge of you.'

So every day is Mother's Day, Muriel thought. Her eyes half-closed, she regarded the old woman. Evelyn reached out and took Muriel under her armpits, trying to pull her to her feet. Muriel allowed herself to be lifted, her body hanging like a sack filled with bricks. Evelyn's chest rose and fell audibly, with a creak that was very like that the furniture made, but which seemed strange from a human person. Her lips turned blue, her face grew pinched, flesh fell away from the bones. When Muriel was good and ready, she put her hands on Evelyn's shoulders and heaved herself upright.

'It'll get worse before it gets better,' Evelyn said. 'I'm only telling you.'

For years she had been of the opinion that Muriel didn't feel pain.

She got bruised and bled, but she didn't feel it like any normal person. What was agony for some could be just a twinge for her. Tonight even her twinge must be regarded.

'I got this dress on the island of Kos,' Elvie was saying. 'We went there on honeymoon. It was very cheap, this dress.' A sort of complacent savagery crept into her voice. 'But I think it's rather special. It's my colour, scarlet. It was too long, you know, so I made them shorten it, there and then. That's what I call service.' She looked around, ready for a challenge. 'That's what's wrong with Britain today.'

'Ah,' Edmund said, 'how does it feel, I wonder, to be twenty.'

'After we'd been to Kos,' the girl said, 'we visited Malta. On both islands we saw all the historic sites.'

'I did the swim,' Frostick said, 'the famous swim. As in history.'

'It's got to be done in armour,' Frank said.

'Where would I get armour from?' Frostick demanded.

'Well, you say swim,' said Edmund, 'you say armour, but I question whether it is possible to swim in armour.'

'Not what you would think of as armour,' Frank explained. 'Not plate armour. A leather jerkin with things sewn on it. Chain links.'

'Oh, that,' Toye sneered.

'My friend fell in the canal wearing her suede coat,' Gail Colman said. 'She sank like a stone.'

Colin pushed his chair back and stood up.

'You can't go to the lavatory, because I'm going.' Elvie Frostick hoisted herself to her feet, looking belligerent. She thrust her chair away and swayed across the room, her face incandescent; it could be seen that she was in fact little more than a dwarf.

Colin edged himself around to Frank and bent over him, whispering.

'Do you think I could make a phone call?'

'Of course.' Frank gestured expansively. 'You don't have to ask permission, you know where it is.'

'I said I was going,' Elvie yelled back from the doorway. She clung to the doorframe like a furious and compressed gorilla.

Colin slipped into the little room that Frank had indicated earlier. It was a junk room indeed, piled high with broken-sided old tea-chests and yellow newspapers. The phone with its stack of director-ies was on a rickety table in the far corner. Colin swore to himself as he picked his way over the rubbish. How bloody impractical and stupid, how exactly like O'Dwyer. All his respect evaporated, replaced by loathing and fear, as if he were compelled to walk a mountain road in the company of a lunatic. He nudged the director-ies aside to crouch over the telephone; no one must overhear. Under the topmost book was a copy of *Playboy* and a volume of *Readers' Digest*. Colin stared at them. He did not know which he found the more shocking. After a moment he recovered himself, but as he began to dial Isabel's number he was appalled to see that his fingers were trembling.

He tried to work out how many weeks it was since he had spoken to her. Suppose her father answered, and she refused to come to the phone? Or she answered herself, and put it down at the sound of his voice? His heart was thumping against his ribs. Is it so important, he asked himself, is it a matter of life and death? He didn't know, his brain was befuddled, he couldn't think straight. He must choose the words, the exact words that would tell her at once –

'Hello?'

'Isabel.'

'Colin? What is it?'

'Listen . . . '

'What do you want?'

'Something's happened, ver – '

'Oh? Something's happened, has it?' Her tone was full of im-patience and mockery. 'Has Sylvia miscarried? Is that it? So you think that now – well, you can't. It's not on, Colin. So if that's it – go to hell.'

He gasped, and suddenly tears filled his eyes, pricking and de-meaning. Where did she learn to talk to him like that? Why did she do it? Was it out of perplexity and confusion greater than his own, or out of some practised hardness inside her? He shuddered, taking a great breath.

'I know where your file is,' he said, as loudly and clearly as he dared.

'What?'

'Your file, your missing file.' As simply as he could, he told her what had happened.

'Wait,' she said, when he finished his account. 'Colin, you've got me out of bed. I can't think straight.'

'You'll have to be quick. I'll have to ring off in a minute.'

'But I went to the garage three times. They denied they'd ever seen it. Then they – but Colin, how could he write a novel? I don't know what you mean.'

'He thinks it's got the makings of a good story.'

'But it's not a story, it's just what people do. It's just a record of what they do.'

'Grist to the mill, he says. Have you ever heard that stupid phrase? What is grist, anyway?'

'Colin, are you drunk?'

'No, not by a long chalk.'

'This isn't some stupid joke, is it?'

'Of course it's not a joke. It's a dinner party. We've finished two courses and I've come to phone you. I've got to be quick.'

'Colin, there's nothing I can do, is there? I mean, if I came and asked him for it . . . do you think – ?'

'I don't think that would be a good idea, because how would you have known, and that involves me – '

'Yes, I see, I do see that.'

'If Social Services asked him for it? If you told them?'

'Don't be stupid, Colin, I'm trying to avoid them knowing, isn't that the whole point? I don't want this case discussed at Social Services. Can't we persuade him?'

'I've told you, no.'

'This is awful, Colin, this confidential information lying about, it could cause the most awful blow-up.'

'I know that, I know, you don't have to persuade me.'

'Do you know where it is?'

'Where it is? What do you mean?'

'In the house.'

'Well . . . yes. Roughly.'

'Then take it.'

'What?'

'Get it for me, Colin.'

'But Christ, how can I – '

'Do you see any other way?'

'No, but – '

'Phone me tomorrow.'

He heard a click. The line was dead. She didn't even say thank you, he thought. And she hadn't told him what the file looked like, or whose name was on it. Presumably he would know it when he saw it. Gently he replaced the receiver. Someone was calling him.

'Sidney! Sidney!' That was Frank. Now Frank thought it was a big joke to call him Sidney. 'Sidney, come for your chocolate mousse.'

At least, Evelyn thought, the turn of events had not taken her by surprise. She had dreaded being roused from sleep, pulled up from her musty undersea dreams to find the girl and her half-born child scraping at the bedroom door. What if there were difficulties? Of course, it had to be considered, she had run over the question in her mind. If Muriel looked like dying, she would fetch the doctor. If it came to that . . . she could not stomach being haunted by that composite creature that would be Muriel and the half-emerged child; no, she could not stomach it. They would want a room to themselves, to hiss and cavort and bang on the walls; ah, the gay young dead. Soon she would be forced to live in the kitchen.

She left the lights burning all over the house. She hoped that it would not attract attention from the outside, but she had enough to do without being hampered by things following her down the hall. She made Muriel a cup of tea and let her have it lying on the-bed. She was the soul of kindness. Then she took out the first aid books and her reading glasses. She boiled the scissors for ten minutes. She did not think they would be much use, but you cannot get scissors sharpened nowadays. In her drawer in the kitchen cabinet she found some lengths of string, which would do for tying off the cord; they were rolled up with the remains of her paper bags, from her tenants' tearing days. She could not see her pile of farthings, and spent a minute or two rooting around for them. She sighed. She would have to ask Muriel about it, when Muriel was more in command of herself. 'I do like everything in its place,' she said to herself. She got ready a blanket for the baby, a bit worn and musty but the correct size; it must have been one of Muriel's. She took up some aspirin and a glass of tonic wine; but when around midnight Muriel screamed out in pain, she lost her nerve and slapped her repeatedly until she lay quiet, with two tears rolling down her grey cheeks.

When Colin re-entered the dining-room, he saw at once that the situation had deteriorated. Several more bottles of wine had been opened, and Charmian had returned to gin; the bottle stood by her elbow. Charmian's precise tones had become even sharper, as if her tongue were edged with glass. Sylvia looked up at him anxiously. He attempted a smile, a reassuring smile; his face felt stiff. Edmund Toye was explaining how after a hard week at the Teacher Training College he liked to support his local football team and stand on the terraces, wearing a cap and bellowing. He described it as a most valuable emotional release.

'A. J. Ayer does it,' he said. 'Logical Positivism.'

'Go on,' Frostick said.

'He's Arsenal.'

Colin took his seat. He pushed his plate away. He certainly wasn't going to eat chocolate mousse. He picked up his brimming glass and took a gulp of dessert wine. He did not notice the taste; it could have been water, or vodka. His throat was dry. Stewart Colman pushed the bottle down to him.

'Refill, Colin. Might as well. When in Rome et cetera.'

Colin noticed that Colman seemed relatively sober still. And Sylvia too; she sat with an expression both hunted and mutinous, which she had assumed as soon as she saw Frank's white shoes and which the meal and the drinks had done nothing to alter. But then, he thought, for what I have to do next it would be as well if they were all drunk. He shifted his attention from his glass to find Charmian's eyes fixed upon him. He lifted his head.

'Do you know,' she said distinctly, 'he hasn't *got* spondylitis?'

'I suspected as much,' Colin said.

'He said it because he thought it sounded clever. In fact it's not an intellectual's disease at all. I should think you might get it from carrying heavy weights.'

'I should think you might,' Colin said.

'In that case it surprises me that half the population of Africa hasn't got it, from carrying things on their heads. It may be that they have. We do not comprehend,' she said, shaking her head, 'we seldom take the time to try to comprehend, the sufferings of the Third World.'

At that moment there was a loud clatter just outside the room, and Elvie stood in the doorway holding by the hand a bald sandy-coloured man of about sixty, with moles and bristles on his shining scalp. He wore sagging twill trousers and a leather-patched jacket. The man's mouth hung open, but it was difficult to tell whether he was inebriated, or meant to utter a greeting, given time. It was possible that this was the only member of the party for which the excuse could be made that, when sober, he appeared drunk. Locked together, he and Elvie staggered across the room towards the table.

Now Charmian displayed the first real sign of animation since her discomfiture over the squid. She sat bolt upright, her hands clasped.

'I say, Yarker. How clever of you, Yarker, to know that we wouldn't get to pudding till midnight.'

'Pudding?' said Yarker. 'No pudding, whisky for me.'

'Oh, you are tiresome, Yarker, we've finished all the whisky.'

'Eh?' said Yarker.

'S'right,' Frank said. 'Colman here's been mixing cocktails.'

'You say cocktails,' Toye put in, 'but does anyone, I wonder, really know the derivation of the term, "cocktail"?'

His glass halfway to his lips, Colin glared at Colman. If Colman had been sampling his own product, his last hope of sane assistance had gone. Elvie had now resumed her seat, and as if in early confirmation of his fears, Colman rose from the table, lurched across to her and pressed his mouth into her stout shoulder. Brian Frostick watched from under lowered eyelids. Gail Colman stared at her husband's strange parti-coloured beard moving across the girl's flesh like some small browsing animal; she pursed her mouth, and sat isolated in a moody silence, looking as if she were accustomed to this and had been waiting for it all evening. When Colman raised his head, a large half-moon of teethmarks could be seen above Elvie's meaty left breast. Perhaps anaethetised by alcohol, she had not made a sound. As Colman straightened up, Gail's fingers crept across the table towards Colin's untouched mousse; she stood up, drew back her arm, and with an Amazonian heave of her bosom lobbed the heavy glass dish at his head. It struck him a glancing blow, and a gelatinous mess slid down his shirt front. He swayed slightly, then stretched his arms wide and thrust his head forward, as if he were in the pillory. 'More, more,' Edmund Toye cried. Her eyes narrowed, Gail Colman reached for the pepper-mill. Sylvia shot out of her chair in alarm.

'My God,' Colin roared, 'you all know each other, don't you? You do this regularly.'

'Let's go,' Sylvia said to him.

'Soon. Soon as we can.'

'Can't we go now?'

Above the general racket, something penetrated to them all simultaneously, a new noise in the room. It was a quiet snuffling, a sighing, a series of little squeaks. It emanated from Mrs Toye, who now sat swaying in her chair, crying softly. Colman realigned himself with the table, stumbled back to it and resumed his seat.

He put his elbows into the debris of the food, and peered closely at Charmian.

'I say, pass the port,' Frank said. 'It's going the wrong way.'

'Shut up, Frank,' Frostick said, with no amiability. Charmian was fumbling for her handkerchief. She found it, then looked at it, bunched up in her fist, as if she did not know how it got there or what it was for. Her eyes had become dreamy and huge with tears, her mouth quivered, and her voice had broken down into a plaintive bleat.

'So delighted, so euphoric,' she said, 'always the same when you're pregnant, you don't want to tell people, tempting fate, you know, not that I expected any trouble but you get that funny feeling and you can't help worrying, but Edmund goes and tells everybody right away. He can't contain himself, bursting with pride, well I think men are, don't you?' Charmian, eyes glazing, addressed the empty air. 'I mean it must seem so sentimental to you, I expect you get tired of people enthusing, but it really is so wonderful, absolutely the most wonderful thing in the world, I remember I absolutely melted when Jerome was put into my arms, and it was the same with Ariana so I know it works with girls too. Oh, and such an absolutely super super feeling, each one like a little miracle, each tiny perfect little finger – '

'She's cracked up,' Frostick said.

' – and each tiny perfect toe.'

Charmian subsided into muffled sobs. The room fell quiet. Then suddenly Frank rose to his feet with a deafening clatter, slapping his palms down on the table; extending one arm, gripping the table with the other, he commenced a repertoire of humming and twanging which Colin took to be the sounds of an orchestra tuning up. Ambitiously extending both arms, he bellowed two lines:

> 'Allons enfants de la patrie,
> Le jour de gloire est arrivé.'

'Can't remember any more,' he said, and sat down abruptly. His whole body seemed to sag, and he made a soft snorting noise. His head lolled, and a trail of spittle ran down his chin. His body lurched over to the left side of his chair, and stayed there, leaning precariously over the arm.

'He's had a seizure,' Sylvia cried, jumping to her feet.

Frostick looked at her with contempt and annoyance. 'He's pissed,' he said. 'He's had far more than we have. He drinks in the kitchen between courses. For God's sake, sit down, woman, and give me the port if you don't want any.'

Charmian was still crying, wiping her nose noisily from time to time. Colin knelt by Frank's chair and took his pulse. He could not find it, but did not assume from this that Frank was dead; it was more a formality than a practical proceeding.

'Sylvia,' he said, 'why don't you take Charmian upstairs, and loosen her clothes, and get her to lie down for a few minutes?'

Sylvia dragged her eyes from Frank. 'Right,' she said. She took Charmian firmly by the arms and raised her from her chair. Mrs Toye suffered herself to be led from the room. Colin saw with admiration that, although Sylvia was trembling a little from the multiple shocks of the last ten minutes, her expression was firm and her gait quite steady.

'Upsy-daisy,' she said to Mrs Toye, when they reached the bottom of the stairs. He heard her retrieve the tiny lady from a tumble, and set her on her feet again. 'Up we go, there's a good girl.'

And up they went. Colin surveyed the wreckage. Frank was still lolling half in and half out of his chair, one knuckle brushing the carpet. Colman and Frostick were mixing port with brandy. Gail Colman had resumed her sulk, and Elvie, whilst sitting bolt upright, appeared only semi-conscious.

Now Yarker sidled up to Colin and took him by the sleeve. He was breathing heavily. Colin saw that his freckled skin was almost entirely covered in fierce ginger hairs like those found in doormats. 'I say,' said Yarker, 'what's all this about Frank having no more whisky! It's nonsense, I say. Of course there must be whisky.'

Colin saw that he must placate Yarker before he would make any progress. He appealed to the table. 'Have you any idea where Frank keeps his spare whisky? Yarker seems to think he must have a supply.'

'Yarker is not known to be wrong,' Toye said.

Frostick looked up. He seemed to be giving the matter consideration. 'We could look for it,' he offered.

'Good idea,' Colin said. 'It's a big house, so we'd better split up.'

'Look, I'll take command of this exercise,' Yarker snapped. 'Volunteers for the study?'

'Me,' Colin said promptly.

'You'll not find it there,' Yarker said. 'He spends too much time in there. If it were in there, he'd have drunk it. Stands to reason. Moral: never volunteer.'

'I don't mind,' Colin said. Yarker glared at him.

'Colman, stand on your feet man when I address you. Kitchens, out-houses, sculleries. Frostick, recce all medicine cabinets. I myself will search the upper floors in their entirety. Toye – oh, leave him, the bloody man's playing with himself under the table.'

Toye's expression had become vague and goatlike, and neither he nor Elvie seemed better than stuporous; Frank snored gently, twitching a little at his extremities. Colin bent down and compassionately eased off Frank's shoes. Then he straightened up, wheeled smartly and trotted off for the study at a pace which brought a bark of approval from Yarker. Softly he closed the door behind him, shutting them all out.

A smell of damp and old papers, and the healing darkness. Colin felt reluctant to switch on the light, but that was ridiculous; he was working against time, he told himself. For good measure he switched on Frank's desk lamp too. He pulled out the first drawer and rifled through it, and then the second. Nothing. On the desk, then, actually on it. All waiting for tomorrow, Frank had said, but how could you find anything under all this rubbish, these press-cuttings turning yellow, these ends of string and scissors, and pile upon pile of the *Readers' Digest,* even in Compendia, even in Condensed Books. Was it possible to do any work in this room? If only she'd told him – what's this? His hand slid over a buff-coloured folder. He swept the debris off the top of it. Opened it, flicked through. MURIEL ALEXANDRA AXON. Yes, this was it all right. Funny, that name sounded very familiar. Where did he know it from? He was beginning to have a headache, and his eyes burned from the cigarette smoke. He rubbed them vigorously. Never mind now, it would come back to him tomorrow, as soon as his head was clear. The important thing was that he'd got the file. He patted the papers back into it and tucked them under his arm. There was a cough behind him and he jumped violently. It was Frank, swaying alarmingly, smiling, his expression sly. 'Ah, Colin!' he said. 'Caught you! Cry down my idea, would you, and then creep in here and steal my file? Thought you'd write it for yourself, did you? Wait till the others hear about this!' He raised his voice. 'Help! Help! Stop plagiarist!'

Colin heard Sylvia's voice in the hall. He held the buff cardboard across his palpitating heart. Frank took in a breath, poised for another roar, but at that moment he lost his balance slightly, and clutched at an armchair to save himself, his head drooping over the back.

'Might be sick,' he said. His head hung.

'Will be,' Colin said. 'Will be bloody sick.' Colin's hand closed around the nearest of the Condensed Books – *Kon Tiki, I Leap Over the wall,* and *Father of the Bride*; he raised his arm high, and with the evening's amassed frustration brought the volume crashing down on the back of Frank's neck.

It must be two o'clock, Evelyn thought. Two o'clock in the morning. She remembered the whisky. It was true that Florence Sidney had not thought highly of it at Christmas, but then the circumstances had been vastly different. Yes, she would go down and get herself a drink of that. The thought was comforting.

She fumbled with her reading glasses, and thumbed over the pages of the first aid book. She turned to Muriel on the bed, Muriel with her damp face, crawling up the side of her glassy pyramid of pain. 'Take quick pants when you are breathing,' she reminded her. 'Short quick pants, the book says. Don't hold your breath like that. You'll stop it coming out. It might as well come, now. We might as well see what we've got.' Muriel didn't answer. 'It says to put newspaper under you, Muriel. It sounds like what you do for dogs, but that's what it says. Or a plastic sheet. I haven't got a plastic sheet, otherwise you could have it, Muriel. I'm going down to the lean-to, to get some newspapers. You'll be all right, won't you? I'll not be long.'

Muriel seemed indifferent. She doesn't seem to care whether I go or stay, Evelyn thought. But it's nothing new, she's always been like that, hard-hearted, independent, going her own way. Evelyn gripped the banister with both hands as she went downstairs, bringing her feet together one step at a time; the pain in her knees burned her, as if the muscles were being torn, and getting downstairs was worse than getting up. When she reached the foot of the stairs she steadied herself with one hand against the wall. I do not seem to feel strong, she said to herself. She forced herself to rest for a moment, and then made her way to the kitchen. The room had a derelict, unused air; the night looked straight in at the window, a blue night with a parched moon. She fumbled in a cupboard for the bottle of whisky, found a cup and poured out the last inch of it. She grimaced as she swallowed it; it burnt her lips and tasted of earth, left her mouth dry. It will brace me, she thought. When she opened the door of the lean-to, a wet and rotten smell rushed towards her, invading the house. Holding her torch carefully she picked her way among her possessions. The newspapers were sodden; she can't have these, she thought, whatever the book says. That is summertime advice, I am sure. On the top of one bale lay the corpse of some small animal, a mouse or shrew, its tiny mouth gaping. I need some air, she thought. She stood at the door looking down over the garden.

How far and giddyingly distant the moon seemed; there were no visible stars. She thought she heard, blown on the night wind, the wailing and chattering of children. Lights were on in the Sidney house, and once she thought that a window opened, and white faces, no bigger than a child's, stared out over the dark gardens. She wondered if they were waiting in the dark for her, amongst the shrubs, around the old coal-bunker, down in the shed where Clifford used to go. Perhaps we should have had more children, she thought, more children of our own. But after Muriel, Clifford had not wanted to risk repetition. He said that he would amuse himself. He would go down to the shed and she must turn a blind eye. A blind eye to whatever he kept in there and whatever comings and goings there were. That what was what she had always done, until one day she had seen the child from next door heading down the path, little Florence Sidney; little Florence Sidney, who was that great hulk of a woman now. She had taken it upon herself to shoo the child away, scold her out of the garden. When Clifford came in for his tea at three-thirty – it was a Sunday – she asked him, 'Do you take children down there?' How her hands had quivered; milk and sugar had gone all over the table. Clifford's face then: 'A blind eye, Evelyn, a blind eye'; the threats in his voice, the promise of a week of bruises, and Muriel tossed into her bedroom unfed and screaming. 'What are children to you?' Clifford had sneered. His own eyes not blind, but pale and rimless, turning now to all the wastage on the table, the messy spillings of her fear.

Years passed like this, the nameable fears giving way to the unnameable, the familiar dread of evening muffled under a pall of fog, of blackness, of earth; all the days lived as if underground, and Muriel, she thought, if I could have mourned myself, if I could have drawn breath, I might have pitied you. She pulled her cardigan around her and turned her cheek from the wind. Time to go back upstairs.

To Colin's alarm and astonishment, Frank slowly stood erect. Colin stepped back. It was beyond his power to deliver a further blow, to knock down a sentient, upstanding Head of Department. But then, as if swaying in some whimsical breeze, Frank leaned sideways, then tottered, then keeled over and crashed to the floor like a dead man.

Giving his victim a cursory glance, Colin secured the file and headed back for the dining-room. Sylvia was coming in from the kitchen with two mugs of black coffee on a tray.

'There you are, Colin,' she said in a matter-of-fact voice.

Colin's chest heaved, sweat ran from every pore.

'These were all the cups I could find that were reasonably clean and fit to use.' She put the mugs on the table and held up the tray. It had once been the lid of a biscuit tin, with a bit of bilious green lino, sugar-encrusted and stained, forming a top to it. 'I wouldn't give this houseroom. It's an education, what people have in their backs. That kitchen makes me heave, all that Italian muck plastered all over the place. I'd have thought he could have afforded decent food. And cleanliness costs nothing. I don't know who's going to have these coffees. Do you want one?'

'We're going,' Colin said.

'I've got my coat.' Tears sprang into Sylvia's eyes, glinting like bayonet points. 'Colin, do you know what he'd done with it? He said he didn't know where to put it. He'd dumped it in his rubbish bin. My good coat. It stinks of tomato sauce and fish.'

'Oh, Sylvia. Oh, love, I'm sorry. I didn't know it was going to be like this.'

'I can't wear it. It'll have to be cleaned.'

'Do you want my jacket?'

'No, it'll do me good to get out in the cold. What's that under your arm?'

'Nothing, just some papers. Come on, let's go.'

Sylvia pulled out a tissue and polished the tip of her nose. 'I'd like to give Frank a piece of my mind.'

'He was drunk. I'm sorry.'

'Where is he?'

'I put him to bed.'

Behind him, from the study, he heard movement and a muffled groan; Frank coming to, or as to as he would come, before morning. He took Sylvia's arm. 'Come on.' From upstairs came a yelp of triumph, and Yarker's voice:

'Well done, that man!'

He bundled Sylvia out of the front door and into the damp air. A pulse hammered in his forehead, his hands had begun to shake again, but free of the smoke-laden fug of the house, he took huge raw gasps as they scurried to the car. All I need now is a flat battery, he thought; expecting the worst, as experience was training him to do. But the engine roared, dreadfully loud, shattering the silence of four a.m. on a dead winter's day.

'In twenty minutes we'll be in bed,' he said.

'You know the way, don't you?'

'Oh yes, I know it now.'

'I wish we *had* got lost. I wish we'd called it off and never gone. It was the worst night out I've ever had.'

'Yes, I know. Try and forget it.'

'We'll never go there again.'

'I'll be surprised if we're ever asked, love.'

'That's something, then. I wonder how Florence went on with them? Perhaps she'll come over and mind them next week, and we could go to the pictures.'

'I don't know. We'll have to see.'

'I'll have to take my coat to the cleaner's first thing. Colin, it was awful, that man Yarker started interfering with her. With Charmian. I was embarrassed. I came out.'

'Yes, you did the right thing. Don't get involved, that's the best.'

They were the only car on the road, an icy ribbon unwrapping beneath them, the fields bare and still, the houses shuttered, the moon riding high and white.

'I haven't been out at this time for years,' Sylvia said, adding, 'thank God, and I don't intend to be again.' She sounded cheerful enough, now that the whole ordeal was over. She stretched, arching her body in the seat, and yawned loudly. 'Is that somebody behind us?'

Colin saw the flashing lights in his rear-view mirror. Sylvia saw them too, looking back over her shoulder. Colin pulled into the side of the road. For a moment neither of them spoke. Then, very quietly, very calmly, Sylvia said, 'It's like a nightmare.'

Colin wound down his window. The young constable whose face loomed up to fill their vision had a paste-coloured face in which freckles bloomed like the raisins in a steamed pudding. Shorn copper bristles extruded from under his cap, and for a chilling moment Colin thought Yarker had pursued him, metamorphosed, rendered youthful the better to hound him down the years.

'Are you aware, sir,' the boy said, 'that your rear lights are defective?'

Slowly, Colin swung open the door and uncoiled himself from his seat. He set his feet as firmly on the ground as he could manage, but it seemed to give under his tread, as if swamp had bubbled through the tarmac. With one hand on the roof of the car he worked his way around to the boot. Something ghastly hung from the policeman's hand, some membrane, shiny and swinging. Colin blinked.

'Would you please, sir,' said the constable, 'breathe into this bag?'

CHAPTER 7

Colin woke up next morning to the sound of Sylvia talking on the telephone. The house seemed strangely quiet. Of course, he thought, the children are still at Florence's. He fumbled on the bedside table for his watch, and when he raised his head a glancing pain swooped through it and settled behind his eyes. Just after noon. He allowed himself to flop back against the pillows. There was a foul taste in his mouth, and he felt slightly sick. I must get up, he told himself, and face things. Get the car; and the file, Isabel's file, is still in the back of it. It came to him in a flash: Axon, Muriel Axon, their neighbours at home. How stupid that he shouldn't have remembered, after all the years that the Axons had lived round the corner; next door, in fact, but because of their front gate being in Buckingham Avenue you didn't think of them being next door. Not that he'd ever known the Axons, but you didn't think of them as the kind of people who were a problem for Social Services. You didn't think of Social Workers operating at all in the Lauderdale Road area, people were generally pretty self-sufficient, they kept their problems to themselves. He had a vague idea that there was something wrong with Muriel, not altogether there, but it wasn't something you talked about. He supposed Mrs Axon was getting on a bit, maybe she did need some kind of help. Hadn't Florence been going on about them a few months back, saying she never saw them out and about? Not that you listened to half that Florence said. Wearily, Colin pushed the covers back and swung his legs out of bed. He sat on the edge of the mattress, rubbing his eyes. With the threat of motion, the pounding inside his skull had increased. Never mind the Axons, he thought, I've done my bit for them. I've got to sort myself out.

He went into the bathroom and cleaned his teeth. His face in the mirror was that of an elderly rake, parched and neurasthenic; as if with Frank's Valpolicella he had drained the dregs of experience. He went downstairs. The living-room was unnaturally tidy; he realised that Sylvia had been cleaning. A sort of exorcism for her, he supposed, driving out the bad memories of Frank's kitchen. Already the foul taste had come back into his mouth, mingled with toothpaste.

Sylvia came through from the kitchen carrying a duster and a tin of spray-polish. She was very pale, and looked suddenly much more pregnant.

'Oh, there you are. I'll make some tea, then. I tried to get you up at ten o'clock, but you were sleeping like the dead.'

'I'm sorry. What a night!'

'You've nothing to be proud of, anyway.'

'I'm not proud. Do I look proud? Oh, for God's sake, let's not have a row.'

'I phoned Florence. I suggested she should bring them over on the bus. She didn't seem keen. She's waiting for you to fetch them.'

'Yes. All right.'

'The police said not to drive till late afternoon.'

'I'll have to risk it, won't I? How am I going to get to the car, is there a bus?'

'You can get the number ninety, and get off at the top of the hill by the Express Dairy. I think you'd better phone your solicitor, hadn't you?'

'Yes.'

'What'll happen.'

'I'll lose my licence.'

He felt almost tearful. Sylvia was treating him as if he were somehow disgraced, and yet he thought that he could have been in a much worse state, and that considering the circumstances he had managed extraordinarily well. Of course, he could not tell her what the circumstances were.

'What was that thing you had under your arm? Was it that file?'

'Yes.' He saw no point in denying it.

'What do you want to go and get involved for?'

'I'm not getting involved. I just want to give it back to the people it belongs to.'

'What's Frank going to say when he finds it's missing?'

'I don't know what he'll say.'

'Well, you've got to face him on Tuesday. Oh, I don't know.' Sylvia said. 'I'll get that tea for us. I think you ought to have an aspirin.'

What day was it? Sunday. You got so mixed up at half-term. The streets had a Sunday quiet. He waited twenty minutes for the bus, his stomach rumbling, his knuckles turning mauve in the raw air. Not raining, thank God. Off the bus, he trudged by a dripping hedgerow, by grey litter-blown fields. At the first phonebox he stopped and dialled Isabel's number. She answered at once.

'Colin here. I got it.'

There was a pause.

'I'm grateful, Colin.'

Isn't she going to ask how? Clearly she's not. All right, he thought, I won't tell her about the party, I won't tell her about the breathalyser, I'll cut her out of my life. But he blurted out, 'It wasn't easy. I had to hit someone.'

'Oh, Colin.' She sounded . . . gratified? Embarrassed? 'Did you?'

'It was Frank. My Head of Department. Isabel, are you still there?'

'Yes, I'm still here. But I can't think of much to say.'

'Shall I bring it to your house?'

'Please.'

'This afternoon?'

'Well, if you can.'

'Will you be there?'

'Yes, I'll be there. But my father will answer the door.'

'But Isabel — '

'I'm grateful. But it doesn't change anything.'

I have to keep her talking, he thought, before I lose her altogether. 'There's just one thing — of course I've not read the file, but I noticed the name, and the odd part about it is that I know the Axons, known them for years. Would you believe it, they live next to my sister, round the corner. The daughter's a bit backward, isn't she?'

'Yes.' He heard tension creep into her voice; she wanted to be rid of him, he thought, she found him a nuisance.

'Will you be making a home visit to them now?'

'I'm in court tomorrow. A child battering case. Tuesday's all spoken for.'

'But you ought to go, oughtn't you, after such a long gap?'

'Maybe Wednesday. I've got the file. That's the main thing. There's no reason for you to worry about it, it's for me to sort out.'

'You know, I've been piecing things together, and I realise you might have mentioned them once, and I just didn't make the connection. We were in the pub, you see, talking – you said you didn't like the case, you couldn't come to grips with it.'

'I can't discuss my clients with you. You know that. The fact that they're your sister's neighbours makes no difference to anything.'

'It's funny, though, isn't it?'

'These things happen. We live in the same town. It's not such a coincidence, really.'

'But I lived in the same town as you,' he burst out, 'and I never knew.'

'Yes, well, now you do. Thank you for getting the file back. Goodbye.'

'Is that all?'

'What else is there to say? The situation hasn't changed.'

'But could I see you, just once?'

'You made your choice, I thought.'

'Shan't I ever see you again, then?'

'I expect you will, sooner or later. After all, as you say, we live in the same town.' A moment's pause, and she put the phone down. Colin came out of the box, and stood blowing his nose. As he tramped towards his car, it began to rain, little grey tears running off his anorak and trickling in his wake.

Evelyn sat in the kitchen staring into her teacup. It seemed absurd that she had suddenly become an invalid, but she felt she had hardly the strength to put out her hand, pick up the cup, and carry it to her mouth. The tea was going cold, her hand shook, the cup rattled in the saucer. The sleepless night had left her drained and muddle-headed.

The baby, which was born before dawn, had been very small. She could not bring herself to look too closely at it. At first it would not breathe. Muriel's eyes signalled something to her. Leave it, she was saying. Shocked, Evelyn gripped the slippery thing and shook it. A thin hopeless bleating came out. A fine idea of Muriel's, the ghost under their feet for years, learning in the parallel world to crawl, walk and talk; and perhaps blaming them for its demise. She ventured downstairs, her flesh crawling, and brought Muriel some mixed biscuits on a plate.

Yesterday Muriel had been bothering her about a pram. As if she could push it about the streets, with her bad chest; as if Muriel was fit to be let out with it.

It was all as complicated as it could be. Muriel didn't seem to have the knack of feeding it. Her milk hadn't come, or the baby wouldn't suck; it would have to have powdered milk out of a bottle, she supposed, but where was she to get such a thing on a Sunday?

'You realise,' she said to Muriel, 'that if I go to the Parade asking for baby's milk, they'll probably ring up the Welfare? I'll have to go where nobody knows my face. It's a lot of trouble. Have another try with it.'

But Muriel yawned and rolled over on to her side and closed her eyes.

All that morning there were rappings and banging at the front door. The screams and laughter of spiteful children rang in Evelyn's ears. She went down the hall at last, and threw the door open; but no one was there.

Florence will be furious with me, Colin thought. He sat in the car outside Isabel's house; his sister had been expecting him for the last hour and more. He pictured his hand reaching out for the ignition key, turning it, engaging gear, moving off down the street. His real hands lay loosely inert, one at his side, one draped over the steering wheel. Driving about and driving about, that is all the last months have been, lying, driving from one set of hostile eyes to another. This is the last time I will have any business on Isabel's street.

The eyes were not really hostile, of course. Just the bored indifferent eyes of strangers, slow to be roused to curiosity, slow to notice anything. Strangers in public houses, strangers by the roadside. He had long ago given up the writing class; he had got nothing from it, no pleasure, no profit.

He was angry; angry that she could now seem so immature, so callous. And she had been trained, he thought, trained to be in charge of other people's lives, selected for it. It seemed that she had set out in their last conversation to demolish the picture he had built of her in his mind. It was not a reasonable picture. But reason has grown tired of its own successes.

Mr Field came to the door. Without his spectacles, he blinked at Colin.

'I think you are expecting me, Mr Field.' He held out the file. 'This is for Isabel.'

'Ah, yes. Yes, thank you.' Mr Field took the file from him and held it carefully in both hands. 'Thank you so much. I hope it has been no trouble to you. Goodbye. Drive carefully.'

Have I failed her, let her down? Did she expect too much? I am too tired to think about it any more. Colin climbed into his car, slammed the door, set the windscreen wipers going. Life came home to him as blind chance and triviality, a series of minute disappointments impatiently endured. I shall never see her again, he thought, as he drove away.

'Monday morning, Muriel,' Evelyn said. 'I should think you'll be up and about later today, don't you?'

She had hit on a brisk and reassuring tone, like the one that the Welfare visitors used. Talk loudly; keeps matters at bay.

The child was not deformed, but she did not take to it. Since its birth it seemed definitely to have changed for the worse. It seemed feeble, and it cried all the time with a noise like the mewing of a cat. It took no notice of them, never smiled. For all the company it was, it might have been inside Muriel still.

'I'm going now,' she said to Muriel. 'It looks like snow. I hope it holds off.'

She took a bus. It was years since she had been in a bus. There was no conductor, and the driver called her lady. She had to give him her money.

'Don't you know where you want to go, lady?'

'Yes, I do. I want to go to the shops in Kenilworth Road.'

Muttering to himself, the driver pulled out a book of fare tables and laboriously followed a column with his stubby finger.

'Fifteen pee,' he pronounced, and rolled up the book and shoved it away. She offered him some coins. 'Right money,' he said, 'right money. No change will be given. God help us.'

'That's all right,' Evelyn said. 'I don't want the change, if it's so much trouble. You can keep it.'

'What do you think I am, a hackney carriage?' the driver said. 'What's up with you?'

'I know what you are, a most ignorant and unpleasant man.' She pulled her ticket from the machine and handed herself down the bus to an empty seat. Her heart fluttered. It was warm and damp on the lower deck, the breath of the swaddled passengers steaming up the windows. She rubbed the pane with her hand, so that she would know when she got to Kenilworth Road. No one bothered about her; an old man with a loose cough, women with string bags, two young lads sharing a cigarette. A girl brought on a big collie dog and took it upstairs; up it ran, its jaws laughing, used to riding on the bus. A nice woman leaned towards her and offered her a mint.

'I heard that cheeky devil,' she said. 'You did right to tell him off.'

'He was very rude, really he was.' She turned to the young woman.

'I'm on my way to the chemists at Kenilworth Road. I'm shopping for my daughter. She's got a new baby, you know.'

'Oh, that's nice,' the woman said. 'I'm expecting myself. Nice to be a grandma.'

'Yes,' Evelyn agreed. 'It's lovely.'

Her eyes were bright when she stepped off the bus. In spite of the driver, it had been a lovely journey, and perhaps she was rather at fault in not knowing the procedure. In the chemist's shop, a girl in a lilac overall was opening cardboard boxes and putting bottles of egg shampoo on a shelf. She smiled over her shoulder at Evelyn. A man in a white coat came from the back of the shop.

'All right, Carol, I'll serve this lady,' he said. 'Good morning, madam.'

'Good morning,' she said. 'I want some milk for my daughter's baby, and a bottle, if you please.'

The chemist seemed most interested, very attentive. He sold her some fluid for sterilizing and carefully explained to her what Muriel would have to do. 'I'm surprised the midwife didn't sort you out,' he said, 'and being your daughter's first, frankly I'm a bit surprised that she's not in hospital.'

'Oh, she likes to be at home,' Evelyn said. 'She wanted it like that.'

'Well, they say it's the modern trend among the young mothers,' the man said, 'and there's a lot to be said for a home confinement. They go in for it in Holland, you know, and they've a lower mortality rate than here. Anyway, you'll have the Health Visitor along, won't you? Any problems, she's your girl.'

Then the telephone rang in a back room, and the chemist had to go. Nodding to Carol, she pushed her purse into her bag and went out. She felt dazed as the shop door closed behind her. She could have stood there for ever, she thought, talking to that considerate man. She hadn't told him that the baby had only been born yesterday, much less mentioned its odd behaviour. Perhaps he could have given her some good advice. She hesitated, wondering whether to turn back. But better say nothing perhaps. We've got this far, managed for ourselves. Her own convictions had carried her forward, her convictions about what was best for Muriel in the long run; and it was she, Muriel's mother, and not the Welfare workers, who ought to know about that. She did not wish to admit to herself that now that the child was born she was confused, beginning to be frightened; menaces from the tenants she had expected, but she had not reckoned on a deep shrinking antipathy to what Muriel produced, the feeling that even their precarious foothold in the house was crumbling further; and that feeling dated, she knew, from her first good look at the baby's face. She began to walk towards the bus stop, as slowly as she could, looking at the people she passed.

There was pleasure in being amongst them, a safety in being on the street. It was a feeling she remembered from before, from the day she got the library books, and stood among the shoppers hurrying to the sales. In the foggy air, in the pavements under their busy feet, she saw for a moment a prospect of release.

She thought she might begin to cry. Tears seemed to choke her, and she put up a hand to unfasten the top button of her coat. She turned back and retraced her steps to the chemist's shop, and stared in at the window. She stared at bottles of nail varnish in glittering racks, at hot water bottles, shelves of toothpaste. I would like to possess all of those things, she thought, all of that shop, everything new and plastic and wipe-clean, and live under those hard striplights. I would not go home when it was time to close. Everyone who wishes could look in at my life; there would be no shadows, no dark corners, no locked rooms.

But now it is time to go home. The baby, which might have changed everything, has brought nothing but the stench of its own peculiarities; that misbegotten, that changeling, that demon-food. She rubbed her eyes with the back of her hand, hoping that no one had noticed her crying.

When she got back the baby was still wailing. She had put it in a big cardboard box, lined with old blankets; it was cosy enough. She bent over it; Clifford stared back.

At ten to nine on Tuesday morning, Colin entered the staffroom, his heart thudding with apprehension. He had decided to say nothing, let Frank take the initiative. He had buttressed himself with no explanations for the assault, being unable to think of any; he would have to go on the offensive if he was tackled, claiming that he was owed an apology himself, and Sylvia too, for having her coat put in the dustbin. The bell was ringing for Assembly; there was Frank, folding up his *Daily Telegraph*.

'Hello, Colin,' he said mildly. He was paler than usual, badly shaven, altogether worn and frayed. Colin's resolve broke immediately.

'About the other night – '

'Yes,' Frank said. 'Splendid do. Good food – if I say so myself – and the best of company. You must come again.'

Colin stared at him hard. 'Oh, splendid do,' he said, with a heavy irony that did not seem to strike home. 'A most civilised evening.'

'Excellent raconteur, Edmund Toye. And young Elvie the life and soul. Sylvia enjoy herself?'

'Hugely.'

'Get home all right?'

'In one piece.'

'Good, good, good. Well, better shuffle off now and sing a hymn, hadn't we?'

Colin followed him. He felt benumbed, stupefied. What had he expected? Perhaps that Frank intended to sue him or at least knock him down, that Mrs Toye had been taken to a psychiatric ward, that Yarker was in police custody. It seemed miraculous that anything short of murder should have come out of such an evening. Perhaps Frank was suffering some type of amnesia. He passed Stewart Colman in the corridor. Colman nodded amiably.

'I say,' he said, 'did you nick Frank's file?'

'Yes. Yes, I did.'

'All part of the fun,' Colman said. 'We had a nude treasure hunt. Looked for it till dawn. What did you want to go rushing off for?

Oh yes, they're all right, Frank's parties, if you can put up with the literary chitchat. That can be a bit of a bore.'

Is this how people live, Colin thought? I must have no idea how people live. At my age . . . He followed Colman.

'Stewart — '

'Got to get along.'

Colin took him by the arm. 'Listen to me.' They came to a halt in the corridor seething with children. 'Was he serious about writing that novel?'

'Good Lord, how do I know?' Sounding surprised, Colman disengaged his jacket from Colin's grasp. 'Doesn't pay to take anything too seriously, you know. Life's too short.'

'Look at it,' Evelyn said. 'You can't say it's human.' It was Tuesday morning. She brought the child over to show to Muriel, pointing out the strange large ears, the wrinkled skin, lifting the flaccid limbs and letting them drop. 'It cries all the time,' she added, unnecessarily. 'You never cried, Muriel. You were as quiet as a lamb.'

Unable to bear the feel of the child's damp skin, she crossed the room and put it back in the box. 'It might be a changeling,' she said. 'I'm not saying it is, but it could be. It didn't seem as bad as this when it was born.'

Of course, she'd not been able to stay with Muriel all the time. Only a few minutes after the birth, she'd gone out to answer a call of nature. And any time, during the night or when she was down in the kitchen putting the kettle on; there was plenty of opportunity for a substitution to be made.

'Because I wouldn't want you to think,' she said generously, 'that it's some shortcoming of yours. Not necessarily. You're bound to be disappointed in it. Are you disappointed, Muriel?'

From Muriel, no answer. Head twisted away. No gratitude for her mother's concern.

'If it is a changeling, you ought to give some thought to getting the real one back. The ones they take lead miserable lives. They look in at people's windows. Their growth's stunted. They're always cold.'

Muriel took the feeding bottle and thrust it at the child once again. The ugly little face contorted, sucked a little, twitched away.

'It's a simple matter, Muriel. You have to find some water, a river or something. Float it along. And sometimes they pick it up and give you your own back. Well, you ought to have something better than this after all you've been through. You're entitled. I'm not saying it always works. There's a risk, of course. A real baby would be nice, though, wouldn't it?'

Muriel seemed dubious. She peered at the baby, as if she thought that, after all, this was her own, this was what she was entitled to. Did they have stores of them, she wanted to know, real babies stacked up by river banks?

'Fairly cunning, aren't you?' Evelyn said in admiration. 'Like to pull a little trick on them, would you? Well, you're right, even if it's not a changeling it certainly looks like one.'

Muriel had always been credulous. Evelyn had noticed that she believed most things she was told. I am perhaps halfway to believing myself, she thought, there are plenty of subhumans planted among the real men and women; you learn about them if you read the newspapers, rapists, vandals, people who make nail bombs. On the bus, she had been reading the headlines, and it made her feel queasy to think about it all.

'A real baby . . . ' she said, her voice softening. 'We could do the place up a bit. Decorate. Perhaps we could have television. Ah, you understand that, don't you?'

She looked down at the baby, and saw Clifford again, sitting behind its eyes; behind the glassy layers the years peeling away. She picked up Muriel's cardigan from a chair, and threw it over the baby's face.

CHAPTER 8

Wednesday. They hadn't slept. The incessant mewing kept them awake. At least it was too feeble for the neighbours to hear. 'We'll not put it off any longer,' Evelyn said. 'We'll take it up to the canal this afternoon. There'll be nobody around. If they give us a nice little baby, Muriel, we'll take it out in a pushchair, you and me. In the spring. We'll go to the Parade.'

More likely, of course, the Welfare would catch up with them and take it away. They couldn't be avoided for ever. Still, Muriel was entitled to a bit of hope. Except for the baby, the house was so quiet. No incursions from the spare room. Everything held its breath. Another lightbulb had gone. The weather was getting colder, and the house was full of draughts.

By now there was no more milk. Muriel had spilled a lot, wasted it, even drunk some of it herself. Evelyn didn't feel up to another shopping trip. It had a strange effect on her, making her speak out to people like that, tell them confidences. Least said, soonest mended. There were people everywhere waiting to report you to the Welfare. Look at that Florence Sidney.

Yes, look at her. Evelyn stood at the window on the landing. What did Florence think she was doing, standing outside by her dustbin and staring up at the roof?

Evelyn stopped at the door of the spare room and listened. She distrusted this unnatural silence. After a minute or two she thought she heard a faint stir behind the door, a grumbling, a low mutter of protest. I'll fetch you a sop, something that's belonged to it, palm you off.

'Well now, Muriel, are you ready?' she asked, going downstairs. 'It'll be dark before long. You carry the box. Sink or swim, we'll have to see. We all take our chances in this world.'

'All right,' Muriel said.

They put on headscarves, and their thick coats. The baby seemed exhausted now, and had stopped crying; it didn't seem likely to attract attention. Evelyn put a towel over its face, and folded over the flaps of the box.

The clock struck half-past three as they set out. It was one of those dank cheerless days so frequent in February and March; the ground was sodden underfoot, the trees dripping, and the sun a white haze low on the horizon. They passed no one on Lauderdale Road, no one on Turner's Lane. From here a muddy path led across an open field. There was a faint scrabbling from within the box, and Muriel tightened her arms around it. She looked about her as she walked. It was months since she'd had an outing, of course. 'Don't dawdle, Muriel,' Evelyn said crossly. 'At my age you feel the cold.'

On the canal bank, their shoes squelched in a mulch of old newsprint and last autumn's leaves. There was no one about. There was a wrecked car rusting away, and broken glass on the path. The water was stagnant, green. A wind was getting up.

When Evelyn turned back the flaps of the box, Muriel thrust her hands out officiously, as if to pick the infant up. Evelyn slapped them away. She removed the towel and the sheet that had lined the box, put them aside and lowered the box on to the surface of the water. She straightened up; her back ached from bending. In the last few minutes it had seemed to grow darker. The wind will push it along, Evelyn thought. They watched the box growing sodden, tipping into the water. 'It must be moving,' Evelyn said. Then darkness sucked it away.

Inexplicably, Muriel leaned down and put a finger into the slime, as if she were testing bathwater. There was a kind of avidity in her face; no doubt she was straining her eyes. Evelyn gave her a clean handkerchief to dry her hand, then took it off her and put it in a damp ball in her pocket.

They waited on the bank for ten minutes. It was quite dark now. 'It must be dead,' Evelyn said at last. 'They won't give you anything in exchange for a corpse. Well, I did the best I could for you, Muriel.' She folded the bedding and crammed it into her shopping basket, and took out a torch to light their way home. 'Kick that box over by the wall,' she said, 'we don't want that.'

Muriel did as she was told, with an energetic boot from her sturdy leg. It will all be as before, Evelyn thought, as they trudged back across the field. As if Muriel had never been pregnant. Back to our old life. Oh, dear God. A sickly fear began to tickle and scrape in the pit of her stomach, then rose and lodged itself behind her ribs. The old life. What have I done? Her heart felt like lead, but molten lead, heaving and pulsating inside its coffin of flesh.

On the doormat there was another card from the gasman. Muriel rushed into the hall as if she had no concept of what might be waiting for her. Perhaps the changeling, come home already. She showed no fear. Sometimes Evelyn wondered at her.

'We'll have our tea early,' she said. 'We'll have corned beef. I want to put my feet up. That walk's taken it out of me.'

There was something she had to do first. She collected together the baby's towel, its blanket, its feeding bottle and the sterilizing solution, and put them in a paper bag. She took them out to the lean-to, and thrust them into a pile of Clifford's newspapers. It gave her a sour satisfaction. Back from the dead, are you? Your own daughter, in your own house. Damn you, Clifford; your handiwork hasn't lasted long.

As she came through to the kitchen, she heard the doorbell ring. It was probably the gasman again, she thought. They'd not let him in the last two times, and he was getting impatient. Well, it could do no harm now, there was nothing out of the way for him to notice. Calling to Muriel to stay in the back room, she went down the hall and opened the door. On the doorstep stood the girl from the Welfare.

Evelyn's jaw sagged. With a bleat of protest she stepped back and made to slam the door. But the girl put up her arm and held it open, a stronger girl than she looked, planting a booted foot on the threshold. She smiled implacably.

'Hello, Mrs Axon. May I come in?' She was coming in, even as she asked, pulling off her woollen gloves as if she meant business.

'I'm sorry to call on you so late, but I did come by just after half-past three.'

'I was out.'

'Yes. I thought you must be,' she said easily. 'How's Muriel?'

Evelyn felt she might suffocate with rage. 'Who notified you?' she said fiercely.

'Notified me?' The girl's face was blank. 'But it's just a routine call, Mrs Axon. You're on our files.'

'But you've not been, have you? Not for months. What have you come for now?'

The girl hesitated for a second. 'No, it's been a while. I've been very busy, Mrs Axon, and – let's be honest now – you don't always let me in when I do call, do you?'

'Why should I?'

'I do want to help you, you know,' the girl said gently. 'You're not getting any younger, Mrs Axon, and I know there are some things that Muriel can't do for herself. You're always hostile, but nobody's against you. Nobody means to upset you.'

'I don't appreciate these visits. I never have done.'

'I know that, Mrs Axon. But I need to see Muriel, so let's get it over with, shall we? Can I put the light on?'

'It's gone. The bulb's gone.'

'Can't Muriel change it for you? She's a big girl. You ought to let her do things like that.'

'Would you like a cup of tea?' Evelyn asked abruptly.

The Welfare woman stopped short, struck by the change in her tone. 'Why, that's very kind of you, Mrs Axon. Actually, no thank you, but I appreciate the offer. I really do.'

She looked very pleased. She thinks it's going to be a new era in our relationship, Evelyn thought. 'My daughter's upstairs,' she said sweetly. 'In my husband's old room. Just one minute.' She opened the drawer of the hallstand, felt about, and pulled out a key on a piece of string.

'You haven't locked her in, have you?' the woman asked in consternation.

'She's been wandering, Miss Field. Wandering off. I don't like to think she might get into trouble, and how else do you stop a grown woman going out?' Evelyn made her voice pathetic. 'I'm getting on in years, Miss Field.'

'Yes, I know that.' The girl was striding upstairs ahead of her.

'She hides from me,' Evelyn said. 'She's always up to something.'

'I told you always to call me if you felt you couldn't cope.' Her voice had an edge to it; Evelyn fumbled with the key. 'I can't live in your pocket, Mrs Axon, and I can't read your mind.'

The door was open now.

'Where is she?' the girl said. 'I don't see her.'

'Hiding again. Under the bed, very likely. In the wardrobe. Go and fetch her out. She won't come for me.'

She stepped into the room, her heels clicking on the floorboards, and wrenched open the door of the huge wardrobe. An empty mothball dimness within, but a space big enough for two. As she bent down to peer under the high old-fashioned bed, her dark hair slid forward over her shoulder.

'There's no one – '

Evelyn stepped out of the room, closed the door and turned the key in the lock. Smiling to herself on the landing, she imagined that she had heard the girl's neck click back as she glanced up in surprise. She waited for the inevitable. Yes, there she was, banging on the door. Predictable as Muriel, and not much cleverer.

'Mrs Axon, let me out. For goodness sake, Mrs Axon. What do you think you're doing?'

The noise hadn't attracted Muriel into the hall. Muriel had many faults, but curiosity wasn't one of them.

Isabel fumbled for the lightswitch. At least there was a bulb in here, though it was dusty and dim, the strength you'd have in a table lamp; unshaded, it cast patchy shadows into the corners of the room. She looked around. Besides the wardrobe, there was a heavy chest of drawers, and the bedstead with its mattress inside a yellowing cover, and a solid bolster lying across it. The top of the chest of drawers was thick with dust, and there were drifts of it under the bed and on the windowsill.

She raised her fist and banged on the door twice, as loud and hard as she could. I might as well save my strength, she thought. By now she had realised that the room was very cold, colder even than the rest of the house. Even in her jacket and scarf she felt it, not icy, but a clammy chill like wet earth. Let me think, she said to herself, let me think.

She thought she caught a movement from the corner of the room. She swung round. Nothing there. Crossing to the window, she looked out. Worse luck, the room looked over the gardens. The light must be on in Evelyn's back room, and so perhaps were the lights in the house next door; a dim glow allowed her to see a little. Could that be Colin's sister's house? Not that it would be any help, if it were. Colin's sister was unlikely to make a habit of gardening in the wet February darkness. It had turned half-past five. Not even hope of a delivery man calling at this time. Besides, could she be seen from the garden next door? Why did I come, she asked herself angrily. That stupid, malign old woman. The daughter will have to go away, and I'll have to make out a very good case to explain why I didn't see the situation deteriorating. She knew why she had come, of course; guilt had brought her back. Guilt, and duty, and an inability to go on living with a set of stupid and groundless fears. Whatever Muriel's problems were, a secret sex life wasn't one of them.

Perhaps if she leaned out of the window and shouted, somebody passing on the street might hear her. Even Colin's sister. She might bring out something to the dustbin. I could shout myself hoarse, she thought, waiting for that to happen.

Or climb out of the window? She wrenched out the handle from its notch half-way up the frame, lifted the metal bar from its peg, and pushed outwards. Nothing. Running her hand over the wood, she could see that it was swollen with damp. The window was quite big enough for her to climb out, if there was anything to hold on to. She pushed the frame with the heel of her hand, but couldn't exert the pressure that was needed. She was afraid to push against the glass in case she went through it; Mrs Axon certainly wouldn't be ready to administer first aid.

She regarded the window again and sucked at her bruised hand. Thoughtfully, she took her gloves out of her pocket and put them on. She could take off her jacket and wrap it around her hand, but she felt reluctant, not only because of the liquid, intense cold, but because she felt irrationally that, with one layer less, her flesh would be vulnerable. There is no point in asking yourself what you are afraid of, she told herself, only know that you are afraid, and then take some action to remedy the situation. What was that? Some sort of rag, lying by the door. She would use that. She scooped it up. It was a pink angora cardigan with shiny white buttons. Even in this light it looked grubby. What a strange garment, she thought, for either of the Axons to possess. If I push that window enough, I'll loosen it, by degrees I'll unstick it, it will give. A faint odour from the cardigan caught her attention, and she lifted it to her face.

Her lips set, and suddenly she began to blush, a deep crimson blush which seemed to wash over her whole body and turn her legs to water. She wanted to sit down, and did sit down, on the bed. To be sure, she sniffed the wool again. It was unmistakable, the sour-sweet baby odour of regurgitated milk.

Then, all those months ago – when she had come to the house and seen Muriel in that peculiar smock; she could hear her own words to Colin, 'For a moment I thought she might be pregnant.' So why, why on earth had she not seriously entertained that possibility? All these months, Muriel had been absent from the Day Centre. No one else had seen her since the old place was closed. And that was months ago, plenty of time. I have certainly made, she thought, a gigantic professional blunder.

But then, people do worse. She tried to comfort herself. She thought of the court hearing she had attended only the day before yesterday. Children go to school hungry and fall asleep at the back of classrooms; teachers are only grateful if they don't scream, start fights, come at them with knives. Children fall into fires. With childish obstinacy, they ram doorknobs into their eye sockets. They fall downstairs with the thumping regularity of prisoners in South African police stations. I can't live in your pocket, Mrs Axon. One of my colleagues returned to its parents a child that is now dead, a snivelling and unappealing brat with impetigo, which I once visited myself.

If Muriel had a child, it would have to be removed at once. But where had she delivered the child? Which hospital? Surely any half-observant medical personnel – but perhaps it had been born here, at home. What an awful thought. It occurred to her that the house was quite silent; twenty minutes had passed; was the baby sleeping soundly?

Perhaps it is dead.

Oh Christ, she thought, if Muriel has a child, who is the father? But I'm jumping to conclusions. A smell of milk on an old cardigan. Does that add up to a baby? And Muriel's strange clothes? Muriel's clothes were strange at any time.

She launched herself up from the bed and flung herself at the door, hammering again with her fists. 'Mrs Axon, let me out, let me out immediately. You're behaving in an incredibly stupid fashion. If you don't let me out someone from my office will come to look for me, so you see it's no use.'

Not tonight they won't, she said to herself. And Evelyn, standing on the stairs, thought, not tonight they won't, and tomorrow's another day.

Isabel turned and flew back to the window. The frame shuddered, free in the middle but sticking at the top and bottom. She reached up and thumped at it. She beat at the wood with a series of sharp heavy blows, and with an involuntary sound of triumph and surprise saw the window give and swing outwards. She stuck her head out, peering into the darkness.

She couldn't see much to help her. There was a drainpipe, but it wasn't within reach. She leaned out further, trying to estimate distances. If she had been locked into the room next door, her fall would have been broken by the roof of the lean-to, but from here there was nothing between her and the flagstones below. If there were a fire, I suppose I'd jump, she thought. But it's suicidal. I could break my back. And if by some mischance there was a baby, and if by some mischance it's dead; who knows? Who knows, besides me?'

She picked up the pink cardigan from the bed and looked at it carefully, turning it inside out. Nothing more, no smell of urine. Quickly, she rolled it up and pushed it into her big bag, averting her face as she did so, as if she did not want to see what she was doing. She placed her newspaper on top of it, and Muriel's file. Would the neighbours know? Possibly, and possibly not; perhaps Evelyn was in the habit of locking Muriel up. If I have the only knowledge, she thought, I may also have the only evidence. She could not picture Muriel surrounded by terry squares and baby bouncers, and little bibs from Mothercare.

She tried to think back over the weeks. When was it, that Muriel had appeared in the smock? The file would tell her the date of her last visit. But no, never mind that; the important thing was to get out of here. Suppose she had made an error, why should she suffer? Why should I? she demanded of the clammy air. They wouldn't let me in, they didn't want me, they rejected my help. I had no reason to expect this, none.

She returned to the window. What can I shout? She felt foolish. Just then, the dim glow strengthened perceptibly; someone had switched on an outside light, not here at the Axon house but at the house next door. She could see a little paved area outside the house, with dim shapes that must be flower tubs. From ground level, she thought, the shrubs and bushes would completely conceal one garden from the next, but from here she could see a long path leading down the lawn between empty flowerbeds. Now a torch beam struck across the path.

She did not shout at once, but held her breath. Someone was definitely coming out into the garden, and she wanted them to spot her, recognise the problem, and get her out with the minimum of fuss. Screams and shouts would only create panic. Just a ladder, that's all she needed, and somebody to hold the base steady. After that, she would be able to find out what the neighbours knew or suspected; they would come out with it without any prompting, once they knew she was from Social Services. Heights did not worry her; she could manage to scramble out backwards, and would be on the ground before she had time to think twice.

A woman, broad and shapeless, was stumping down the path. Halfway, she stopped and turned back to the house. That must be Colin's sister, surely? It would be more reassuring to call to her by name. Explanations for that could come later. As she leaned out, another torch beam crossed the first. Colin came down the path and joined his sister.

I can hardly believe my luck, or lack of it, Isabel thought. The pair below shone their torches up at the roof. What were they doing? From Florence she caught the words, 'Guttering looks dubious too.'

From Colin, 'Better in daylight, Saturday.'

And from Florence, 'But a loose slate might –'

'Help me,' she yelled. She hung out of the window. 'I'm locked in here. I'm locked in, help me get out.'

Startled, their heads jerked up. The torch beams swept over the trees and fences till they rested on her face.

'Good God!' Colin said. More loudly, 'What are you doing?'

'What?' Florence said. 'Who is it? Do you know her?'

'I'm a social worker, Miss Sidney. These mad women have locked me in.'

'I'll be right there,' Colin shouted. He approached the fence. 'Hang on, I'll be right there.'

'No, go round. Fetch a ladder and come round the drive.'

His face was in shadow. 'Florence, have we got a ladder? We haven't got a ladder,' he yelled back. 'Hang on. I'll be there in two minutes.'

'It's no use, they won't let you in.' Too late. Colin scrambled and heaved himself over the fence, crunching wood under his feet. 'You stay there, Florence,' he called. 'I'll sort this out.' His arms flailing, he crashed through the Axons' shrubbery and was lost to view around the side of the house. Isabel heard him banging on the back door.

'Stay in sight, please,' she called to Florence. 'Please stay where I can see you. I'm sure they won't let him in.'

Florence's voice was piercing in the gloom. 'Ought I to call the police?'

'No. No, don't do that. Please keep your torch on me.' She admitted it, the words sticking in her throat; again a brush at her hand, a twitch at her skirt. 'I'm afraid. I'm frightened. Please don't go.'

'Of course you are,' Florence boomed. 'They frighten me too. We'll soon have you out, don't you worry.'

Getting no reply from the back, Colin ran around the house and rang at the front door. He put his thumb on the bell and held it there, and hammered on the door with his other hand. Quite obviously they were not going to let him in. The back door would be the easier option; never mind what's happened, he thought, she must be got out first.

He twisted the knob of the back door, rattled it to no avail. In a frenzy, he rammed his shoulder into it; he withdrew, gasping with pain and rubbing his bruised arm. He stepped back, preparing a great kick that would splinter the wood or break the lock; heard a bolt slide, and presented the sole of his shoe to Muriel Axon's grinning face.

'Miss Axon, I have to come in.' With difficulty, he steadied himself. Muriel stood in the doorway, a strange gaunt figure, her eyes vacant, her large feet thrust into fluffy bedroom slippers.

'Muriel,' a voice called from inside. 'Muriel, don't unfasten that back door, don't you dare.'

Something like a mad excitement came into Muriel's eyes. She pulled a handkerchief from her sleeve, extracted something from it, and dropped it at Colin's feet. He bent down for it.

'This the key?'

She nodded, and dropped back to let him pass. He hustled through the kitchen and into the hall. The layout of the house was not hard to imagine. As he reached the foot of the stairs, a figure appeared from the back room, an old woman with a face like clay. He stopped short. She looked harmless and feeble. She smelled, he thought. They both smelled, of must and poor nutrition and neglect. In a second he took in the desolation around him, the peeling wallpaper, the caked mud on the parquet floor.

'I told you, Muriel,' Mrs Axon said. 'You always do the opposite of what I tell you, don't you?'

'Mrs Axon, what are you up to?' Alarmed as he was, he tried to moderate his tone. 'Why have you locked Miss Field in the bedroom?'

'Oh, you know her, do you?' the woman said, with a hard sneer. As if to back her up, Muriel sniggered loudly. Colin started towards the stairs, Evelyn following him and pulling at his arm.

'I've got the key,' he said, trying to shake her off. 'It's no use, I'll have to go up, I'm afraid.'

She hung on grimly, her hand scrabbling at his collar, her weight holding him back. Dragging her with him, he mounted four steps into the darkness.

'You'll let them out,' she gasped. 'Don't for heaven's sake let them out.'

'What?' He twisted round, trying to hold her off. 'Who else have you got locked up?'

She reached up and fastened her hand over his face, jabbing him in the eye with her forefinger. He swore. 'Let me go, you silly bitch, you nearly had my eye out. I'm coming, hold on,' he yelled up the stairs. With an effort he shook Evelyn off and gave her a push. She lost her footing and slid halfway down the stairs, her breath jolted out of her in a cry. At the top he turned and saw her ready to come after him, her hand on the banister ready to haul herself up, her jaw set like someone facing the Matterhorn. Suddenly a hand shot out and wrenched her savagely sideways, slamming her face into the wall. She did not make a sound. Her hand knotted into her mother's clothes like someone controlling a puppet, Muriel hauled her upright again and let her go. Evelyn's mouth opened for air. Her face, so far as he could see, wore an expression of amazement; but it was dark, he could not see very much. She put one hand to her chest, buckled at the knees, and slid down the last half-dozen steps to the hall floor, where she lay untidily on her side, one arm flung out.

Colin leapt down the stairs three at a time and hunched himself over the body. He knew, quite certainly and without investigation, that she was dead. Without touching, he stared at her for a moment, then jumped up and ran back up the stairs. 'I'm coming,' he called. He pounded along the landing and turned the key in the lock of the room at the end. Isabel stumbled out, straight into his arms, almost knocking him down. He held her gingerly, and then forced her away from him, gripping her by the upper arms.

'You don't know me,' he hissed. 'You don't know my name.'

Drunkenly, she nodded. She pressed her fingers, which were stiff and blue with cold, across her mouth. 'I'm going to be sick.'

'The bathroom's there.' He released her and started down the stairs, hearing her retching and shivering behind him. Florence had come in. Solid and square, wearing her gardening coat, she blocked the hallway. Muriel peeped over her shoulder at Evelyn's body.

'Colin?'

'Yes. I'm here. Coming down now.'

'There's no light in here. What's happened?'

'Mrs Axon's collapsed. It's all right, Florence, here I am.'

'Is the young lady all right?'

'She's fine, she's behind me now.'

'She's dead, isn't she?'

'I think so.'

Isabel appeared on the stairs, her handkerchief dabbing her mouth. 'Call an ambulance,' she said. She began to come down, tottering like an invalid. Colin was afraid to touch her. She squatted by Evelyn and picked up her wrist.

'Do you think we could give her artificial respiration?' Florence said. 'We could massage her heart. My brother here, Mr Sidney, once took a first aid course.'

'You can try if you like,' Isabel said.

'Turn her over,' Colin grunted. 'Straighten her legs out, Florence. That's it, now I need to raise her shoulders a bit.' He stripped off his jacket, wadded it up and pushed it under Evelyn so that her head dropped back. He fished in her open mouth, trying to bring her tongue forward.

'Unblock the airway,' he said to himself. 'Remove any dentures.'

'I always knew something dreadful would happen in this house,' Florence said. 'I've always hated this house since I was a child.'

'Never mind that now. Go for the ambulance,' Colin said. He leaned forward and sealed his mouth over Evelyn's. By the front door Muriel watched him, her legs planted apart and her face absorbed.

'Now, Muriel,' Florence said. She spoke distinctly, as if to a foreigner. 'Now Muriel, your mother's had a bit of an accident. I'm going to call an ambulance. I'll go out the front,' she said to Colin, 'it's quicker.' For a moment Muriel stood blocking her path. 'Now, Muriel,' Florence said again. Her eyes focusing, as if she had only just seen her, Muriel stepped aside. The front door clicked shut after Florence.

Isabel looked down, frowning. 'I think you're wasting your time.'

'There's no heartbeat,' Colin said. He bunched his fist and brought it down on Evelyn's breastbone. 'It's no go,' he said. 'Nothing.'

'Get up then.'

Colin levered himself up to a kneeling position. Gently he removed his jacket from under Evelyn's shoulders, steadying the head reverently till it rested on the hall floor.

'What happened?' Isabel's tone was dull, as if she could barely be troubled to frame the question.

'She was coming after me. Trying to drag me back. I must have pushed her. It wasn't intended. Not hard. She just slipped back a few steps, she wasn't hurt, she was coming up after me again.'

'She didn't die of being pushed. She's had a heart attack.'

'Muriel banged her against the wall. It must have been quite a knock.'

'Did she now? Yes, well, you can see that. She's got a bump on the head too.'

'She'll have done that when she fell.' Colin rubbed his back. He put his jacket on. 'Ought we to cover her face?' He was surprised at how little he felt; no shock, no revulsion, just a kind of numb practicality.

'If you like. I imagine there'll be an inquest. You'll have to give evidence.'

'Will it come out, about the file? I mean, all those months — '

'No, I'll say they refused to let me in. I had no reason to make them a priority. I have a full caseload. Of course they'll criticise the Social Services. It's the rule these days. Never mind. Personally, I've had enough.'

Colin nodded warningly in Muriel's direction.

'Oh, Muriel doesn't know what day of the week it is. Do you, Muriel?'

Muriel gaped at her. Isabel took her eyes from Muriel's face. 'What on earth are you doing in that overcoat, Muriel?' she said sharply. 'Where did you get that?'

'She had it on when she let me in,' Colin said.

'Take it off,' Isabel said. 'Let me have a look at you.'

Obediently, Muriel unfastened the coat, a dark flapping garment of old-fashioned shape and cut. She slipped out of it, held it in one hand, looked around her and finally hung it tidily on the hallstand. Isabel ran her eyes over the girl's body; bare-legged, thick-waisted, her breasts shapeless inside an old stained pinafore.

'What is it?' Colin said. 'What's the matter?'

'Nothing.'

Muriel glanced up the stairs and along the hall, rested her eyes on each of them in turn, and spoke, very softly. It sounded like 'Victor of the field.' Isabel had so seldom heard Muriel speak that she could not be sure what she had heard, or that there had been anything at all. 'What did you say?' Her voice was urgent. She looked up into Muriel's face and saw there for an instant an expression of extraordinary lucidity and calm. Then Muriel turned, stepped over her mother's body, and shambled off towards the kitchen. Colin blundered after her. Muriel picked up from the table a piece of bread and jam – which she must have been eating, he thought, when I came to the door – and began to chew at it, laughing quite loudly, and once offering him a bite. Ten minutes later, the ambulance arrived.

CHAPTER 9

The many marks of violence on Evelyn Axon's body, some recent, some quite old, were carefully enumerated in the post-mortem report. Cardiac arrest had killed her; she had been alive when the left side of her face had struck the wall with some force, but dead when the right side of her skull had struck the hall floor. I wonder how they can tell that, Colin said to himself, as he came out into the fresh air. He looked at his watch; twelve-thirty, nice time to get some lunch.

He had needed to take the morning off work for the inquest. There was a reporter from the local paper present. What would Frank O'Dwyer make of it? They were sure to put HEART ATTACK MOTHER WAS BEATEN, CORONER SAYS, or BEATEN MOTHER DIED OF NATURAL CAUSES. Perhaps he had no gift for headline-writing.

Frank had made no more references to the night of the dinner party. He obviously didn't remember being hit on the head. If he'd found a lump next day, he'd obviously put that down to natural causes too. Colman had not said anything either, except 'bit of a bore'. As if such Charenton junketings were what you got every time you accepted a dinner invitation. But possibly, Colin thought, it was more his memory that was at fault. Already he could see a tendency in himself to confuse the two incidents, to impose on Frank's drink-sodden features the expression of astonishment he had seen on Evelyn Axon's face as she died. Or thought he had seen. Perhaps it had not been there, and perhaps the party had not been as bad as he thought. Perhaps I have a tendency to dramatise things, blow them up out of proportion. He could not ask Sylvia for her reminiscences; she had said it would suit her best if the evening were never referred to again. The loss of his driving licence was breeding much inconvenience for the family. Everything has been out of perspective since last September, he thought, and that dinner party was not the worst of it.

A weak sun was struggling out as Colin and Florence came down the steps.

'You gave your evidence very well,' Florence said. 'Very lucidly.'

'Florence, I'd like to have a word with the young social worker. Will you just wait for me?'

'Miss Field? I'd like to speak to her myself. I want to know what will happen to Muriel.'

'Muriel? Why?'

'We *are* neighbours, Colin, after all. Or have been, all those years. I'd like to visit her.'

'She might not know. She's resigned, after all. I'll ring them up about it, the Social Services Department. No, you stay there, I won't be two ticks. I'll have to dash.'

'All right, Colin,' Florence said, and stood on the steps looking after him uneasily, her stout handbag dangling from her wrist.

He caught up with Isabel in the car park. She heard him behind her, and walked back to meet him.

'It wasn't too bad, was it?' he said. 'It's all over now.'

He saw a sullen young woman with a pale face and sharp nose, drably dressed in office clothes, with legs disproportionately thin. Last winter's ghost burned feebly behind her eyes, almost extinguished.

'Like spring, isn't it?' she said, making an effort at a smile. 'No, it wasn't too bad. I'm out of it now, anyway.'

'What are you going to do now?'

'I'm going to work in a bank. It will suit me, don't you think?'

'Well, it'll be less complex. Less wearing, I should think.'

'No emotional upheavals or moral dilemmas.'

'I'm sure you'll get on. You're a clever girl.'

'I may not be, you know. I may be most extraordinarily stupid.'

'Forget it. If you made a mistake – '

'Yes, it's too late. I know it's no use crying over spilt milk, but it is a very common and understandable thing to do.'

'She was elderly. You couldn't prevent her having a heart attack, could you?'

'No.' Her eyes searched his face. 'I couldn't help her and I couldn't really help Muriel, and there was no one else, was there?'

'Well, you could have helped me.'

'Oh, perhaps. How is your wife?'

'Sylvia?'

'Have you another?'

'No, of course not. I was just surprised at you asking after her. She's fine, thanks.'

'I'm not her enemy, you know.'

'No . . . of course not. My sister, she's blaming herself a bit. For not knowing Mrs Axon was ill. She told me she'd not seen them for months. I didn't take any notice. Now she's worried about Muriel.'

'Muriel's all right.'

'Do you know what'll happen to her?'

'She's in a supervised hostel. Sheltered accommodation. She's no danger to anybody.'

'Can't they — well . . . examine her? Find out what's the matter?'

'Yes,' Isabel muttered. 'I expect they'll examine her. But as for what's the matter — I don't know.' She turned away and closed her eyes with a tired frown, trying to obliterate once and for all the memory of Muriel's face in the dark hall, for five seconds, perfectly lucid and perfectly sane. Perhaps a trick of the light, she had said to herself, light or the lack of it.

'Are you all right? Do you feel dizzy?' Colin touched her elbow timidly, as if she were a stranger in the street.

'Yes. I'm all right.' She moved away from him. 'Will you be taking any evening classes this year, Colin?'

'Yes. I'm taking Do-It-Yourself. We want to move, you see, we need more room, and our only chance is to get something going cheap that needs a bit of work. I was thinking, actually, Mrs Axon's house will have to go up for sale, won't it? I mean, Muriel won't be coming back to live by herself, I shouldn't think, so they'll have to put the money in trust for her, or whatever they do.'

Isabel stared at him. 'You must be mad.'

'What do you mean?'

'You're not really thinking of buying that house?'

'Why not?'

'Didn't you feel the atmosphere?'

'Atmosphere?' He laughed. 'There's no atmosphere. Give it a good clean-up, slap a bit of white paint around, it'll be completely different.'

'You'll never clean it up. The smell – '

'It smelled of mould.'

'It smelled of misery.'

'We'll get rid of that.'

'Oh, you're planning to be happy, are you?'

He looked away. 'That's perhaps too much to ask.'

'I cannot understand how people can give up on life as you do. You used to talk as if you were looking for the Holy Grail.'

'It was a phase.'

'You got a quick poke in the back of a parked car and you said it had changed your life.'

'I thought it had.'

'Tried and failed, is that it? A lifetime's excuse for not trying any more. Ultimately, Colin, they'll find your body and bury you.' She turned away, pulling up her collar and knotting her scarf against the wind. 'Anyway – the house. I wouldn't call myself over-endowed with imagination, and I wouldn't buy it.'

He followed her. 'Do you know something about the Axons that you aren't telling me?'

'I don't *know* anything.'

'The Axons – you see, if only we had known what their lives were like . . . '

'Well, there are a lot of things we don't know, and choose and prefer not to know.' She hesitated. 'Goodbye, Colin.' Slouching, his face set, he watched her walk away between the line of parked cars.

When she had driven off he turned and went back to Florence; he found her on the steps where he had left her, a glassy tolerance in her eyes, and her handbag on her wrist, like the Queen reviewing a parade.

CHAPTER 10

Many months had passed. It was September again. Colin stood by his new double-glazed french window, the part product of his second mortgage; and stared out over his crepuscular garden, open and breathing like a ploughed field. The scent of autumn earth carried into the house.

He had never known what the police had been looking for, when they turned over the garden, and he was not sure whether they had known themselves. Still, a few timely words from his solicitor had reduced the purchase price still further, and Sylvia had not been sorry, she said, to see the back of some of those evergreens. Sylvia had been extremely sensible about it all, putting her back into weeks of cleaning without a word of complaint. Even Florence, who had not been keen initially, had to admit they'd changed the place out of all recognition; two rooms knocked into one downstairs, the fireplaces pulled out, and all the ceilings painted eau-de-nil.

Sylvia sat behind him, placidly knitting, the picture of domestic contentment.

'Draw the curtains, love,' she said.

From upstairs, Alistair gave an earsplitting yell. The baby began to cry, and Sylvia thrust her needles into her ball of wool and heaved herself to her feet.

'Just as I'd settled him,' she said. 'I don't know what's the matter with Alistair. He wants a good slap. I think the devil's got into that child since we moved house.'

She bustled out, yelling at the child as she clumped up the stairs. Perhaps he's unhappy at the new school, Colin thought. He heard Sylvia administer the slap, heard Alistair's wail, the louder shrieking of the baby, and Sylvia's voice rising over all. The noise, the sheer noise level defeats me, he thought, the classroom all day with the five minutes anarchy between every lesson, the traffic rattling the staffroom windows, the pneumatic drills on the bypass, the screaming baby all night. How that child screams, worse than all the others put together, I've never heard anything like it.

Just now, when it was going dark, he had been touched by the depression that crept up every day at this time. It was a new kind of gloom, more akin to fright than misery; a tightness round the heart, a tension at the back of the neck. It was not circumstantial, not related to the delinquent children or the size of the mortgage. He had consulted the doctor; free-floating anxiety, the man had called it. Offered him Valium; Valium, he felt was for women. He took it for a week and found himself bursting into episodes of florid rage; he threw it away. He had little fear of the future now, for he knew what the future held; an infinite series of evenings like this one, the same vague dread touching his heart. It would seem infinite, of course, because he would never be able to look back and say, 'That was the last one.' Suicides never realise it, but no one experiences his own death; we only experience in retrospect. Those were the kind of speculations that ran through his mind a lot these days; he was thinking over a lot of things that had never bothered him before. He had begun to wonder whether his blood-pressure was up, and to worry about air-crashes; not that he ever travelled by plane.

Perhaps I need to make some noise of my own, he thought. He went to the radiogram and eased out of the pile of records the one Isabel had given him for Christmas. She had not written on it of course, not even 'To Colin with best wishes'. There was no written evidence, and really no evidence at all, of that segment of his life. He put the record on the turntable, and, on impulse, opened the french window and stepped out into the garden. A large waxen moon illuminated the rutted earth and the two apple trees near Florence's fence, ancient trees bearing tiny acid fruit. They can come down, he thought, before Alistair breaks his leg. He shook himself, under the moon, trying to hustle the dread off his shoulders. His feet sank into the soil and from the house behind him the music bounded out into the twilight, thumping and swooping, wave after wave of *The Washington Post*.

P.S.

Ideas,
interviews
& features...

About the author

2 An Outsider's Eye: Louise Tucker talks to Hilary Mantel

6 Life at a Glance

8 Top Ten Favourite Novels

9 A Writing Life

About the book

10 The Woman in the Hall by Hilary Mantel

Read on

14 Have You Read?

18 If You Loved This, You Might Like ...

An Outsider's Eye

Louise Tucker talks to Hilary Mantel

How did you start your first novel, and how long did it take?

The first novel I wrote was not the first I published. I began *A Place of Greater Safety*, which is a novel about the French Revolution, in 1974, which was the year after I left university. I had completed two drafts by the end of 1979. It then gathered dust on a shelf until 1991, when I tidied it up for publication (and retyped the enormous MS) in the course of a summer when I survived on very little sleep, permanently distorting my work habits. My first published novel, *Every Day is Mother's Day*, came out in 1985. It took me around two years, on and off; I changed country part way through, moving from Africa back to England and then on to Saudi Arabia.

Nothing's ever been straightforward, but why should it be? The writing of the story becomes part of the story.

You have lived abroad and in various parts of England. Where is home, and why?

I have lived in the south-east since 1985, but still somehow feel this is a temporary arrangement. But the north-west, where I grew up, has changed a good deal. So I don't know where I belong, or even if it's in England at all; but I don't mind that. I think it's good to have an outsider's eye. And the past lives in people, as much as places. I like to know where I come from, but it doesn't dictate where I may go.

What did you want to be when you grew up?
A man.

What, or who, made you a writer?
Circumstance and chance; poor health, unfitting me for more active trades; the desire to read books that didn't seem to exist, and wouldn't exist, unless I wrote them.

The supernatural, in all its manifestations, has featured in many of your books. Does it personally as well as professionally fascinate you, and if so why?
When I was a child I believed our house was haunted, and so – worryingly – did the grown-ups. I was often very frightened, and the imprint of that fear stays with me; but I try to use it constructively now. The good thing about being a writer is that you take your bad experiences and make them pay.

The book is set in the seventies, a decade of drabness and misery in England, which is how it is portrayed. Is that how you experienced it, and was that what you were aiming to create?
It probably wasn't all drab and miserable. But I think my book offers a fair picture of the part of the country it's set in. The North/South divide was very pronounced then. I deliberately didn't name the town, but made it typical enough of the North-West/Midlands. I chose the year 1974 very deliberately, not just because that was the year I was involved in social work, but because it was a year when professional practice was subject to a huge reorganization, and specialists gave way to 'generic' social ▶

> 6 The good thing about being a writer is that you take your bad experiences and make them pay. 9

3

An Outsider's Eye *(continued)*

◄ workers. Reorganizations, both bureaucratic and philosophical, increase the potential for the kind of confusion that the early part of the story catalogues – files lost, responsibilities shuffled off. Isabel, my social worker, does her best; but she's beset by difficulties of her own, in the shape of her old father who tends to go walkabout; in dealing with the Axons she's up against a problem the nature of which she can hardly guess, and which may not be amenable to social work as it was practised; and, most importantly, she has severe doubts about the value of her own trade.

Christmas at the Sidneys' is reminiscent of Mike Leigh, director of films like *Abigail's Party, Secrets and Lies* and *Life is Sweet*, a wickedly funny scene but full of pathos. Do you consider his work, if you know it, to have an affinity with yours?
The first Mike Leigh work I saw was *Nuts in May,* and it made me very happy indeed. And *Topsy-Turvy* is one of my favourite films.

Life, thinks Colin, is 'a series of minute disappointments impatiently endured', and certainly in his family and marriage that seems to be the case. Were you explicitly commenting on married or family life through your depiction of the Sidneys?
Bad marriages are much more fun to write about than good marriages. I have a sneaking sympathy for Colin. The early seventies, when the book is set, were years when feminism became a profound and active force in society. But who would speak up for

the badgered, dutiful young husbands, ground down by their wives' desires to procreate at all costs? Sylvia is one of those women who get married just to have children. Thereafter the man is a source of income, perhaps, but also a bit of a nuisance.

Single motherhood, I think, can be an honest choice, and it is available to women now, as it wasn't then. The managing, humourless, unimaginative sort of woman that Sylvia represents was a very familiar type to me when I was growing up.

When Colin discovers that Frank has the Axon file he says, 'These are real people. You can't make their lives public property.' How do you, as a novelist, come to terms with using real people, albeit often only the suggestion of them?
Because it is 'the suggestion', I don't think there is a problem. I admit, though, that in this book, especially in the dinner-party scene, I am quoting, rather than inventing. I did sit through a selection of similar occasions, which I stored up for further use. Did the people I'm quoting ever recognize themselves? Maybe; but of course they'd be too ashamed to complain. On the whole, the real people you slide into fiction don't notice unless the portrait is flattering.

On the same subject, when you wrote your memoir *Giving Up the Ghost*, was it hard to switch from creating characters to a world full of real people?
Not at all. When you are intensely engaged with a novel you think of 'my people' not ▶

6 Good fiction expands our sympathies, asks us to consider people and places and circumstances very remote from our own. Much wickedness stems from our failure to imagine other people as fully human. 9

An Outsider's Eye *(continued)*

◄ 'my characters'. You know they aren't real, but you deal with them as carefully as if they were.

What do you think the purpose of fiction is, if any? Is it simply entertainment or does it have a moral dimension too?

I think good fiction expands our sympathies, asks us to consider people and places and circumstances very remote from our own, and asks us to consider how we would act and what we would feel if we were in their shoes. Much wickedness stems from our failure to imagine other people as fully human, and as our equals. So, yes – I think fiction does have a moral dimension. But of course, if it is not also entertaining, no one will read it and it will have no effect at all.

What has been the most satisfying part of your career? And the most frustrating?

This may sound childish, but I will never forget the day on which I learned my first novel was accepted. I was in Saudi Arabia at that time; an airmail letter brought the news. It was early afternoon. I opened the letter and when I tried to speak, my mouth moved but no words came out. Until then, I thought that it was only in stories that people were 'speechless with shock', or 'dumb with delight'.

Each novel breeds its frustrations. But frustration is usually the prelude to a breakthrough. When I'm in the process of frustration, I always manage to forget that.

Who are your influences?

I don't write novels about pirates or Highland

rebels, but I think Robert Louis Stevenson formed my notion, as a child, of what a story ought to be like.

What do you do when you are not writing?
When would that be? Writing is not a trade that gives you holidays. In *Who's Who* I put my 'recreation' as 'sleep', but that's not wholly true, as I do a lot of work during dreams.

What are you writing next?
I have a long-term project, a short non-fiction book called *The Woman Who Died of Robespierre*. And I am working on two novels. *The Complete Stranger* is set in Africa during the late 1970s. *Wolf Hall* is a big novel about Thomas Cromwell. ■

Top Ten Favourite Novels

Kidnapped
R.L. Stevenson

Huckleberry Finn
Mark Twain

Another Country
James Baldwin

Things Fall Apart
Chinua Achebe

The Good Soldier
Ford Madox Ford

Blood Red, Sister Rose
Thomas Keneally

I, Claudius
Robert Graves

Effi Briest
Theodor Fontane

Sword of Honour trilogy
Evelyn Waugh

Angel
Elizabeth Taylor

A Writing Life

When do you write?
Whenever an idea strikes.

Where do you write?
Wherever I am. Usually on public transport.

Why do you write?
Good question. Habit/need to earn
money/curiosity about what I will say
next/hope of doing something good.

Pen or computer?
Pen first, as I write all ideas first in notebooks.
But the screen seems as natural as paper.

Silence or music?
Sometimes I put on music, but I screen it out;
I only hear it if my writing is not flowing.

How do you start?
With spirit and dash, but with an error; I
usually rewrite the beginning.

And finish?
Softly: I have to go back after a few days, and
work it up.

Do you have any writing rituals?
None.

Who is your favourite living writer?
Oliver Sacks.

If you weren't a writer, what would you do?
I'd be a spy.

The Woman in the Hall

By Hilary Mantel

Every Day is Mother's Day was the first novel I published. I wrote the beginning in Botswana, accompanied by the evening whine of mosquitoes, and the closing chapters in Saudi Arabia, in a lightless room where an air conditioner throbbed and groaned. The middle of the book I wrote at a kitchen table in Windsor, with a view of the castle framed by the window. Windsor, a prosperous and pleasant town, was so far from the England I describe in the book that it too might as well have been a foreign country.

It's sometimes easier to recall home when you're far away from it. It rises up before you in almost hallucinatory detail. When I wrote the novel I was casting my mind back to an earlier phase in my life, before I went to Africa. Soon after I left university I became a social work assistant in a geriatric hospital. It was in Stockport, and it occupied a grim building, a former workhouse, which it shared with a psychiatric unit. Case files were my preferred reading in those days; one learned the stories not only of elderly clients, but of their families, and not only of their present, but their past; hard lives, very often. It was part of my job to visit elderly patients in what we now call 'the community'.

One day, in one of the more reassuring and tree-lined roads of my territory, I got lost. The road numbering had confused me. I rang what I thought was the right doorbell, and a smiling elderly woman answered, an old gentleman in a cardigan shadowing her.

'Don't worry, that's always happening,' she said. She told me where I ought to be, and as I was apologizing, and backing away, a dark shape appeared at the end of the hall; it was a bulky, hostile-looking woman in middle age. She didn't come to the door; she just watched me. 'We used to have visits from the hospital,' the old lady said. 'Our daughter was on the other side. You know. Psychiatric. But she's all right now.'

I said my goodbyes. Off I went, down the path of their neat detached house. No problem, I said to myself, they're obviously coping, they seem happy. But I had found it hard to pluck my eyes away from the younger woman, the daughter. It wasn't that I was afraid of the 'other side', the psychiatric hospital; far from it. My own difficult medical history made me both informed about issues of mental health, and profoundly sympathetic to those carrying the stigma of psychiatric problems. But the woman in the hall . . . though I hadn't seen her clearly, and perhaps just *because* I hadn't seen her clearly, something about her had troubled me profoundly. But I said to myself, the household is fine; the trouble's all in your head.

I found the correct address, where I should have been all along, and approached a flat-fronted stone cottage, a small cottage with a single window right by the door. I knocked, waited. Nothing. I was used to long delays, for an elderly and perhaps sick person shuffling to answer. After a time I knocked ▶

> ❛ I always worried that my well-intentioned ring or knock would cause some frail client to hurry, trip, flip downstairs, break something, go to hospital, and die: cause of death, social worker. ❜

The Woman in the Hall *(continued)*

◄ again. Again, nothing. This delay was long enough to create unease. I always worried that my well-intentioned ring or knock would cause some frail client to hurry, trip, flip downstairs, break something, go to hospital, and die: cause of death, social worker. There was always, too, the possibility that a client couldn't answer the door because she had been taken ill. I tried to look in, but the room was dark. I knocked again. Then a gnarled hand appeared, seemingly from mid-air. Slowly, it waved before the window; it quivered in mid-air *and knocked back*.

Today was getting worse and worse. I felt that I had fallen into a ghost story. What did I do? I expect I went to a phone box, rang the hospital, checked out the situation; I had already worked out that there must be a bed below the window, just out of my line of sight, and that the hand belonged to an old person lying on it. The rest of the day, I've forgotten. Nothing remarkable happened. But those linked two occurrences stuck in my mind, and I couldn't dislodge them. That was where the novel started – though I didn't know it at the time. What you might call the 'inciting incident' seldom, for me, appears in the novel itself. It just sets a mood, raises a question.

Muriel Axon is, of course, a product of my imagination, and the key to her character is that she has no imagination of her own. That, I think, may be where 'evil' comes from: the inability to comprehend others as fully human. Muriel can't empathize with other people; her mother, Evelyn, has hardly set her

❝ Muriel doesn't fully understand the laws of cause and effect and she lives in a world stripped of all day-to-day certainties. ❞

an example. But both mother and daughter have their strange kind of pathos. And their strange kind of comedy, too, I hope. Muriel is not suffering from any defined condition. What she lacks is a 'theory of mind' – or perhaps she has a theory of her own. She doesn't fully understand the laws of cause and effect – as, of course, we 'normals' think we do – and she lives in a world stripped of all day-to-day certainties. How far Muriel is responsible for the dark events that surround her is something I leave to the reader to decide. ■

Have You Read?

Other books by Hilary Mantel

Vacant Possession

In the sequel to *Every Day is Mother's Day* Muriel Axon re-enters the lives of Colin Sidney and Isabel Field. It is ten years since her last tangle with them, but for Muriel this is not time enough. There are still scores to be settled, truths to be faced and a certain amount of vengeance to be wreaked.

Giving Up the Ghost

A wry, shocking and unique autobiography of childhood, ghosts, illness and family. From childhood daydreams to the reality of family secrets, her father's mysterious disappearance and an adulthood blighted by medical neglect, Mantel uncovers the losses that wrenched her from the patterns of the past and drove her to forge her own path.

Winner of Mind Book of the Year 2004.

The Giant, O'Brien

Charles O'Brien flees Ireland for England and, he hopes, a future as a sideshow exhibit. But his enormous size attracts the attention of John Hunter, celebrated surgeon and anatomist who buys dead men from the gallows and babies' corpses by the inch. Hunter is determined to dissect this giant, but Charles needs to keep body and soul together in order to reach heaven. This book is based on the true story of an eighteenth-century Irish giant, Charles O'Brien, who was, despite his best efforts, eventually dissected by the surgeon John Hunter. His bones still hang in the Museum of the Royal College of Surgeons in Lincoln's Inn Fields.

A Place of Greater Safety
'Household names come out of households,' said a perceptive reviewer of this novel of the French Revolution. Great historical figures have their private – even their hidden – lives. Robespierre, Danton and the journalist Camille Desmoulins are the three main figures in this novel; in five years of revolution they lived as hard as most people do in a natural lifespan. Their lovers, wives, sisters lived with them; in some cases they died with them.

Fludd
Fetherhoughton is an isolated village, poor and superstitious, located in the north of England in the 1950s; it is earthy, stolid, yet it seems adrift in its own dream. Father Angwin, gentle and anxious, is a parish priest who has lost his faith. His only (chaste) bond of sympathy is with Sister Philomena, a passionate young Irish nun. But she is a prisoner in the convent, and he is a prisoner of habit. One stormy night a stranger appears at the door of the priest's house, wrapped in a black cloak and carrying a black bag. Who is Fludd? Is he a curate? Is he an angel? Is he perhaps a devil? Or is he something stranger than any of these? 'I have come to transform you,' he says. 'Transformation is my business.'

Winner of the Winifred Holtby Prize, the Cheltenham Festival Prize and the Southern Arts Literature Award.

Have You Read? *(continued)*

A Change of Climate

Anna and Ralph Eldred live happily in the Norfolk countryside. To the outward eye they are a contented, middle-aged couple who have raised four happy children and devoted themselves to helping others. But in the course of one summer their peace is almost destroyed, as echoes of their early career in Africa come to haunt them, and it becomes evident that, in their present life, something or someone is missing.

Eight Months on Ghazzah Street

Frances Shore is a cartographer by trade, but when her husband's work takes her to Saudi Arabia she finds herself unable to map the Kingdom's areas of internal darkness. The streets are not a woman's territory – confined in her flat, she feels her sense of self begin to dissolve. She hears whispers, sounds of distress from the 'empty' flat above her head. As her days empty of certainty and purpose, her life becomes a blank – waiting to be filled by violence and disaster.

An Experiment in Love

It was the year after Chappaquiddick, and all spring Carmel had watery dreams about the disaster. Now she, Karina and Julianne were escaping the dreary north for a London University hall of residence. Awaiting them was a winter of new preoccupations – sex, politics, food and fertility – and a grotesque tragedy of their own.

Winner of the Hawthornden Prize.

Learning to Talk
A semi-autobiographical collection of stories
drawn from life in the 1950s in an insular
northern village. For the child narrator, the
only way to survive is to get up, get on, get
out.

If You Loved This,
You Might Like . . .

The Giant's House *by Elizabeth McCracken*
Peggy, a lonely and socially inept 28-year-old librarian, becomes friends with an oversized 11 year old, James Carlsson Sweatt. A strange relationship develops between these two people at odds, socially and physically, with the world.

....

The Lady in the Van *by Alan Bennett*
For several years Miss Shepherd, a homeless old lady, lived at first opposite, then in Alan Bennett's driveway. This is the sometimes hilarious, sometimes heartbreaking story of their relationship.

....

Puffball *by Fay Weldon*
Richard and Liffey, a young married couple, follow their dream of moving out of London to a country cottage in the middle of Somerset. Richard continues to live and work in London, coming to stay with Liffey at weekends. But Liffey's pregnancy, the odd neighbours and Bella, Richard's lover in London, all threaten the rural idyll she has imagined for so long.

....

Cold Comfort Farm *by Stella Gibbons*
Neighbours you can get away from; family is not so easy to escape. When Flora is orphaned and left with very little she goes to live with her relatives, the Starkadders, at Cold Comfort Farm. But the chaos of their lives is such that she can't rest until she brings order. Or tries to.

Behind the Scenes at the Museum *by Kate Atkinson*
The day-to-day life of Ruby Lennox's dysfunctional family is both humorous and tragic, from the runaway great-grandmother through two World Wars and Ruby's own conception thanks to a few pints of bitter. But deep within the family stories a dark tragedy is buried.

Dog Days, Glenn Miller Nights *by Laurie Graham*
Birdie lives in a high rise on the Fruit Bowl, a rough council estate in the East End of London, and longs for some action. But when the estate overheats in the summer she gets more than she bargained for.

The Rotters' Club *by Jonathan Coe*
The 1970s are brought to life in all their undesirable glory – strikes, IRA bombs and terrible music – through the story of the coming-of-age of four adolescent boys in Birmingham.

The Prime of Miss Jean Brodie *by Muriel Spark*
Spark's black comedy about a Scottish teacher who invests all her energy in tutoring a select group of girls is the best introduction to an oeuvre of witty writing that spans several decades.

If You Loved This, You Might Like . . .
(continued)

Abigail's Party

Mike Leigh's 1970s classic film about an excruciating evening in the suburbs is both a comedy and a tragedy of manners.

BOOKSHOP

Other titles by Hilary Mantel available from Harper
Perennial at 10% off recommended retail price.
FREE postage and packing in the UK.

Vacant Possession
ISBN: 1-84115-340-0   £7.99
....

Eight Months on Ghazzah Street
ISBN: 0-00-717291-5   £7.99
....

Fludd
ISBN: 0-00-717289-3   £7.99
....

A Change of Climate
ISBN: 0-00-717290-7   £7.99
....

An Experiment in Love
ISBN: 0-00-717288-5   £7.99
....

The Giant, O'Brien
ISBN: 1-85702-886-4   £6.99
....

Beyond Black
ISBN: 0-00-715776-2   £7.99
....

Learning to Talk
ISBN: 0-00-716644-3   £6.99
....

Giving Up the Ghost
ISBN: 0-00-714272-2   £7.99
....

Total cost _____

10% discount _____

Final total _____

To purchase by Visa/Mastercard/Switch
simply call **08707 871724** or fax on **08707 871725**

To pay by cheque, send a copy of this form with a cheque made
payable to 'HarperCollins Publishers' to: Mail Order Dept
(Ref: B0B4), HarperCollins Publishers, Westerhill Road,
Bishopbriggs, G64 2QT, making sure to include your full name,
postal address and phone number.

From time to time HarperCollins may wish to use your personal
data to send you details of other HarperCollins publications and
offers. If you wish to receive information on other HarperCollins
publications and offers please tick this box ☐

Do not send cash or currency. Prices correct at time of press. Prices
and availability are subject to change without notice. Delivery over-
seas and to Ireland incurs a £2 per book postage and packing charge.